Breaking Protocol

T. James LeDoux

Published by Alpha Group 3 LLC

Paperback book edition created 2018

ISBN 9780985226688

BISAC Classification: Fiction/Thrillers/Espionage - FIC006000

Cover picture: Big Ben and Parliament Building with layers opened to expose code sheet under picture, code discovered and letter depicting threat to U.S. security.

Dedications

To my beautiful wife, Marilyn, whose patience, proofreading, attention to detail and advice did much to help make this book a reality.

Table of Contents

Chapter 1

Court of Inquiry

"Relax and calm your mind. Forget about yourself and follow your opponent's movement." - Yip Kai-Man

Admiral Evan Roedl looked over the members of his specialized team, identified as the Creative Access Team 205 or better known as CAT205, as they waited in the hallway. "They certainly are a bunch of rogues," he thought as he looked them over. "But they're my rogues."

The corridor of the basement of the facility was painted in yellow and lighted with florescent lights. The ceiling was about fifteen feet high and had numerous pipes running along the length of the ceiling with labels on them showing some pipes with 'water', 'gas' and 'sewer'. The floor was cement with a table sporting a phone and a check-in log sitting near the main entrance to the inquiry room. In the hall, two armed Marines stood by the door to the inquiry room and two other armed Marines were next to the small group of people waiting to go into the room to continue testimony on an operation that took place in Iran some seven months previously.

The person nearest the door was Jim Lawson. He looked at the Marines, wondering if they were there to protect the proceedings or to arrest those in the hallway after the inquiry board found the group negligent in the performance of their duties. Now a Navy Lieutenant, he was a second class petty officer with a rating of Intelligence Specialist when he was selected for the mission to get documents from a research center in Iran. He was successful and, as a result, was promoted to Lieutenant after the mission. At five feet, nine inches in height, light brown hair, a fair complexion and a good physical build, he had no problems keeping up with the hectic demands of the Navy. He spoke English and Russian, having just graduated from the Russian language training school at the Defense Language Institute in Monterrey, California. Before entering the Navy, he attended Carnegie-Mellon University with a major in electrical engineering but had to leave in the last semester of his senior year due to lack of funds as he refused to indebt himself with a student loan. Once he left college, he joined the Navy, attended the US Navy's 'Navy and Marine Corps Intelligence Training Center' at the Naval Air Station Oceana Dam Neck Annex in Virginia then was sent to the aircraft carrier USS Theodore Roosevelt. While on the Roosevelt, Lawson was instrumental in identifying threats to the Roosevelt while they were in the Persian Gulf after which he was selected for the mission in question. This inquiry was looking into the facts and results of that mission. Lawson, known for his attention to detail and recognizing patterns in people's actions and events, was sought for his opinions concerning motives and outcomes. He exhibited a sense of authority that kept other intelligence officers wondering what his real rank was.

Next to Lawson was Nick Myers. He was an MIT Graduate with a Master's degree in wave energy technology and, as a highly skilled electronics technician, he had an ability to fix anything electronic with a minimum of tools. Besides being able to program at assembly-level code by looking at the machine code on a computer and modifying it, he was also an expert at fixing communications and cryptographic equipment. With a normal physical build, his five feet, nine inch frame exhibited the wear of his thirty-two years of experience. Being black and from East Boston, he had experience getting out of trouble by using logic, which worked most of the time. He revealed a level of brilliance at an early age which resulted in a four year scholarship to MIT in Massachusetts upon his graduation from high school at age 17. His grasp of advanced mathematics and technology was so extensive that several major corporations working on leading-edge automation got into a bidding war to get him. He chose the Navy instead. He spoke English with a slight Bostonian accent, Russian and Farsi. He was a Christian that had planned to be a minister but events changed his plans. He had refused to be promoted to being a naval officer because as he explained, "Officers do nothing but paperwork and I only want to work on the newest technology." He was part of the team that worked with Lawson to get the Polevsky Papers at the Iranian research facility and to destroy the munitions shipment bound for Gaza that was part of the operation, called 'Tin Cup', under scrutiny by the board.

Standing next to Myers was Master Gunnery Sergeant Arnoud 'Gunny' Glendenning. Whereas most Master Gunnery Sergeants would be called 'Master Gunny', Glendenning wanted to be called 'Gunny' because, according to him, calling him 'Master Gunny' took up too much time in a critical situation. A career Marine at six feet, one inch tall with dark brown hair, blue eyes and a moderately rugged build, he spoke English and Russian with an Irish accent. Going by the book, he was always impeccably dressed in uniform and held all enlisted personnel to the rules, no exceptions. Experienced in weapons, security and combat, he previously maintained security records and directed weapons maintenance for all personnel in the Kennedy Irregular Warfare facility. He was an expert with both rifle and pistol. A

Marine Colonel on the shooting range commented one time that Gunny 'could shoot the eye off a fly at one-hundred yards'. His demeanor seemed to indicate that he was a typical Marine but his instincts and quiet character demonstrated a level of maturity and wisdom that helped keep those he worked with out of trouble. He was part of the team that worked with Lawson and Myers to get the Polevsky Papers and destroy the ammo dump in Iran.

Standing farthest from the door was Beth Norman. A U. S. Navy Commander, Beth Norman was a rather attractive woman with an ability to remain unseen even in a small group. After graduating from the U.S. Naval Academy, she spent several years working as a liaison officer within the Defense Intelligence Agency (DIA). For the past two years, she worked closely with Admiral Roedl, head of Office of Naval Intelligence's Special Operations Group. Her personality allowed for her to not draw attention to herself which made her one of Admiral Roedl's best spies while also having the ability to speak both English and Farsi. She had brunette hair with a captivating smile and was five feet, six inches tall. She had developed a good friendship with Lawson and was concerned that their friendship would be tested by any operation which they could be jointly assigned. Lawson saw her as a paradox. He told Myers one time that she was like a cat. Very caring and compassionate but could kill without hesitation if it meant not doing so would cause a mission to fail. They both respected each other's opinions and advice.

Finally, facing them was Admiral Evan Roedl. He was a Rear Admiral Upper Half with two stars on his epaulettes. At six feet, one inch in height, he tended to loom over those he commanded. He was meticulous in his appearance, work area and expectations. At the same time, he was inclined to go rogue when the rules got in the way of his operations, which tended to irritate other officers in the Navy and Marine Corps. A graduate of Notre Dame with a Masters of Business Administration from Harvard, he started his career in the U. S. Navy later than most but moved up quickly to his present rank. As head of the Special Operations group at the Office of Naval Intelligence, he was known for getting things done. The current inquiry was into his methods and his team's actions in acquiring a document belonging to the Russians that was generated at an Iranian research facility. Many of the officers familiar with the operation that occurred six months previous felt that his actions put the US on the edge of a major conflict. Tensions settled down but the opinions did not.

"You must remember that this is an inquiry not a courts martial," Admiral Roedl told his people before they went into the inquiry room. "Events have changed the scope of this inquiry in the past twenty-four hours. Be flexible and don't let the inquiry board get to you. You performed an unsanctioned protocol in your last mission. Based upon our meaning of the expression, 'Unsanctioned' means that you operated without explicit official permission. You had permission to perform the mission, but no rules or reporting instructions. Working with a 'Protocol' means you were supposed to have a preset set of steps or sequences required to perform a function but there was no protocol for what you were doing. In other words, you weren't following any prescribed rules. However, what you did is within the typical venue of an intelligence operation, so don't let them push you into thinking you did something wrong. Everyone understand?"

Everyone nodded agreement as they turned to leave the hallway to go into the inquiry room while Admiral Roedl turned to leave the building.

U.S. Navy JAG Judge Mark Henderson looked around the inquiry room as the Marine guard pulled the door closed after the judge and two others entered the room. Henderson was a naval officer with the rank of captain in his forties. A short man with a slender build, he was no nonsense with a history of wanting only facts with no unsupported opinions. He was joined by two other officers, a Marine Corps colonel and a Navy lieutenant commander making up the three person board of inquiry.

"All rise," called out a U.S. Navy Yeoman as the judge moved toward the bench at the front of the room along with his two associates. Everyone stood up as the inquiry board moved to sit down. Once they took to their chairs, the other occupants in the room sat.

The room was a high-security inquiry room used for evaluation and judgments provided for actions taken by U.S. military personnel in highly classified operations. The room had no windows, two steel doors, the main door manned on the outside by a Marine guard with the room having desks and chairs set up in a classroom-type environment with a long table at the front of the room where the inquiry board sat facing the witnesses. It smelled musty with the mix of different perfumes and colognes and the light smell of cigarette smoke coming off of the uniforms of those who were previously smoking outside the building. The lighting gave a glare that was somewhat subdued by the monotonous gray walls. There was one podium facing the judges' table where those testifying would stand while being questioned. A large video screen hung on the wall to the left side of the room which allowed everyone to see anything needing to be displayed. The only notes taken were those done in writing by the judges. Nothing else could be taken from the room. There was no court recorder and no documents, except those in the judges' possession or being shown on the video screen.

"For the record, it is 09:00 hours on February 1, 2016 and we are continuing the inquiry into the actions taken in Iran. So we will continue with the events surrounding the acquisition of documents taken from the Sheysheh Research Facility in Iran on July 31st, 2015. Those documents being referred to as the Polevsky Papers and shown as exhibit H on the screen," Judge Henderson stated as he opened the third day of questioning in the inquiry. Everyone looked to see a display of the first page of the document being shown on the screen. The document was written in the typical East Slavic Russian text.

"Will Lieutenant James Lawson please take the stand?" Judge Henderson called out while looking up from his notes. "I remind you that you are still under oath," he continued.

"Yes Sir," came Lawson's response. The judge looked back down at his notes.

"Let's see," the judge started, "I see that from the casualties to the Iranians and Russians during your operation in Iran against the Sheysheh Research Facility and the munitions storage area, we have...215 dead from the destruction of the ammo dump, another 87 wounded. We also have 36 dead resulting from the actions at the research facility, 27 dead from the action by your team to get back to the Whiskey November pickup point, 4 dead at one of the radar sites and 9 dead from various helicopter shoot downs. That's a total of 290 dead for a mission that was supposed to be simply to get a document and destroy an ammo dump. Did I miss anything?"

Lawson stood frowning for a moment then replied, "You forgot the casualties at the army base when the munitions storage building was destroyed."

"I did not forget that," the judge retorted. "That was a Kurdish action and, even though it was meant to aid you in your escape, it was performed strictly by Iranian locals. But for your interest, estimates place the loss of life there somewhere between 150 and 175 Iranian and Russian personnel."

Lawson just nodded his head as the judge proceeded to look back at his notes.

"Do you think the goals of the mission justified the loss of life in this situation, Lieutenant?"

Lawson began to feel a slow anger build up but kept his composure. "Sir, when I went into the operation, I expected there might be casualties."

"A simple yes or no should suffice," the judge quickly responded, cutting off Lawson's answer.

"If I may, Sir," Lawson continued as though he was unaware of the judge's order. "There were many things that could not have been planned and things changed radically throughout the operation. Furthermore, the fact that we've delayed the Russians the ability to build such an advanced weapon for anywhere from 2 to 3 years, I feel, made the cost worth it. How many more thousands if not tens of thousands of lives may have been saved because nations still have their airpower to defend themselves. If the Russians had mass produced that weapon, they would be able to take out any aircraft or missiles in their vicinity. Add on top of that that the Iranians would have working models which would have made them much bolder in going after their enemies."

"Mr. Lawson," the judge shouted, "you are not in the position to make policy. What I just heard from you is that you deemed you had the authority to take these actions as your own policy!"

"No, Sir," Lawson quickly responded, "I was given wide latitude to get the documents. I was following orders. If I was influenced by policy, it was the military policy of accomplishing the goal of the operation at all costs. The Senior Command knew that this was a suicide mission. They didn't expect success but they knew they had to try. They picked me because I had enough knowledge of the intelligence gathered in this part of the world to know what would come next if the Russians and Iranians were successful with this development. I also knew that anything short of the success of this mission would radically raise the level of sword rattling. It would embolden the Russians and Iranians and put Israel into a position where they would have to take military action to defend themselves. Sir, with the conditions in the world today, we are a hair trigger away from someone making a mistake resulting in war on a major scale. I took the oath to protect the constitution from enemies both foreign and domestic very seriously. I was doing what I had sworn to do."

Judge Henderson watched Lawson's expressions as Lawson gave his explanation. Henderson looked over his notes once more. "I appreciate your passion, Lieutenant. Your explanation does carry significant weight. In your situation, policy has a lot of gray areas. By the way, what is CAT205?"

Lawson shifted in his chair before he answered, "CAT205 is the designation for the team I am responsible for. CAT means 'Creative Access Team' and 205 is the next sequential team number given out. Our team designation is a new one since all the other teams had a 'GOT' designation meaning 'General Operations Team'."

The judge looked once more at his notes then looked up stating, "I have no further questions. You may step down."

Lawson went back to his seat while looking for expressions from his other team members.

"Will Second Class Petty Officer Nicholas Myers please take the stand," the judge called out as he watched Myers rise from his seat and go to the podium.

"Please raise your right hand," the judge ordered. Myers raised his right hand. The judge continued, "Do you swear that the testimony you're about to give is the truth, the whole truth and nothing but the truth?"

After a short pause, Myers responded, "No".

The judge looked up from his notes then to the other people in the room. He was in a state of confusion. No one had ever refused to take the oath and now he was at a loss as to how to react to this turn of events. What just happened?

"You did understand the oath you were asked to take, did you not?" the judge pressed.

"I understood perfectly well," came Myers response, "and the answer is still 'no'."

Henderson looked once more around the room. "We'll take a 15 minute recess while I try to sort this out," Henderson said as he slammed down the gavel.

The attendees exited the room to the outside hallway then were escorted by marine guards to use the restroom or get drinks from the vending machine in the hallway. After approximately 10 minutes, they returned to the secure room to continue. Once the board members entered the room, Henderson continued his questioning of Myers.

"Let me get this correct, Petty Officer Myers," Henderson began. "Are you saying that you refuse to take the oath and if so, what is your reasoning?"

Myers stood at the podium looking over each of the board members while he gathered his thoughts. He could tell they were not happy and, in fact, greatly dissatisfied by his refusal to take the oath.

"With full respect to your position and rank and that of your role as an honorable judge, I am refusing to take the oath because of the conditions given in it," Myers replied. "I am asked to tell the whole truth. I might be able to do that if I was allowed to do so but this board has full control over what they will allow me to say. As such, the potential of me telling the whole truth is very limited. I am not going to pledge to do something when it is out of my control to do so. Furthermore, even if I'm saying I will just tell the truth but am not allowed to give the criteria for the reasons for my statements, then you'll only hear part of the truth which may make it appear as though it is a lie. I will not put my reputation in jeopardy or face the potential of perjury because I was not able to provide the facts supporting my statements. One additional item, why is it we must take the oath if the only option is to say 'yes'. This appears to be a little disingenuous if the only option is to answer a question that should have more than one answer available. If it only allows for a 'yes' then it is not a question but a command that I will tell the truth regardless of what my answer concerning what the oath would be."

Henderson leaned over to his associates as he whispered and they answered back. It was obvious to all that they were in quandary on what to do about the situation. As Henderson looked back down to his reporting sheet for actions taken, he saw the box on the sheet with the statement that 'the witness had taken the oath'. How was he to check the box if the witness refused to take the oath?

"Your argument has some validity," Henderson stated as he proceeded with his thoughts. "My problem is that I must check the box on this document saying that you took the oath before we can proceed. Yet if you don't take the oath then we can't proceed. It's a Catch-22 situation."

"Might I suggest, Sir," Myers responded, "that you contact the commander of JAG to see what he thinks is the best solution to the problem."

Henderson looked over the room with his gaze falling upon Lawson. "You're a smart man, Lieutenant Lawson. How would you resolve this dilemma?"

"Well, Sir," Lawson replied, "why not check the box then write down next to the box about Myers' actions and concerns." There was more whispering and discussion between the members of the board as Lawson continued. "You see Captain, the document is merely a form you must fill out. It doesn't appear to be an order but rather just a checklist."

"Are you an attorney or JAG officer?" Henderson shot back.

Lawson smiled at the question. "No I'm not, Sir. With due respect to you, I answered a question you posed to me. If that solution doesn't appear to work, might I suggest that you go back to Petty Officer Myers' suggestion."

"Your solution appears to be workable," Henderson said sheepishly as he recognized that Lawson had an air of authority about him that went way beyond his rank. Henderson was beginning to like this guy, the type of guy that doesn't back down because he deals with the facts of the present situation and knows he's on firm footing. "I'll use your suggestion and make notes next to the item on the sheet." Henderson proceeded to write as Myers waited at the podium.

"Petty Officer Myers, I'm Colonel Jacobs," the Marine Colonel of the inquiry board interjected. "What was your part of the mission?"

Myers looked down at the podium as he thought through his answer. Colonel Jacobs was a tall, well-conditioned Marine that was well known in the fleet. Myers had met Colonel Jacobs, at that time Major Jacobs, while they were both on the aircraft carrier Harry S. Truman early in Myers' Navy career before Myers went to the USS George Bush. Jacobs had the ability to see little details that made it hard for anyone to get some falsehood past him. Jacobs reminded Myers of the personality of Lieutenant Lawson, always thinking one step ahead of the current situation, two peas in a pod. However, with Lawson, it was about five steps ahead. Myers was thinking of how interesting it would be to get Lawson and Jacobs in the same room.

Myers looked back up from the podium. "My part of the mission was to support Master Gunnery Sergeant Glendenning in destroying an ammo dump of weapons and explosives that were being sent by Iran to the Gaza Strip."

"It appears that you destroyed more than the munitions," Jacobs continued. "It also seems that you were working way outside your normal functions based upon your rating and your history. Why did they pick you?"

Myers began to realize that the question wasn't so much about him but about Admiral Roedl's decision to put him on the mission. Admiral Roedl commanded the operation called 'Tin Cup'. Myers turned to look at Lawson. He could see that Lawson had come to the same conclusion that this appeared to be a witch hunt to get Roedl removed from his command.

"They picked me because they knew they would need someone to handle the electronics portion of the mission. Since we didn't have any tool kit or equipment to carry out the mission, we had to improvise from what we could find."

Jacobs looked down at his notes and continued, "I remember you on the aircraft carrier. You fixed a problem we had with the phalanx weapon system. You're the guy with the advanced engineering degree from MIT. What would be so important that they would take a man of your capability and risk it on just blowing up an ammo dump?"

Captain Henderson broke into the conversation as he could see the questioning getting out of hand. "Colonel," the Captain started as his gaze rested on Jacobs, "I'm not going to have you bring your personal battles into this inquiry. We'll get a chance to question Admiral Roedl as to his reasons when we call him to testify. Now, if you have somewhere important you are going with this questioning, please proceed. Otherwise, we need to continue."

"I'm finished," Jacobs responded as he leaned back in his chair, his focused stare going first to Myers then to Lawson. Lawson recognized this man was very political and a problem.

"Petty Officer Myers, what was the reason for the large loss of life at the ammo dump?" Henderson asked while looking at Myers then at Lawson. Henderson could tell that Lawson had the capability to verbally take Jacobs apart if Jacobs were to question him. Henderson was not about to let that scenario play out.

Myers adjusted his neckerchief on his uniform as he began to answer. "The loss of life was purely coincidental but it was definitely to our benefit. The detonation took place as the Iranian force was overrunning the ammo dump. We had to destroy it at that time because it was the first chance we had to initiate the explosion without killing ourselves and, if we had waited, we would have been captured and our setup would have been discovered and disabled. The mission would have failed."

"Thank you Petty Officer, you may step down," Henderson said while looking at Colonel Jacobs. "Admiral Roedl will be here in half an hour so we are going to move our schedule around. We will have Master Gunnery Sergeant Glendenning testify after Admiral Roedl. We'll take a twenty minute break and continue at 10:40 hours. Might I remind the witnesses they are not to talk to each other during the recess." With that the gavel came down after which Henderson motioned to Jacobs to come with him.

While the others went down the hallway to the vending machines, Captain Henderson and Colonel Jacobs went into the private conference room. Henderson motioned for Jacobs to sit.

"Jack, what were you doing in there?" Henderson barked as he turned to face Jacobs.

"Well, Mark," Jacobs responded, "I don't like the way Roedl does his business or how his teams work. They don't follow protocol, they have no rules and they lack any sort of military discipline. Roedl doesn't supply his people with the proper materials or equipment to carry out their missions and this mission put us on the edge of a shooting war with Iran because of the large loss of life."

"I understand your concerns," Henderson replied. "You must keep in mind that this is not an inquiry to determine what they did wrong in the last mission, even though that is what it appears to be. We have to determine their capability as a team to carry out the Operation Scarborough requirements. They have demonstrated that they have the skills to get accomplished whatever is placed before them. Admiral Roedl is somewhat rogue but, in the world of intelligence operations, we can't have an all-military, by-the-book commander running the show. The enemy will always be one step ahead of them. Not an acceptable outcome."

Jacobs thought about Henderson's comments then continued his concerns. "There has got to be better planning. We have no idea what Lawson or Myers or even Norman is going to do and whether we will get the outcome we want. They must come up with a plan that we can feel comfortable about!"

"OK, you want to have some control over the operation, I understand that" said Henderson. "The problem with that approach is our bureaucracy. If a plan is produced, it will pass through the hands of the reviewers and logistics people at the Pentagon. That means that there will be numerous people that will see the plan and the risk of exposure is high. If we don't know the plan, it does not have the risk of finding its way into the hands of our enemies. Besides, it would take them several days to approve the plan and we don't have that luxury."

Jacobs nodded his head in agreement even though he felt this went against the best traditions of the Marine Corps.

"Might I add something else for you to consider?" Henderson asked then continued without waiting for a response. "Lieutenant Lawson is someone you don't want to lock horns with. You may have the advantage of rank, by a wide margin, but Lawson is no respecter of rank. He respects character. If you get political with him he will shred you like a discarded classified document. He thinks on his feet, is very creative and, as Admiral Roedl has said, appears to be three to four steps ahead of the thinking of those opposing him. You know Commander Blaine Samoylev over at the ONI?"

Jacobs nodded his head 'yes'. "I worked with him on the Defense Intelligence Committee's internal mole problem last year. Nothing gets past that guy. I also heard rumors that he took out the Russian agent 'Tripoli'."

"What you say is true," Henderson replied. "Samoylev is quite capable. However, Lawson brought him down a couple of pegs when Samoylev challenged Lawson over Lawson's view of how a mole in the ONI was going to get out of the building. According to a couple of officers in the Special Operations Group at ONI, Roedl threatened to bust Samoylev back to Lieutenant if Samoylev kept interrupting Lawson's explanation of how he thought the spy would get out. Turns out Lawson was right on target as to the plan and had analyzed the situation beyond what anyone had thought was actually happening. Lawson is not political in any way. He hates the politics of the military. He just wants to get the job done and I dare anyone to keep him from his goal."

"So You're saying he's kind of like Greg Boyington and the VMF214 turmoil in the World War II Pacific war?" Jacobs questioned.

"Worse," Henderson replied. "Unlike Boyington, Lawson has all of this advanced technology at his disposal and he knows how to think and how to use it. Now, it's about time we got back out to the room. I feel we've got enough information to move forward. What's your assessment?"

Jacobs walked around the room for a couple of minutes, thinking about the options. "I say we go with the team we've got. Myers and Norman appear to be the technical brains on this effort. If what you say about Lawson is true, he appears to be the person to drive this effort forward. Gunny Glendenning has the maturity to keep the other three under control. Gunny's twenty-two years of experience in the Marine Corps and his knowledge of the legalities of military regulations gives me some comfort that there is someone there to rein the other three in if things get too chaotic. We've got three, maybe four days to find out why those pictures are so important. I say go." Upon hearing Jacobs' remarks, Henderson realized that Jacobs' assessment was from a military rank perspective and not a capability one. "Quite a useless piece of information," Henderson thought to himself.

Henderson rubbed the ribbons on his uniform as he looked at the clock. "Let's get back into the room." They both walked out the door, joining up with the Marine security detail to go back into the inquiry room.

Chapter 2

Scarborough

"You can use all the quantitative data you can get, but you still have to distrust it and use your own intelligence and judgment." - *Alvin Toffler*

Admiral Roedl had arrived and sat down in the row of chairs closest to the front in the spectator area. As everyone assembled in the room, Henderson addressed the group. "We don't need to have any further testimony. I would like to request that Admiral Roedl, Commander Norman, Lieutenant Lawson, Gunny Glendenning and Petty Officer Myers remain here. The rest of you are dismissed. That includes our inside Marine security people."

With Henderson's order given, everyone except those he named left the room as Henderson motioned for Admiral Roedl to take over the meeting. Roedl stepped up to the inquiry board table and sat down in front of a laptop computer. Keying in some data from the keyboard, the video screen in the room came alive with a picture of Big Ben and the parliament buildings in London, England. He looked at the individuals in the room then spoke. "You were all called together to be the core of an operation called 'Operation Scarborough'. Commander Norman will be in command of this effort. She may task the team members as she feels fit. As with all of our operations, she may transfer command to one of you other members during certain parts of the operation as she sees fit and may take back command when she feels it is necessary. Any questions on the command structure?"

Everyone looked around to see if there were any issues to Admiral Roedl's command setup then waited for him to continue. "The first picture you see here," he said while pointing to the Big Ben picture on the screen, "was captured yesterday. Captain Henderson is handing out the memorandum letter created last night that will help you get a basic understanding of the issue."

Henderson gave each person a copy of the letter, reaching Lawson last. He leaned over to Lawson as he gave him the paper and whispered, "This concerns North Korea. These pictures mean something to them. You're to manage the cryptology portion of this effort to find out what these pictures mean." Lawson nodded his head as he took the letter.

The letter read,

"Issue: Digital pictures being sent to North Korea by individual or Individuals located in the U.S. Capitol building. Importance of pictures is unknown.

Details: Fort Gordon NSA Cryptographic Listening Post retrieved three digital photos being sent from Congressman Jules Latershan's office to a senior military officer in the North Korean intelligence branch. Photo 1 is of the Parliamentary Building with Big Ben in London. Photo 2 is of the outside of a store in Paris. Photo 3 is of a fire department in New York. What the significance or intent of the photos is unknown.

Needs: (1) We need to determine if Congressman Latershan is responsible for the transmission of those photos or if someone else as hacked his system and IP address. (2) We must find out what significance these photos have and what they are being used for. Are these targets or something more sinister. (3) We believe we are limited in time to get answers. The fact that the three photos were transmitted in the past 10 days implies something is to happen soon. Urgent to act on it."

After a couple of minutes Roedl spoke, "Now that you all have had time to see the contents of the letter, here is what I need from you. Commander Norman and I have already discussed the components of this effort. As you can see, there is an issue about the pictures in question going to North Korea sent from California Congressman Jules Latershan's office in the House of Representatives building called the Rayburn building. Latershan in on the House Intelligence Committee, so it is critical that we find out if he or one of his staff is feeding information to a North Korean General that is in charge of their weapons technology and testing group. The messages also appeared to be forwarded to a Chinese Colonel in the Chinese foreign intelligence branch according to Josh Henry. This appears to prove that China is helping North Korea."

"Josh Henry?" Henderson exclaimed. "How is he involved in this operation?"

"He's not," Roedl answered. "I merely asked him to see if the messages went anywhere. He checked the dark web and found this evidence. Now, this team will occupy one of the offices in the Rayburn building, Room 2337, on the third floor near the congressman's office. The person normally occupying that office went on a two week vacation today so you shouldn't be interrupted for the time we have to do this. Any questions so far?"

'Gunny' Glendenning was first to respond. "What is the level of security for these offices in the Rayburn office building?" Everyone turned from Gunny to the Admiral to hear the answer.

"Each room has a key-code pass card," Roedl explained. "You put your card in the slot at the top of the keypad and it will let you in if your code matches. Each one of you will get a card. The code has been changed so that only you assigned to this operation can get in. The present occupant of that room cannot get in until he receives a new key card. If he requests one, Commander Norman will have to approve his request before he will be issued one. This will give the team the opportunity to get everything out of the room that belongs to us before he goes in. One other note, all the rooms have a code entry slot on the telephone to use the phone. It's a secure line environment. You are not to use someone else's card, only your own to make any calls. Also, the phone line is the only access you have to go outside of the facility on your computer. You will have to insert the card into the phone and enter your passcode on the computer screen to get any outside data connection. The security system registers each call and the number dialed when using the phone and any IP addresses when you go out on the internet. Any other questions before I continue?"

They all nodded 'no' as Henderson interrupted with his comment, "You all understand that this has the highest security priority. Nothing leaves this room and you only have conversations about this subject in Room 2337 or the Admiral's office at the Kennedy Irregular Warfare Center. By the way, Room 2337 will be swept for bugs and wires every day. Is all this all understood?" Everyone said 'Yes' in unison.

It was Myers that put a can of worms into the discussion with his comment which left everyone wondering as to the safety of their effort. He said, "You all do realize that the newest bugging equipment captures video and conversations without actively transmitting until it has collected about ten minutes of conversation then sends it in a quick burst that takes thirty seconds to a minute based upon the closeness it has to a cell tower. So sweeping a room once a day is useless except for the cheaper bugs that transmit all the time. You have to have an active monitor in the room that is constantly looking for frequencies emanating from the room so these bursts can be captured. It's also possible for the device to activate when someone is using their cellphone nearby where the bug locks on the phone's signal and sends the burst on the same signal the phone is using."

In Lawson's estimation, the look on everyone's face after Myers finished was priceless. It reminded him of a person walking out to a parking lot to find their car was no longer there…panic. It was Roedl that got them back on track.

"OK, everyone, let's settle down," he shouted as conversations were going on around the room. "Let's deal with this operation and I'll ask Captain Henderson to address the issue brought up by Myers' concerns. Any other questions before we continue?" It was Lawson that provided the next interruption.

"I have a concern," Lawson started. "With your permission, Admiral, I like to know the people I'm working for or with. We may be devious to those on the outside of our operations but we have to have absolute honesty when we're dealing with one another."

"Do you feel that someone in this group is not playing well, Lawson?" Roedl interjected.

"Well, Admiral," Lawson quipped, "Captain Henderson is known around here as a senior JAG officer and headed up our inquiry. However, everything I've seen of him today reeks of intel not lawyer. Who and what is he?" Roedl looked at Henderson while Henderson smiled.

"Didn't I tell you, Captain, that Lawson would see through you?" Roedl said.

"Yes, you did, Admiral," Henderson responded. "For everyone's information which stops at the door of this room, I do the job of a JAG officer but I'm actually a deep cover intel officer. I do a lot of work inside the halls of congress and the departments attached to the White House as a JAG officer but my primary job is to look for disturbances in the force as a Star Wars fan would say. In other words, a spy looking for a spy. That's why I'm involved in this operation. Any further questions?" No one responded.

Admiral Roedl continued as he switched from one picture to another, "Back here at the ranch, we were talking about this picture of Big Ben. There are two other pictures. This one of a retail shop in Paris, France and this one of the 21st Fire Department Engine Company in New York City. We need to find the significance of the pictures."

Lawson and Myers started whispering back and forth as Roedl and Henderson looked on. After a moment, Roedl interrupted them, "What has got you two in such a deep discussion?"

"Well Sir," Myers answered, "We think the photos may be their own answer. Are these photos digital in their original format or have they been modified before you got them?"

Henderson looked at the screen then replied, "These are in their original format, just as we received them from Fort Gordon. Why do you think the pictures are the answer?" Myers looked to Lawson to carry the conversation forward.

"We think we might be able to prove if these pictures are just someone's curiosity or something more. Do you have PhotoEngin2 photo editor on your computer?" Lawson said while walking to the laptop computer on the table.

Admiral Roedl moved the mouse and clicked on an icon on the computer. "This computer has the full version of PhotoEngin2. What do you want to do?" Myers and Lawson continued their discussion. Finally, Lawson took the computer mouse from Roedl.

"I am going to work on the Big Ben picture since that was the most recent one you got," Lawson instructed while he opened the picture, and saved it under a different name so that, if he damaged the original beyond repair, he would still have a copy. "First, I'm going to make a backup copy of the Big Ben picture then I'm going to open the photo editing program and try some things on it." Roedl looked at Lawson then at Henderson. Henderson nodded 'yes' so Roedl told Lawson, "go ahead and do what you were going to do. I'll assume the risk if something goes wrong. We're not connected to any wifi or internet connection so you should be able to do your thing without a hidden Trojan horse getting into the network."

Lawson opened the file for the picture using the photo editor. The picture of Big Ben with the parliament buildings came up within the editing box of the software on the screen. Lawson was about to click on the picture when Myers stopped him and said, "If you're going to take any action on the picture, you may want to drag the picture rather than delete the suspected layer you're on. Deleting it may delete the whole picture if it's not in layers. It's a 'TIFF' file extension so it should support layers."

Lawson looked at the picture and realized Myers was right. Clicking on the picture and selecting the 'Select Layers' option, Lawson moved the pointer to the right and, as he did so, the top layer of the picture in blue color moved off of the main picture as he moved the layer to the right, exposing a red-colored layer. He clicked on the red layer and moved it to the right and as he did so, moving the layer exposed a green-colored layer underneath the red layer. Then he moved the green layer off of the main picture area. Underneath the green layer was a text table of 49 rows each with 29 columns made up of five-digit numbers. The first row, first column number was '21398'. Both Lawson and Myers looked at the data table while Roedl and Henderson watched the main video screen to follow what they were doing.

Chapter 3

Have a Little Faith

"Man is not what he thinks he is, he is what he hides."
- André Malraux

"That's incredible what you guys just did in a ten minute period. I'm impressed," Henderson said while looking at the screen. "How did you figure this out?"

Myers looked up at the screen on the computer and responded, "Lawson mentioned that in his intel training class they talked about using pictures to hide code underneath the picture. It was a gamble but it made sense. The bigger problem is going to be figuring out the code. We've got some ideas on how to do it but we're going to need unmodified copies of all three pictures. How soon can we get them? We'll also need a computer the 'Basic' language application and a 'C' language program."

"I'll request the pictures be sent to you on a jump drive by courier," said Henderson.

Roedl immediately raised a red flag. "That will take days to go through the approvals and security validations to get them the files. We need this stuff now! There is only one way for them to get them now and that is to take this computer with them."

Henderson looked disturbed at the suggestion but realized that was their only option. "You realize we have to get this past the security outside and we are in violation of about eighteen federal and military codes if we do so. Are you willing to stake your career and, possibly, your freedom on this venture?"

"So," Roedl responded, "How did this computer get in here?"

"A Marine Security guy brought it in."

Roedl smiled for a moment then looked at Gunny Glendenning. "How long would it take you to go back to your berthing area to get your dress blues and get back here?"

Gunny looked at the clock. It was 11:20 AM so he figured the traffic would not be bad. "About half an hour, Sir." Gunny had been around Lawson long enough to know that to accomplish anything, you had to break the rules. However, there seemed to be a lot of rules about to be broken. He knew this was a gamble but what if the code was something indicating lives would be lost if they didn't act. He knew he was about to break his twenty-two years of Marine discipline. The book just got thrown out.

"You better get going," Roedl said while his face showed his appreciation for what Gunny was going to do. "Change over into your dress blues at berthing and bring your sidearm that goes with that uniform when you come back. Here is the entry card to get back in the facility and here is the one for this floor. They have your picture and ID on them. Don't ask how I got them, just get moving."

"Aye, Sir," Gunny said as he headed for the door. "Ye be hoping my angel takes the lead on this one," he said in his Irish lilt as he opened the door to be escorted out by Marine security.

Lawson knew Gunny would get some static from the commissioned officers at the Basic Officer's Quarters (BOQ) where he was staying since he was a senior enlisted Marine and the officers didn't like it when an enlisted person was forced upon them for berthing. It also irritated the officers that Gunny had a room to himself when the junior commissioned officers had to live two to a room. So, Gunny would have to consider the time it would take for him to face the scrutiny he would get from the admissions desk at the BOQ facility every time he went in.

Henderson looked at Roedl as Lawson sat down and started laughing. Henderson turned to Lawson and began to wonder what just happened. Lawson looked at Roedl and said, "You knew this was the only way to get the pictures without the delay, didn't you? Seeing you had the entry cards already made up, I'll bet you've got a letter pinned to Gunny's uniform at the BOQ that authorizes for him to take possession of this computer and all its contents."

Roedl looked awkwardly at Lawson like he had just got caught stealing money out of his dad's wallet. "I knew that once those pictures were sent from Fort Gordon to the Fort Belvoir, Virginia, it would take us a minimum of a week to get copies of them and they would, most likely, have been data compressed for storage. That would have made it impossible for you guys to do what you did today. As for a letter authorizing Gunny to take possession of the computer and contents, it's in his dress uniform hat. He should have no problem getting the computer out of here because the letter is signed by the Chief of Naval Operations."

Henderson sat down and exhaled as he began to see Colonel Jacob's previous concern about Roedl. "You guys really don't know what a Naval Regulation is, do you? Commander Norman, how can you quietly sit there when you see all that's going on? Do you feel they are justified in their actions?"

Norman thought over Henderson's question for a moment then replied, "I wrote the letter Gunny is going to use to get the computer out of here. By the way, the CNO would have to be included in your concerns because he signed the letter after he was told what we planned to do. You see, Captain, sometimes the rule book gets in the way of keeping America safe. I gave my oath to protect and defend the United States. I don't recall any part of that oath saying that I will follow a law that prevents me from keeping my oath."

"Justify it however you want, Commander," Henderson said while walking toward the door. "I will have to report this to the FBI."

"Go ahead and report it," Roedl responded. "When Seattle or New York gets hit by a nuclear weapon from North Korea and several million people die, you sleep well. Your conscience will somehow justify your interference."

Henderson stopped at the door and glared back at Roedl. "You don't know if this code has anything to do with a nuke attack!"

"And nobody except the North Koreans and possibly one mole in the Rayburn building knows if this could be a presage to an attack," Norman said while watching Henderson. "It appears that all three pictures could be targets. Big Ben and parliament are obvious targets. All three pictures are targets North Korea has threatened to strike. Are you still willing to gamble on your assumption that this code has no real significance?"

Lawson stepped back into the conversation, "Remember your history Captain. There were a number of indicators just before the attack on Pearl Harbor that were ignored, most of them because people didn't want to go outside the rules. And one other question, what if Greg Boyington had not broken the rules and took over the VMF214? My guess is that the battle in the slot, Northern Solomons and Guadalcanal would have taken much longer. Boyington's pilots reduced the number of Japanese planes by 94 which had an impact on the outcome. And that was just one of the many squadrons in the area."

Henderson removed his hand from the doorknob. "Jacobs brought up Boyington earlier. How much of a possibility is a threat coming from the messages in these pictures?"

Lawson could see Henderson struggling with the decision of what to do. Myers broke in to the conversation to add his voice. "The odds of it being a message that tracks us to war may be low but the problem is that we don't know the odds right now because we don't know what the message says. I'd say the odds are not the problem but the risk is. By not knowing, we are sitting just like Washington, DC was on December 5th of 1941, two days away from the Pearl Harbor attack. They had time to act but very few people wanted to risk their careers, their lives or their sacred honor when the news on the tensions was staring them right in the face. We have some parallels to that event. First, the US and Britain had levied heavy restrictions on Japanese steel and rubber before World War II. The embargos put Japan in a position where they had to do something. We're doing that with North Korea. We have put heavy sanctions on them and the same problem we had with Japan exists. Removing the sanctions allows for North Korea to accelerate their weapons development. Same issue we had with 1940 Japan. Second, Japan was a rogue nation that had aspirations of controlling the Eastern Asian area. North Korea appears to be on the same course. I don't want to have taken no action because I assumed the messages in these pictures have the better chance of being harmless. The actions and evidence of North Korea's actions we see today don't give us that confidence."

They waited in the room for the next ten minutes in idle conversation while Lawson had turned off the main screen and was looking at documents on the computer screen. One document caught his attention. Its cover page was labeled 'SECNAV M-5510.36 Department of the Navy – Information Security Program'. An idea began to form in his mind as how to get the computer and the associated pictures to Room 2337 without violating regulations. He motioned for Roedl to come over.

"Admiral," Lawson began, "Does Gunny have a DD-2501 courier authorization card?"

Roedl looked at the screen. It was a long time since he had read the Information Security Program document in detail. Lawson's question offered an avenue to get the computer and associated photos out of the room without violating U.S. code or regulations. "This might work," Roedl observed while looking at the screen. "The photos have not yet been classified. Fort Belvoir will probably take several days to do so. As such, the photos we have don't have any digital classification stamps on them. So at the present time, only the computer is classified as 'Top Secret'. Gunny can transport the computer as he is cleared to handle and move top secret materials as part of his role at the Kennedy facility. All he needs to provide is a 5511/10 form which is the record of receipt and show his courier card. Since I just gave him a new card two months ago, his picture should well match how he looks now. Good catch, Jim."

Commander Norman whispered something to Myers. Myers went over to the computer then realized that the pictures were not on the computer but on the jump drive plugged into the computer. He was sure that the paperwork to obtain control of the computer did not include control of the jump drive. He started clicking furiously on the mouse buttons as he moved the mouse around. Lawson saw Myers activity but knew that other things were more pressing for action as Roedl stepped next to Lawson. There was a knock on the door and the Gunnery Sergeant in charge of the Marine guard detail outside opened the door. "There's a Marine Master Gunnery Sergeant out here that says he has orders to take the computer. I need to talk to one of you."

Roedl put his hand on Lawson's shoulder. "You need to go out there to resolve this problem," Roedl said. "Colonel Jacobs is in charge of Marine security for this facility and he and I don't quite see eye to eye on things. If I negotiate the release of the computer, it will give Jacobs new ammunition to interfere with our efforts, maybe even stop us. The Marine guards have changed personnel due to the change of the watch. Gunny left before they changed and since it's after noon, the guards out there have not seen Gunny Glendenning or know what he looks like so they don't know that he was previously in this room"

"Good point, Sir," came Lawson's response. "It's a good decision for me to handle this because while Myers was on the stand, Jacobs questioned him in a way that made it obvious he was going after you. Henderson stopped Jacobs from continuing the questioning because you were not there to defend yourself. It was obvious in the inquiry that Jacobs put a target on your back and was out to get you." Lawson stepped out the door into the hallway, leaned back on table that the phone and sign-in board was sitting on and proceeded to hear the concerns.

The Marine Gunnery Sergeant of the security detail was holding a sheet of paper in his hand. "Colonel Jacobs says that the computer is not to leave the room under any circumstances", he said while showing Lawson the paper. "It says here that Master Gunny Glendenning is to take the computer and transfer it to some undisclosed location. I can't allow that to happen based upon my orders."

Lawson looked at the paper. It was a written authorization for Glendenning to take possession of the computer. "Who's signature is this at the bottom of the authorization?" Lawson asked. The Marine guard looked at the sheet and winced.

"It's signed by the Chief of Naval Operations," the guard replied. "But if I turn the computer over to the Master Gunny, the Colonel will have my ass. Besides, Jacobs says that Admiral Roedl's people are devious enough to provide a false document with forged signatures to get what they want."

Lawson smiled and handed the guard the phone handset. "You have the CNO's number on your call list. Put your phone card in the slot and give him a call. Verify he signed it." The guard looked around at the other marines on his detail while recognizing he may not be a Gunnery Sergeant for long. He put his key card in the phone slot, dialed the number and waited.

"Good afternoon, Ma'am," he said into the phone receiver. "I need to get verification from the CNO on a letter I received." After a moment, he spoke once more, "I understand he is not to be disturbed." Lawson tapped the guard on the shoulder causing the guard to say, "Just a moment, Ma'am."

Lawson looked down at the authorization sheet and said, "The person answering the phone is probably the CNO's admin. Ask her to check the list of authorizations signed by the CNO for authorization ID 'AU20160131162001A' on the list and verify it's been signed off by the CNO." Lawson handed the sheet to the guard.

The guard asked the question concerning the authorization list, waited for almost a minute, then responded with, "OK, I guess the order is real." He turned to Lawson and asked, "Is it OK for me to keep this authorization. It's the only thing protecting me from the Colonel." Lawson looked at Gunny Glendenning, saw that Glendenning had a copy of the authorization and nodded 'yes'.

Lawson stepped back inside the room. "Get the computer and let's go", he said while Myers was shutting down the computer and disconnecting its power source. Handing the computer to Lawson, Myers went out the door first with Lawson, Roedl, Norman and Henderson following.

As Lawson started down the hallway, a voice behind him shouted, "Stop there, Sir!" Lawson looked back to see the Gunnery Sergeant facing Lawson while his hand was on the top of his weapon in the holster and he was setting the phone handset back down. Lawson figured the Marine had just talked to Colonel Jacobs, so Lawson waited as the Marine approached him.

"You have authorization to take the computer but not the jump drive," he said while pulling the memory device from the side of the computer. "Great," Lawson thought as the Marine took the jump drive. "The computer does us no good without the photos on the jump drive."

Roedl looked at Lawson and said, "Let's go, we're done here," as they all proceeded down the hallway. Lawson was at a loss on what to do next. Meanwhile, Myers was smiling at Lawson and Roedl as they continued out of the building.

"Don't you guys have a little faith," Myers bantered. "You all act like this is the end of the world."

"You back on that 'let's have a little bit of faith' trip, reverend," Gunny Glendenning chided while Lawson looked around and could see how depressed everyone was. Gunny knew Myers well, having spent a lot of time with him on the aircraft carrier George Bush and of Myers' close walk with Jesus Christ. He trusted Myers to always be honest with his opinion but this opinion seemed strange, even for him. "I admire your faith but they have the jump drive and we don't."

"I copied the photos onto the computer," was Myers response. Everyone stopped in their tracks.

Roedl was first to respond. "That's impossible. These secure computers don't have the ability to copy anything from any of the USB ports and we had no connection to the internal network."

Myers smiled as he took the computer from Lawson. "This piece of equipment is just that, a piece of equipment. It only does what we tell it to do. I got the photos into the computer."

"Please explain how you circumvented the security measures, particularly the measure that restricts moving anything into the computer from a USB port," Henderson questioned.

"It's easy," Myers explained. "They removed the 'cmd.exe' file that opens the 'Command Prompt' screen from the 'C' drive. However, they did not remove the recovery drivers from the 'D' drive. I pulled code from one of the drivers and changed the code to reactivate the USB data handler for copying data from an external device on the USB. I put the photo files into a folder under documents called 'Travel Itinerary 6-23-15' so if the Marine detail had someone that could verify the photos weren't on the system, they wouldn't find the photo files. I set the folder attributes to 'hidden' so that a directory search of the photo file names would show 'no results'."

"Could you say that in a language we can all understand," Norman requested.

"Sure," Myers responded. "I changed some code on the computer that allowed for me to copy the files off of the jump drive. End of story." Everyone laughed as they headed for the parking area.

"Everyone meet me in one hour at the Rayburn building, room 2337." Roedl said as he headed toward his car. "That includes you, Henderson. Everyone change into civilian clothes. And Lawson, Gunny will take control and provide security for the computer." Everyone acknowledged Roedl's order as they headed for their cars.

Chapter 4

The Room

"Everything we see hides another thing, we always want to see what is hidden by what we see." - Rene Magritte

Lawson walked down the hall on the third story of the Rayburn House Office Building. After a few wrong turns in the confusing building arrangement, he finally arrived at room 2337 and knocked on the door as he looked at the nameplate showing the name 'Rod Lavlery' just above the pushbuttons for the passkey entry device. As he was looking at the nameplate, the door opened with Commander Norman holding the door from the inside. She just smiled as Lawson stepped into the room. He could see that Admiral Roedl, Captain Henderson and Petty Officer Myers were there. They just nodded acknowledgement as he walked in.

The room was larger than he thought it would be. There was a heavy computer desk facing the window, a bookcase with numerous books against the left wall, two document safes next to the desk and under the window, a whiteboard against the right wall, a coffee maker at the far corner of the right wall with a detailed map of the world above it, a refrigerator at the near corner of the right wall and stacks of books and documents against the same wall the door was on. There were six chairs in the room which Lawson thought was unusual. The room had one eight-foot fluorescent overhead light that was turned on by a switch near the door on the same wall as the bookcase. The desk was clean except for the phone and a large video monitor. The room was painted off-white with the typical commercial false ceiling. He then noticed the electronic device sitting on top of the bookcase, the active bug scanner. He also noticed the books in the bookcase, books on accounting, science, history and math. There were also several books on computer programming and help books for some commonly used applications for creating documents, spreadsheets and presentations. A lot of the books appeared to be college textbooks. He figured that the occupant of the room was a recent college graduate, someone just breaking into the political landscape.

Lawson nodded at the Admiral then stepped to the window to see lawns and flower gardens in his view. The bushes stretched along the edge of the building with the well-manicured lawn taking up most of the scene going to Independence Avenue. Lawson turned to look at the others in the room.

"We're waiting on Gunny before we start," Admiral Roedl stated as everyone waited. Just as he said that, a knock one the door drew their attention. Commander Norman opened the door to Gunny Glendenning swearing something about a drunk having designed the building. Even though he was familiar with the building, he was always getting lost in its confines.

"Sorry I'm late," he said while he walked in with the computer under his arm and still wearing his dress blue uniform, "Too many wrong turns."

He sat the computer on the desk as Norman checked the door to make sure it was closed. Everyone was smiling as, they too, had difficulty navigating the hallways of the building. Admiral Roedl motioned for their attention. Once they were facing him, he handed out a plastic card and a small piece of paper to each of them and proceeded to give instructions.

"These are your entry cards to get into the room. The entry pad requires that you first put the card in slot above the pad then, within sixty seconds, you must enter the four-digit code you have on your paper into the keypad to get in. You have thirty seconds to open the door, remember that if you're carrying a bunch of stuff. No sharing of cards or codes with each other. Memorize your number and if you forget your number, you have three tries to get it right. I suggest you stop after two tries and wait for one of your team members to arrive to open the door. If you fail after three tries, the room is locked down until the Capitol Police can come, verify your authorization to enter and open the door for you. That can take up to three hours to happen. Everyone with me so far?" Everyone nodded, then Roedl continued.

"There are two safes in here. Your safe is the one on the left, the one on the right belongs to the present occupant that's on vacation. Don't mess with it…hear me, Lawson. I heard what happened on board the Teddy Roosevelt between you and your captain. "

Lawson gave a guilty grin. "Yes, Sir,"

"Your safe has some advanced capabilities to protect our effort. Use it for any sensitive information or evidence. Forget about the rules concerning putting only 'Top Secret' documents in it. Anything of value to this effort goes in there when no one is going to be in the room. The safe must not be moved. A GPS device is built into the unit and if the safe is moved more than six inches, you'll have a Marine security team coming through your door within a couple of minutes. The facility will instantly go into lockdown the moment it is moved which will make a lot of congressmen very angry. To get into the safe, you must put your card into the slot on the front of the safe and punch in your four-digit code. The safe registers each entry made and the person entering it. It also takes a picture of you as soon as you put your card into the slot, even if you don't enter."

Myers stopped the Admiral's instructions. "I worked on these safes aboard the George Bush. If you enter the wrong code on the keypad three times, it will pull your card into the safe and won't give it back."

"Glad you brought that up, Myers," Roedl said while pulling an item out of his pocket. "That was a point I wasn't familiar with. Now, everyone, this is a panic button that stays in this room. Put it somewhere that makes it easy to reach. If someone tries to break into the room while you're in it or you find yourself in a situation where someone outside of the team is trying to interfere with efforts or wants to confiscate your materials, grab this device and press the button. You'll have half of the Marine Corps here within minutes."

There was a knock on the door which seemed to irritate everyone but Roedl. Norman opened the door to a man carrying several garment bags with suits, shirts and ties in them. Roedl motioned the man in. "Now, to all of you, we don't want you to be coming here in uniform. You need to blend in with the environment. Almost everyone wears suits and ties in this facility. It's congress and this is a congressional building. Lawson, Myers and Henderson, these suits, ties and shirts are for you. Your names are on the garment bags and the clothing has been made to fit you perfectly. Norman, your garment bag has three different outfits, shoes and blouses. All of you, do not go out and buy other clothing to work here. Each of your outfits have components built into them that allows for special readers to verify you. This is essential to get you into some secure areas immediately."

"Sir," Lawson interrupted, "Why aren't we working in a SCIF room rather than here?"

Roedl thought for a moment then responded, "For any of you who don't know, a SCIF is a sensitive compartmented information facility. They are rooms specially built to protect conversations and electronics from outside interception. It is usually the only rooms authorized for the discussion of highly sensitive information and there are several in this building. However, since we are also trying to find out how the information is getting out from this facility to North Korea, this is where we must work, near the congressman in question."

Lawson took a closer look at the room while Roedl turned to have a discussion with the man bringing in the clothing. Lawson noticed that the room and desk were devoid of any pictures except the map on the wall and a small picture of a sailboat taped in the upper left-hand corner of the whiteboard next to the coffee maker. He stepped over to the refrigerator and looked inside. The typical menu of a computer geek … old pizza and cold beer.

Admiral Roedl interrupted his thoughts as the admiral continued his instructions. "Gunny will remain in uniform as he has been assigned as a military defense security rover. We made sure that Congressman Latershan received a top secret document that he has to maintain under his control. It fits within his job description since he's a member of the Congressional Intelligence Committee. This means that Gunny has to check the congressman's office once every four hours during working hours and recheck his office once the congressman leaves to ensure no classified documents are left out. He will be also observing activities in the congressman's sphere that may tell us who is sending out the information and how it's getting sent. Lawson and Myers will be working to break the code so they'll spend a majority of their time in this room. Norman is in charge and will be wandering the halls of this facility while making contact with different individuals. She will be in this room each morning and afternoon to get updates from you two and Gunny which she will then discuss with me at the Kennedy facility. We have three, maybe four days to find out what these pictures mean and what is going on between the congressman, his staff or some other entity and North Korea, any questions? Oh, one side note, to get to the outside on the phone or with the computer, you must put your keycard into the phone slot. And don't forget to retrieve your card from the phone before you leave the room. You will not, under any circumstances, go outside of our internal network. No internet! Use your phones if you need to get internet access."

They all agreed to the Admiral's terms as he and the wardrobe guy turned to open the door. Once they left, Myers booted up the computer.

Gunny, Lawson, Norman and Myers were looking at the screen as Myers pulled up the page with the code numbers on it. "I think the first thing we must do is write a program to convert all of the numbers on the page to ASCII code." Lawson agreed.

"What is ASCII code?" Norman asked while looking at the screen.

"It's the code that computers use to translate a number to alphanumeric characters by the computer," Lawson began. "The computer converts the numbers we see on the code sheet into characters that can be displayed or printed. The computer can really read only ones and zeros. The ASCII code gives us numbers that, when broken down to ones and zeros, translate into readable characters. An example is, let's say we 'want the letter 'A'. An 'A' is ASCII code '65' as a decimal number converted by the computer to '1000001' in binary ones and zero numbers that the computer 'can read. A 'B' is ASCII code '66' or '1000010' and so forth. It's the way we communicate to the computer and it communicates with us. With me so far?"

"I think so," Norman said as she nodded her head.

"What will that give us?" Gunny asked.

"It might be that the message is buried as an ASCII message in the groups of numbers you see on this page. There are forty-nine lines, each row made up of twenty-nine columns consisting of five-digit numbers," Lawson explained. "That gives a minimum of one-thousand, four hundred and twenty-one characters. It's a good place to start as the numbers…" At that moment they all turned toward the door as they heard a click of the lock on the door releasing, a beep and the door opening. Admiral Roedl stepped back into the room carrying a gym bag. He sat the bag down with a 'thump' on the desk. Reaching into the bag, he pulled out holsters and pistols for each of them.

"These are .38 caliber pistols," he said while handing each of them a weapon and holster. "The weapons we picked are small so that they can be hidden inside your waistband. Have them on you at all times." Next he handed them each a pack of bullets held in groups of five rounds in a plastic holder. "These are speed loaders. You push the spent cartridges out of the weapon, like this, then, using the speed loader, load the new rounds into the weapon like this," he said while pushing a lever on the cylinder of the weapon that removed all of the bullets from the gun's cylinder. All of the bullets fell out of the gun at the same time. He lined up the bullets in the speed loader to the openings in the cylinder and pushed the speed loader plastic piece to move the bullets into the cylinder. Once again, the bullets all moved into the cylinder at the same time, releasing from the plastic holder. Completing that motion, he flipped the gun to the side causing the cylinder to snap back into the body of the gun. "You are now loaded with a fresh set of rounds."

Each of the members took their weapons and put them inside their belts. "One more thing," Roedl continued, "always wear your suit jackets when leaving the room. Everyone wears suits in the building so it won't be out of place. You need to do this to ensure that no one knows you are carrying a weapon. If you need to go into any of the other federal facilities, show them your federal security ID so that they won't create a scene about you carrying a weapon. Everyone understand?" They all nodded 'yes'.

He looked around at each of them. "Lawson and Gunny, you two are the history geeks," he said while looking at the screen. "I want you to go over to the Library of Congress as soon as I leave here and check on the historical use of pictures overlaying code. We also need to get the latest information on crypto techniques to see if there are new methods of hiding coded messages." They both nodded affirmative. "One other thing, when you are talking to each other, call each other by last names. Don't use any identification of rank as that will raise suspicions. You can call

Master Gunnery Sergeant Glendenning 'Gunny' or 'Master Gunny' as that would be normal for him as a Marine rover but it's also acceptable for retired Marines of that rank. Just for your info, he likes to be called 'Gunny' rather than 'Master Gunny'. The rest of you are last names only. And don't salute me if you see me or each other. Now, you have some work to do." With that, Admiral Roedl stepped out the door, leaving all of them in thought.

"Gunny," Lawson said, breaking the silence, "we need to get over to the Library of Congress."

"On your tail," Gunny said as they both walked out the door. Myers and Norman continued with the ASCII code conversion effort while Lawson and Gunny went on their way.

Once Gunny and Lawson left, Myers continued to work on creating the computer program that would convert the code page numbers into ASCII code. As he did so, Commander Norman brought up a question.

"What is your impression? With the Admiral giving us weapons, do you think he knows of a threat to us that we should know?"

Myers stopped his typing and looked at Norman. He could tell she was serious about a question he hadn't given any thought to. "You've been thinking about this possibility for some time, haven't you?" he said as he turned in his chair to face her.

"I've been thinking about it ever since we had problems getting a copy of these pictures," she responded. "It seems there are people that want to delay us in finding answers. That's all."

Myers thought for a moment then said, "It could be that someone is trying to delay us or that we are seeing the politics of Washington rear its ugly head. There's too much ego and pride in this city and not enough common sense."

While Norman and Myers were talking, Lawson and Gunny had changed to suits, arrived at the Library of Congress and were inside the display areas. Gunny was looking at an original copy under glass of Thomas Paine's 'Common Sense' booklet while Lawson was talking to a Library aide. After a short discussion, he came over to Gunny. "One of the senior library attendants will be helping us in a moment. What are you looking at?"

"The Revolutionary War brochure 'Common Sense'," Gunny answered. "Truly a trigger document that helped get the Revolutionary War moving. It's funny that such a small and simple document could generate such a reaction. It's also funny how it seems that's one characteristic that's lacking in this city." Lawson laughed then turned to a lady touching his arm.

"Mister Lawson?" the lady stated, "I am Kinder Amquist, the librarian for the historical section. Admiral Roedl from the Kennedy Irregular Warfare Center made arrangements to provide you with several books to complete your research. If you come over to the reading floor desks, I will show you where the books are."

Lawson and Gunny followed her to the reading area. It was a large, circular area inside a rotunda layout with many desks arranged in a circular pattern. Each circular row was laid out so that there was room for people to easily move between the rows and desks. The reading area was open to the top of the dome, three stories up, that had large arches at the top being supported by massive, dark marble pillars and smaller, more numerous arches on the next floor down. Around the external areas of the reading area were displays of rare books and historical collections. Looking from the reading area, a person could see the other floors going up on all sides. The architecture, stairs and floors consisted of exquisite polished marble surfaces with oak and mahogany book and display cases. To Lawson, it had a sense of perpetuity and a lasting existence.

They arrived at a desk in the reading area with 'reserved' signs on three of the desks adjoining each other. On the desks were stacks of books. "The Admiral picked out these books for you to do your research," she said while pointing to the desks. "Evan said you may need more books but getting additional books may take some time as they may be stored at one of our off-site locations." They thanked her as they proceeded to look at each of the book spines for titles.

"Evan?" Gunny blurted. "The Admiral's first name is Evan?"

"Yes," Lawson quipped. "He told me that the first day I came on board. When I asked him his first name, he said it was 'admiral'. Later he told me it was 'Evan'." They both laughed which brought glares from other people nearby, a typical library.

Lawson grabbed a book on cryptograms while Gunny began sorting through the history books. He finally landed on one book that caught his attention, 'Charlemagne'. Gunny always had a strong interest in history which was obvious when a person saw his living quarters. He was constantly ordering history books online from booksellers. It was one area where he and Lawson shared an interest. They had many discussions on historical events and why people made certain decisions that affected the outcome of a particular event. Gunny liked Lawson's application of historical lessons to the problems they faced.

Gunny and Lawson spent several hours going through the books when Lawson brought up a point from the crypto book he was reading. "It appears that a common practice in doing pictures overlaying codes was that something in the picture would provide some information on how to decode the message underneath," he whispered to Gunny. The comment drew Gunny's attention.

"You saying that the London picture may have some relationship to the code page we found?" Gunny inquired while looking up to see Lawson looking at his cellphone. Lawson just nodded 'yes'. Gunny went back to his book while thinking about Lawson's observation.

After a few minutes, Lawson broke Gunny's thoughts once more. "Since we are dealing with numbers, it seems that we should be looking for numbers in the pictures," said Lawson. Looking around the room to ensure no one was close enough to hear their conversation, Lawson continued. "We have the Big Ben clock in the London picture, the phone number on the outside of the building in the Paris picture and the number '21' in the New York picture. That appears to be one common element to all three pictures."

Gunny agreed then said, "Don't turn around, but there is a guy across the floor that has been watching us for some time."

Without turning around, Lawson replied to Gunny's observation. "I know, I've been watching him."

"How have you been watching him if your back is to him?" Gunny quizzed.

Lawson pointed to his phone. "It makes a nice mirror when it's turned off." Gunny just shrugged his shoulders and turned back to his book while glancing up once in a while to see what the man was doing.

"You know we should be getting back to the room," Gunny observed while looking at the man across the room. "I've got to do the checking of the congressman's office for classified documents and it's near closing time for the day for the staff. I've still got to get back into my uniform." With that comment, they closed the books, shuffled them around so that no one could determine what books they were looking at and headed out of the library.

The walk back to the Rayburn building was short as the library was situated on the same street as the office building.

While Gunny and Lawson were in the Library, Myers and Norman were in room 2337 as Myers was finishing up the program to convert all of the numbers on the code page to ASCII characters. Once Myers ran the program, they scanned the page for the converted code. One line stood out as the message was easy to pick up. On line ten of the code page was the message 'OUT FEB 1'. Norman looked at the screen as she contemplated the message.

"So, that was easy," she said while trying to discern its meaning. "Could it be something going on or some recommendation to the North Koreans to do something on February 1st?"

Myers leaned back in his chair. "Maybe it's a recommendation to the North Koreans to move something from under cover on the 1st or maybe something we're doing on the 1st." They debated the possibilities for the next two hours on the date but couldn't come up with any solutions.

"You know that message means today as this is February 1st so whatever it is probably already happened. Maybe 'FEB' means something other than a date," Norman said in frustration.

"Welcome to the world of code breaking," Myers replied. "Finding the code is half the job, determining what it means is the other half."

"A question," Norman posed. "You showed me that there are ASCII codes for each letter the screen shows, what about numbers?"

Myers pulled up a list of ASCII characters on the computer. "There are unique ASCII codes for each character we can print. There are the capital letters A through Z, small letters a through z, numbers 0 through 9, punctuation such as asterisks, periods, exclamation marks, spaces and so on. There's also ASCII codes for non-printable commands such as new paragraph, underline, bold and italics, to mention a few."

"But what about the numbers?" Norman repeated.

"Ok," Myers continued. "A zero is an ASCII number forty-eight, a one is an ASCII number forty-nine, a two is an ASCII number fifty. This continues in sequence all the way to number nine that is an ASCII number fifty-seven. The computer reads each ASCII value and presents its equivalent character to the screen."

"So from what you say, if I enter hit the number six on my keyboard, the computer sees that as a fifty-four in ASCII," Norman expounded. "So it's a code the computer can interpret and converts it back on the screen in something that we can interpret."

"You got it," Myers acknowledged.

They continued working on the code message and the possibilities with no other viable possibility than it was a message with the date. They also looked at the other converted characters from the code sheet, trying to find any pattern that would give them more information. After several hours of frustration, they heard a beep at the door followed by Lawson walking into the room.

"Gunny has changed into his uniform and is busy doing his security rounds," Lawson said as he entered the room. Myers was about to show Lawson what they had found when the active bug monitor beeped several times and turned on indicator lights showing that it had gone into 'jamming' mode. "Something is transmitting a fast burst message," Norman said as she pressed buttons on the bug monitor. "Everything that can transmit over the air waves for about four rooms around us will not be able to send out their messages. The monitor will jam signals in the area, preventing the message the bug is trying to send from going out. This will force the bug to keep retrying to transmit which will allow for us to identify where it's transmitting from. Whatever it is that is transmitting, it's not a cellphone. It must be a bug. The locater indicator shows it to be pretty close."

Myers looked at the small screen on the bug monitor. "It indicates that the bug is located about ten feet from the monitor in this direction," Myers ascertained as he pointed toward the stack of books against the wall. Both Myers and Norman began going through the books to see where the bug was located. Lawson stood watching for a moment as Myers and Norman would open a book and thumb through the pages then set the book down. Lawson motioned for Myers to hand him a book and, once receiving the book, Lawson took the book and checked the cover followed by feeling the binding. Both Myers and Norman stopped to see what Lawson was doing. Then they realized that the bug may be small enough to have been put into the spine of the book.

"Either the book will have the center of some pages cut out to put the bug in or it will be present in the spine of the book," Lawson instructed while putting pressure on the spine of one of the larger books. "If it is in the spine, it will have to be one of the larger books, one that's a hardback as a paperback has no room in its spine to embed a bug with the burst transmitter. Even a micro-sized bug would be too large to fit in any other type of book spine due to the size of the transmitter and battery."

They were about halfway through the books when Norman found the bug in the spine of an accounting text book. Cutting the spine and carefully removing the bug, she handed it to Myers. He examined the device, removed a small cover on the bug and pulled out a battery typically used in a hearing aid. Once he pulled the battery, the active bug monitor on top of the bookcase went back to search mode and the screen displayed the message 'scanning'. At the same time, they heard a beep from the door as Gunny walked in from his security rounds. Seeing the books scattered all over the floor Gunny figured something had just happened.

"Just found a bug," Lawson said while Myers held it up for Gunny to see.

"You were right about using them using a burst-mode bug, Myers," Norman commended. "I'll get this over to the lab at the Kennedy facility and see what they can download."

"The question that seems obvious," Lawson began, "is who had access to this room outside of us and when did they bring the book into the room. You see, I looked at the books when we first came into this room for the first time and I don't remember any accounting books in the stack. All the accounting books are in the bookcase. It struck me that there were only books on the natural sciences in this stack. Did any of you move any books?" They both nodded 'no' as they all looked at one another while they realized the impact of Lawson's statement. Someone outside of their team had access to the room.

Gunny broke into the conversation, "I have to get out of my uniform but before I do, my two cents is that we have been exposed. Someone or some group is tracking us which is becoming more apparent with this bug and the guy watching us at the Library of Congress this afternoon."

"What guy?" Norman questioned.

"We had a guy watching us the whole time we were at the library," Lawson interjected. "He was a professional, using the camera on his computer to watch us. My guess is that, based upon the quality of his computer and the built-in camera, he had zoom capability which allowed for him to see the contents of the pages we were reading, at least my pages."

Commander Norman switched to her military officer mode. "I'm taking this information over to Admiral Roedl along with the bug. I want everyone to be especially alert. By the way, Myers found a message on the code page and we haven't come up yet as to what it means. Lawson and Gunny, what have you got?"

"This is ye bailiwick," Gunny said in his Irish jargon to Lawson as Gunny opened the door to leave while Norman looked questioningly at Lawson.

Lawson watched Gunny leave then responded, "He goes into his Irish mode when he's stressed. Now, as noted before, it appears that all three pictures have something in common, they all have numbers in them. The London picture has the clock, the Paris picture has a phone number and the New York picture has the number of the fire station. I think we should consider the numbers represented in the pictures and see how they relate to the code page. By the way, Norman, doesn't the access pad on the outside of this room keep a registry of all persons entering the room? You might want to pull that up before seeing Roedl."

"Good point," Norman responded. "I'll check the security logs downstairs on the way out."

After Norman left, Myers and Lawson looked at the 'OUT FEB 1' message on the code sheet. "This appears to be what the North Koreans were getting from someone in this building," Myers said while looking at the code. "We have several opinions on what it could mean but have no reference point to see what it relates to."

"It's too easy," Lawson replied. "If I'm taking the time to hide a message, I'd make sure that the message was encoded and difficult to find. I think this is a red herring to stop us from looking further."

Myers saw Lawson's logic. It was too easy. "Maybe we need to use your idea about the numbers in the picture," Myers opined. "It wouldn't hurt us to dig a little further. Let's see what the clock on Big Ben shows?" As he said this he was opening the computer file showing the picture.

They both looked as Lawson read the clock hands. "It shows 4:43. Now the question to be answered is it AM or PM. We don't know when the picture was taken and it appears to be taken at either dawn or dusk. The time of 4:43 in the summer would match when dawn was when it is shown in the picture and it could be just as well dusk in the winter time. Seeing that there is no snow and the river appears to be free flowing with no ice along the edges of the Thames, I suspect it's early morning in the summer."

"If that is the case," Myers chipped in, "and it was dawn then the number on the hour hand is four. However, if it was in the afternoon, the hour hand would represent sixteen in military time. Being that it appears to be morning, let me see what is in the fourth line of the code."

"That seems to be the logical use of the number." Lawson agreed.

"One more thing," Lawson added. "We need to look at just the last two digits of each five digit number. That matches with the format they used to create the ASCII message you found earlier." Myers agreed. Counting four lines down on the code page, Myers started looking at the results.

Myers stated his observations, "The first ASCII character is nothing. The second character is the number '0', third is a '1', fourth is nothing and the fifth is a '4'. The sixth and seventh characters show nothing then the eighth character is the number '2'. Then there is nothing followed by two number '5's, another blank followed by a number '7'. So what we have is 'blank, 0, 1, blank, 4, blank, 5, 5, blank, 2'. The next time a number shows up on the line is at position 34 where we see the number '6'. So we have numbers at positions 2, 3, 5, 8, 10, 11, 13, 21 and, possibly, 34."

Lawson looked at the number stream which, taken in sequence, came out as '01425576'. They both looked at the number while wondering what it meant.

Lawson pulled out his phone. "Since we can't get on the internet on the computer, I'll do the search from my phone." Bringing up several screens on his phone, Lawson entered '01425576' and told Myers of his results. "I see an algorithm for brown rust disease control, a part number for a grommet and something referring to grain yield. Nothing that remotely relates to anything North Korea may be interested in except maybe grain yields but that doesn't approach the need for coding the information."

They were both at a loss as Myers commented, "Then the number we came up with may not be the message. I've seen a similar pattern like this before with the numbers on the code page but I don't know where. It may have been something I had to do at MIT or it might have been something I did on board the aircraft carrier. Whatever it is, it's way back somewhere in my mind."

As Myers was finishing his comments, Norman came back into the room. "Admiral Roedl is out for the evening. He'll see me at 07:00 hours tomorrow morning. I told him about the bug and the guy watching you guys at the library. I also gave him my progress." As she spoke, Gunny came back into the room in his dress uniform and a phone key card in his hand.

"I had to redo my rounds and I'm glad I did," Gunny said while waving the phone key card. "Congressman Latershan left his card in the phone and he is definitely gone for the evening. He also left his computer logged in which means anyone could get to his documents and email on his computer. I guess that since you need a pass card to get into his office, he probably feels it's safe to leave everything on even though he's out of the office. By the way, he did lock up the top secret document."

Norman and Lawson looked at Gunny then at each other. "Is it possible that someone got into the congressman's office after hours?" Lawson asked while looking at Gunny. "If so …,"

Then Norman interrupted, "We can see who used their card to get into his office by checking with security to see who entered on August 31st." Lawson shook his head in agreement.

"How many times have your changed your clothes today, Gunny," Lawson quipped as Gunny winced.

"If you're a Marine there are times you may change five or six times a day based upon the demands of duties. It allows you to see if everything still fits or if you've gained weight during the day." Everyone laughed at Gunny's comment. Gunny just frowned and sat down.

Myers drew all of their attention to the code page on the screen. He explained the finding of the message 'OUT FEB 1', Lawson's theory about the hour hand on Big Ben showing which line to read and the results of the ASCII characters on that line. As he was speaking, Norman left the room to stop by security to see what the register showed for who had logged into room 2337.

"I believe that Lawson's assumption about the hour hand on Big Ben showing the line is correct as we have a much greater incidence of characters showing up as numbers on that line than anywhere else except line forty-three where the positioning of the numbers on the line have some similarities," Myers stated as he explained the findings to Gunny. "We have numbers in line four at positions 2, 3, 5, 8, 10, 11, 13 and 21. I know I've seen a pattern like this before but I don't know where."

"I've seen similar patterns like that as well," Lawson broke in. "I haven't seen it in the intelligence training I had but it was something during my college years. I am not sure what it was. Look, we're not getting anywhere right now. We're all tired and we're grabbing things in the dark without giving it some thought. Why don't we start again tomorrow morning." Everyone agreed. They put the materials in the safe and left the room for the night.

Chapter 5

A Glimmer of Hope – Day 2

"Failure is where success likes to hide in plain sight" - Scott Adams

Norman came into the room at 12:30 PM after she met with Admiral Roedl. He reminded her that they only had a few days to figure out what the North Koreans were up to. After she entered the room she looked around to see that Lawson and Myers had been working on trying to find a solution to the number '01425576' they uncovered the night before. They had already struggled for almost three hours as they took the numbers and tried them in different applications such as telephone numbers, part numbers, airline flight codes, technical report numbers and computer-aided design codes used for manufacturing. Nothing seemed to fit. Unable to come up with any solution, they headed off to lunch with Lawson feeling that they were losing traction on an answer and running out of time. Norman noted that when she came into the room, they had left the room unattended with the computer still on the desk, a definite breach of security.

Once they all returned from lunch, they found Gunny had just gotten back from his rounds in the Rayburn Building. Norman handed him a sub sandwich and a drink as she scolded them for leaving the room without locking everything and erasing the whiteboard.

Following some terse moments of the reprimand, she leaned over to Lawson and whispered, "I think I was followed by two different people on my way here."

Lawson looked at her and realized the level of threat was increasing. "We need to do something about the situation," he said while thinking about their options. "You shouldn't be going around the city by yourself."

Seemingly apparent that she ignored his comment, she went over to the screen and looked at the number sequence. "You know, when I was at the academy, we had a class on 'Universal Mathematics'," she said while looking at Myers' notes on the screen. "We learned about how certain patterns were seen in nature such as plants having 2, 3, 5 or 8 leaves on a stem, how the galaxies exhibit a mathematical process with the way the that the arms of the galaxies extend or how a conch shell rotates out from the center."

"You went to the academy?" Lawson asked as he grasped how little he really knew about her.

"Yes," Norman responded. "I graduated from the Naval Academy in 2008. Now, if I recall correctly, the name of the mathematical formula was called the 'Fibonacci Sequence'." Both Myers and Lawson started laughing.

"Excuse me, Commander," Lawson said while repressing his laughter. "I just had to laugh because the answer was so simple and we had it staring at us the whole time. The pattern does appear to be a Fibonacci sequence with some additional numbers thrown in. If we were to just pay attention to the positions on the line that match those of the sequence, we should probably be able to ascertain what the code is." Norman agreed.

"What is a Fibonacci sequence," Gunny asked.

"Well," Myers responded, "you take a zero and a one and add them together, what do you get?"

"A one," Gunny replied.

"And what is the highest number of the two numbers you just added together?"

"A one."

"So you take the highest number of the two numbers you just added together and add that number to the result you previously got. So adding the highest number, a one, to the result which is a one gives you what?"

"A two," Gunny said in an irritating voice thinking that Myers was treating him like a two-year old.

Myers, realizing that Gunny was perturbed with the question, said, "Please bear with me on this Gunny and it will make sense. If I take the highest number from the previous addition we just did together, which was a one, and add it to the result of the previous addition, which was a two, the result is a three. Now going a step forward, if I again take the highest number from the previous addition, which was a two, and add it to the result of the previous addition, which was a three, I get a five. Doing the next calculation, three and five gives me an eight. Then, five and eight gives me a thirteen, and so on. With me so far?"

As Myers was saying this, he wrote on the whiteboard,

$$0 + 1 = 1$$
$$1 + 1 = 2$$
$$1 + 2 = 3$$
$$2 + 3 = 5$$

$$3 + 5 = 8$$
$$5 + 8 = 13$$

"I think I get it," Gunny responded. "So the next calculation would be adding eight to thirteen which would be twenty-one, then adding thirteen to twenty-one would give me thirty-four. Am I right?"

"You got it," Norman said. "Now let's get the sequence going and find out what we've got."

With that, Myers pulled up ASCII numbers using the Fibonacci sequence. Going to each position on the code sheet based upon each it respective number in the Fibonacci sequence, he evaluated the last two digits of each five digit set of numbers to get its ASCII value until the tenth iteration of the Fibonacci sequence where it seemed to stop. Characters after that were letters or blanks. Lawson walked to the whiteboard and proceeded to write the equivalent characters represented by the ASCII numbers they discovered. Myers called out each number as Lawson wrote until they had the whole number written out, digit by digit.

'0142764331' was written on the board. Gunny was looking at the screen with Myers while Lawson and Norman looked at the resulting number on the board.

"Ten digits," Lawson said. "What do we know has ten digits?"

"A telephone number," Gunny said. "You know, three digits for the area code and seven digits for the local number." Lawson thought about it while everyone agreed.

"It sits up there as a good possibility," Lawson said while looking at the white board.

They continued looking at different options the number could be used in. After hours of conversation and experimentation, Gunny made the observation that they were running around in circles with no anchor. Lawson thought it interesting how often Gunny used naval terms to describe civilian situations. Everyone appeared to be struggling with the activity of the day. Finally, Lawson spoke up.

"It's 8:30 PM, sorry 20:30 hours," Lawson said while sitting on the desk and looking at Norman. "I say we call it a night and start again tomorrow morning." Everyone agreed.

"I have a 07:00 hours meeting with Roedl at the Kennedy facility," Norman said as she got up. "Captain Henderson should be in here tomorrow morning around 09:00 hours. Just a word, I checked on anyone entering this room since we've been here yesterday afternoon. Nobody unauthorized has coded in yet Lawson is sure that accounting textbook wasn't there when we first came in. Keep on your toes. The Admiral wants you to keep your weapons within reach, even when you're sleeping. We don't know what level of threat this is to you but a high-tech bug ending up in this room says someone is getting serious. Gunny, I understand you are to meet Josh Henry at Theodore Roosevelt Island at the statue of Roosevelt at 07:30 tomorrow morning. Is that true?"

"Yes, Ma'am," Gunny replied.

"Tell Josh 'hi' for me," Norman requested. "He worked at the Defense Intelligence Agency with me when I was a lowly Lieutenant JG. He's a great guy and knows a lot of the people in

Washington that are on staff to different congressmen and congresswomen. He probably has some good background on Latershan's staff members."

"Yes, I know him," Gunny answered. "We called him 'Mister no routine'. He always said that we should never follow a routine that someone else can pick up unless we want them too."

"Always go out of sequence," Both Gunny and Norman said at the same time, laughing once they said it.

"That was his favorite piece of advice," Norman added. "So, apparently you know him quite well."

"Like I said, I know him. So, why am I meeting him out there?" Gunny asked while Myers and Lawson turned their attention to Norman's answer.

Norman shuffled her foot for a moment then responded, "I want this to stay strictly in this room. Josh Henry came to Admiral Roedl and myself this morning with some disturbing notion that someone had the capability to launch a nuclear strike against Iran without chain of command or launch code approval. Josh has always been very accurate in his assessments and very calm. However, this time we noticed he was out of character and thought he was just being paranoid with all the North Korean stuff going on. But one thing registered in his conversation that caused us both not to just write off his comments. Josh goes to a cyber café in Reston, Virginia as a way of getting the scoop of what is being discussed in the corners of the web. He said he overheard talk of by those in the café of a person claiming he could break the launch codes and sequence for entry to a US or UK nuke. We wouldn't have given it much credence as people in these cyber cafes always seem to brag about botched and imaginary adventures and hacking that level of security would require so many breaches in both our technological and human processes as to make it highly improbable. However, it's the name of a person that came up that caught our attention. He has a dark net pseudonym called 'Hotrod Lincoln'. This dark net guy has been very effective in carrying out his plans and his bragging has teeth in it. He seems to have inside information on new government technology developments. Josh says that he thinks he knows who 'Hotrod Lincoln' is but doesn't want to be seen talking to us. According to Josh, apparently our little group is a hot topic on the dark web. From what he hears, they think this team is a group of hackers going after dark web users and criminals. Even though the rumor is not true, they believe it. With that said, any questions?" Everyone nodded 'no'. "Head home and get some rest."

With that, everyone packed up except Myers as he was looking at the code on the computer. Lawson wrote down the number they came up with and put it in his pocket, just in case. As Lawson was getting ready to exit the room, Gunny stood up.

"Wait a minute," Gunny exclaimed. "Josh Henry's favorite advice about going out of sequence. Maybe he's not the only one following that practice. Write these numbers on the board!"

Lawson looked at Gunny then the others as everyone came back into the room. He figured that sometimes someone sees something no one else does so maybe Gunny found something. "Go ahead Gunny."

"Here are the numbers," Gunny called out as he looked at the code page. "I feel like I'm calling out a bingo night." Everyone laughed then waited as Lawson went to the whiteboard with the marker. Gunny continued, "Numbers from the code sheet are 71048, 36349, 33752, 84450, 45955, 32154, 00652, 98851, 09251 and 87549. Now look at the third digit of each five-number group. Notice that each of the third digits are unique, they go zero through nine. We may be looking at the right numbers, they're just out of sequence based upon the third digit in each number. Set the sequence up according to the third digit of each number and let's see what we've got."

Everyone stood amazed at Gunny's observation. Lawson was first to interject. "Gunny, this isn't the first time you saw a pattern hiding in plain sight. Remember when I had a handful of vehicle keys and was trying each one in the ignition? You grabbed the keys and handed me the correct key saying that 'this is the military. The number on the key matches the number on the vehicle'." Gunny smiled at Lawson's comment.

Norman went to the whiteboard and asked for Gunny to call out the numbers in the order of the third digit to make the number sequence. Gunny proceeded to sit down in front of the computer screen and read off the sequence to Myers as Myers called out the ASCII character represented in the number Gunny told him. When it was finished, Norman had written '0631214437'. They all sat down and decompressed from the effort taken to get this far.

"Now we may have something …," Lawson said while looking at the whiteboard."

Gunny interrupted, "This looks familiar. I order books all the time and this appears to be an early ten-digit ISBN number used to identify a specific book as it starts with a '06' which I saw quite often as the starting of an ISBN number. This is before they went to a thirteen-digit number that's used now.

Myers went to a search engine on his phone and entered the number they came up with. "I find a number of references to a book that shows up called 'The Huns' by E. A. Thompson."

"I remember that book," Lawson said as he looked at the screen. "We had to read that book in history class when I was in college. It's quite a good book on Attila the Hun and a very interesting read. It's worth a try to see if this book has anything to do with the code. Myers, can you get on a bookseller website and order it for overnight delivery?" While Lawson was talking, Myers was furiously typing on his phone.

"I don't need to order it," Myers said. "There is a bookstore near Georgetown University not far from here that carries it and they have copies in stock so I'll stop by there on my way in tomorrow morning to get a copy. I figured with a college nearby, the bookstores in the area would carry books used in the classes. I also recall that we had the same book in history class at MIT so I figured that the book is probably still used as a tool in classes today. It's a perfect book for code generation as it has a wide selection of letters and numbers within its pages."

"Are we sure we want to jump this fast on the first discovery of this number or should we dig more into it?" Norman asked.

"Well," Myers interjected, "we at least have one possible reference point with the number and a book. Since the book is a possibility and we haven't got it yet and it may take time to get it, I think it's a good idea to at least get the book to cut down any delays."

"Agreed and good point," Norman concurred.

"Good job," Lawson said as Norman took the computer and papers off of the desk and placed them in the safe.

"Let's get out of here and continue tomorrow," she said while Lawson washed down the whiteboard with a bottle of whiteboard spray cleaner and a paper towel. Once that was finished, they all left the room to go about their evening plans.

Chapter 6

Opposition

"The enemy is anybody who's going to get you killed, no matter which side he is on." - Joseph Heller, Catch-22

Lawson left the room with Norman as Gunny followed behind. "What are you going to do tonight, Jim?" Norman asked while Lawson checked his pistol and put it back in the holster.

"Don't know," He responded, looking at her while she checked her cellphone. "I guess I'll go back to my quarters unless you got some other idea."

"Why don't we go to that little Chinese restaurant, you know, just off of Independence Avenue on Pennsylvania Avenue," she said. "I know it's a walk but their food is good and we haven't had much of a chance to talk since we got here."

Lawson looked back at Gunny as he smiled. "Well, it is cold outside but these coats should be ok for the walk," Lawson observed. "I'm up for it after this day, let's go."

They walked out of the building as Gunny watched them go. "Kids," Gunny said as he watched them go out the door. "The streets aren't safe around here but they're armed and smart. I guess I should get something to eat."

Norman twisted her arm around Lawson's as they left the Rayburn building and slowly walked past the Longworth and James Madison buildings. The night air was cold and there was the smell of moisture in the air as they looked at the buildings under the lights of the street. Some of the buildings were brightly lighted at the entryways and became darker the farther one got away from the entrances. Looking to the left, Lawson could see the Capitol Building, encased with scaffolding for a dome renovation effort, and the park area with its trees and walkways between him and the Capitol building. It was quiet.

"How do you feel about our relationship," Norman questioned while watching Lawson scan the U.S. Capitol area.

Lawson stopped in his steps and looked at Norman's face in the light from the buildings. There was an inquisitive look on her face as he realized once more how beautiful she was. How did he ever get involved with her? She was distracting but, he had to admit, it was very fulfilling to have a person of her grace and beauty show an interest in him.

"I think we have a good friendship that has the potential of becoming something more intimate," he responded and, while doing so, began to wonder if too much of his analytical character ended up in the answer. She smiled at him, pulled his arm against her as they both continued their walk.

After entering Pennsylvania Avenue, they walked past the entry to a bank when Lawson stopped. As he stopped, the sound of footsteps in the distance behind them stopped as well. Lawson looked back to see who was there but no one was to be seen. They continued walking about twenty steps when Lawson stopped again.

"Someone's following us," he said while looking in Norman's eyes and holding his face close to hers.

"I know," she whispered. "I also noticed three people about four doors up, standing in a doorway. They may be waiting to get into a restaurant but I could swear I saw a gun barrel poke out from one of their hands."

Lawson continued to hold her close, hoping those watching would think they stopped to have an intimate moment. Looking around the street ahead of him, he softly spoke, "Occupied taxi about half a block away on the opposite side of the street." At that moment, they were both startled by the sound of someone locking a door on the front of one of the nearby restaurants.

"It appears that someone else sees a threat developing," Norman whispered back as she drew her pistol from her belt. "What's your plan?" Lawson looked around at his surroundings.

"Keep watching behind us toward Independence Avenue while I watch the guys up ahead and the taxi," Lawson remarked as he developed his plan. As he said that the three men started turning toward them. Lawson estimated they were about forty to fifty yards away. "They're moving toward us," he instructed Norman as Lawson and Norman moved closer to the wall of the bank.

"Who are they?" Norman questioned. Lawson made a quick assessment of their actions. Looking at how the three men moved, Lawson could see they were professionals.

"They're not a street gang," Lawson replied. "They've moved into a staggered single file mode, spreading out as they move."

"The person following us just came into the open," Norman reported, "No he's not," she exclaimed a moment later as she saw the man fall.

"Taxi is starting to move," Lawson proclaimed as he continued to watch the three men slowly moving closer. Moving his weapon from his right hand to his left hand, Lawson then used his right hand to move Norman nearer to the wall of the bank. "Entrance to the bank, twenty feet back," Lawson said. Norman could see the entrance portico inset that would give them about five feet of cover as the doorway was set back from the street with granite walls to each side before getting to the main entrance. Lawson stepped up in front of her and against the wall making it difficult for those in front of them or in the taxi to see her move. Once she made her move, Lawson stepped slowly backward until he could slide into the portico. Once he disappeared from the view of those approaching, the three men stopped and looked at each other. They immediately began to move for cover when a large-caliber rifle shot rang out.

"Where'd that come from?" Lawson asked. Norman looked at him and shrugged her shoulders. Seeing the taxi approach to where they would have not cover if the driver opened fire, Norman swung from her position, stepped out from the entryway and fired twice rapidly into the taxi and jumped back into cover. The taxi rolled to a stop with the driver pushing his door open then falling on the ground. Lawson looked to where the three men previously were and could see one man lying on the ground, obviously the result of the rifle shot. Just as he pulled back to the cover of the bank entry, he heard a noise behind him. Leveling his weapon at the new threat, he saw four men in strike-team gear come around the corner of the bank, the lead man motioning for Lawson and Norman to stay in place while running past the entryway. Lawson and Norman had no time to react as the strike team went past the entryway and up the street. Moments later a furious exchange of muffled gunfire was heard, then silence.

More footsteps then "So how was the Chinese food," came Gunny's voice. "I thought you might need some help to get to the restaurant."

"Well, we haven't actually had a chance to order yet," Lawson quipped as he helped Norman up. Lawson saw movement out of the corner of his eye and in one quick, reactive move, fired two shots toward the form standing at the edge of the bank. The man staggered forward, the weapon in his hand firing full automatic into the ground. Everyone dropped to the ground as bullets were ricocheting everywhere. Once the body fell to the ground the firing stopped.

Gunny walked over to the lifeless body. "Definitely not one of my guys," he said while frisking the body for an ID. "He's a contractor for the Defense Intelligence Agency." He looked up to see the strike team commander walking back toward them.

"We got the same result with one of the others, Gunny," reported the commander of the strike team. "They may all appear to be linked to the DIA with their IDs but, what is curious, of the guy I just checked, I don't find him as having access when I pulled up his name. He doesn't exist. My guys are checking the others. You all need to get out of here as you appear to be targets of a professional hit team. That includes you, Gunny."

"Ok," Lawson queried, "these guys were waiting for us, they knew we would be here. How is that possible if Norman and I didn't know we were coming here until just before we left the Rayburn building? Is there another bug in room 2337?"

"Like I said, we can take it from here, Gunny," the strike commander offered.

"Thanks, Chuck," Gunny replied. "We've got some digging to do back at the ranch." With that, Gunny, Lawson and Norman headed back to Room 2337. While on the way, Lawson called Myers to join them there.

They arrived at the room at 9:45 PM to find Admiral Roedl sitting in a chair waiting for them. As they entered the door, Myers came up behind them questioning for the reason for him being called back.

"Close the door," Roedl order in a terse, commanding voice. "I got a call from the Scarborough Marine Commander that they got an 'Attack Imminent' alert. I knew it had to be my team engaged in some risky behavior. You people think you can just wander off by yourselves without considering the magnitude of what you're working on and who else may be interested?"

Lawson was quick to answer, "Before you get on our case, Sir, don't you think it would have been in our best interests to know the level of threat we were dealing with. You hand us weapons but that's not enough to say there is a threat. After all, we are all required to have weapons on us in the warfare facility, yet the threat there is very low. We need to know what's going on behind the scenes!"

Roedl stood up from the chair and faced Lawson. It appeared that Roedl was going to take Lawson down, possibly even charge him with insubordination. His next action surprised them all.

"Lieutenant Lawson," Roedl began, "you have every right to be angry. Your neck was on the line out there and I apologize. The command group in charge of this mission felt we needed to keep the team out of the loop on the threat level as they felt that it would be a distraction to you all getting to the bottom of what these pictures meant. I see we were wrong."

Norman was next to speak, "Admiral, before we talk any further, Lawson brought up a concern out on the street that we need to address. He said that these guys were waiting for us as if they knew where we would be. We didn't know where we would be until we were in the hallway. So how did they know enough in advance to set up the blind-chase scenario?"

Roedl gave a confused looked at Norman, "What's a blind-chase scenario?"

Norman looked at Lawson to provide the answer. "Well, it's like this," Lawson explained. "When I was in intel class several years back, the instructor talked about how tigers in Southeast Asia team together to catch deer. They have one tiger at one end of a small valley while three or four tigers wait at the other end of the valley. When the deer go for the watering hole, the one tiger spooks the deer causing them to run away from the tiger but toward the other end of the valley where the other tigers are waiting. The result is obvious. That's the blind-chase scenario."

"Is that what you saw?" Roedl asked, turning to Gunny.

"To a 'T'," was Gunny's response. "It was a classical blind-chase setup. One guy behind them, pushing them along into the waiting arms of the other three ahead of them. In the Marines, we might use a blind-chase to push the enemy into an ambush or to initiate a capture. I think these guys were going for a capture as they were well within range to take Norman and Lawson out using their weapons and they appeared to have no snipers on the roof which would have been normal for an ambush."

"Lawson, you've got something?" Roedl inquired as Lawson stood up looking toward the door.

"Yes, Sir, there is something I just realized," Lawson expounded. "We were picked up by a bug, all right, but the bug wasn't in here. It's in the hallway. The door to this room was already closed and we were in the hall when Norman and I talked about going to the Chinese restaurant."

"That's right," Gunny added. "Now that I remember, we were halfway down the hallway before you decided what place you were going to."

"One question, Gunny" Roedl said. "What made you decide to call up the strike team? That's pretty serious action to take on a whim. Did you know there was a threat to Norman and Lawson?" Gunny sat down in a chair as he thought over the events leading to his decision.

"Well, as we left," Gunny started, "Myers and I got talking about the issue that we may be targets of the people on the dark net. Myers said he wasn't comfortable about us walking around Washington, DC at night. Then he said something about things not feeling right and Lawson told him just before we left this evening that threats may be closer to us than we think. That got me thinking that the two people that would have all the information on what we're doing just went for a stroll in the city. No better target. I figured I'd follow them and keep the response team's number ready to dial on my phone. When I saw a man come out of the shadows at the Longworth building and proceed to walk in unison to Lawson's and Norman's starts and stops, I called the response team leader and asked him to meet me on a scramble basis. Once he and his team got to me, Norman and Lawson were already in front of the bank. We checked to make sure there were no snipers on the rooftops then set up our positions. We had to take out the guy following them first, which Chuck did with a silenced pistol shot. We couldn't set up the team on the other corner of the bank until he was out of the way. We saw the three guys come out of the shadows and move in a tactical approach mode then, when the cab started moving toward Norman and Lawson, I knew it was a catch-and-grab scenario. That's when I shot the guy in the front of the group approaching Lawson and Norman using the response team commander's M-14 rifle. The rest is history."

"All right, I want to know what triggered you to get that higher sense of a threat, Myers," Roedl said while looking at Myers.

Myers pulled himself up in the chair, "Lawson keeps feeding me information on things that seemed out of place," Myers explained. "The list is long. Questions on the dark web, three pictures showing up in messages to North Korea all at the same time, Congressman Latershan's staff being involved in some way, the guy in the library, you giving us weapons with no explanation, even this thing with Gunny going to meet with this guy Henry tomorrow morning. They all seem disjointed but, as Lawson says, they all seem to be connected in some way. Now this event tonight says there is more than just a code breaking effort in all this."

Roedl paced across the room a couple of times while looking at a text on his phone then spoke, "There is a lot more than you are seeing. We're not sure as yet how the pieces fit but we sense that something major is about to happen. The Joint Staff feels that we're no longer in control of events, those events are beginning to carry us along and we are just becoming spectators in what may be a major worldwide incident. We just don't know yet what it is but everything seems to point to the picture you're trying to decode. That's why it's essential that you keep your focus on what you're doing. In all this, we are convinced that someone or some group in our government is determined to keep you from discovering the facts. Why? We don't know. We fear it is something far more sinister than Washington politics but Washington politics is one of the drivers."

"A coup, perhaps," Lawson remarked.

"There are elements of that conclusion that fits but there is other evidence that says otherwise," Roedl responded. "It's possible that it is a shadow government operation, time will tell. Look, we're beating a dead horse now. Why don't you all head home. Gunny, 07:30 hours meeting with Josh Henry tomorrow morning."

"Yes, Sir," Gunny acknowledged.

"Lawson, Norman, stay behind," Roedl instructed. Everyone left while Lawson and Norman remained in their chairs.

Roedl reprimanded them as they sat. "I'm not pleased with what you two did tonight. I don't mind you developing an affectionate relationship with each other but that stops at the door or while on a mission. As long as a mission is active, personal relationships end for the duration, is that understood?"

Norman looked at Lawson and nodded to him. Lawson began his explanation, "We're sorry, Sir. We couldn't tell you what we had to do because we had no place to talk to you that was secure. Norman was hoping to talk to you this evening but you were not available so we had to act as we knew we weren't going to be able to leave the building, individually or together, until we confronted this threat."

"Ok," Roedl responded, "it appears things are not as they seem. What threat?"

"No, Sir, things aren't as they appear," Norman answered. "As to the threat, when I came in to the Rayburn building this morning, I noticed that two different people seemed to show unusual interest in me, enough so that I told Lawson about it. He thought they might be setting me up for a trap so we both agreed that it was not safe for me to head home tonight. I called first before going in to meet you. I would've gone in if you were to meet me but, with your sudden change in schedule, I wasn't going to risk going in and I wasn't going to tell you what was going on over the phone."

Roedl turned to Lawson, "Your part in this Lieutenant?"

Lawson leaned back, "Well, Sir, when Norman came to me and said she was being followed, we knew the only thing to do was to flush the one or two people out. Otherwise, we were individually prime targets for either a hit or capture. We figured that, since we were both armed, we had a better chance of eliminating the threat together. We decided on the Chinese restaurant then realized that taking the walk instead of the car was the best chance we had of flushing them out. We didn't bank on them having a full team operation, which wouldn't have happened unless they knew our immediate plans, though we did anticipate that the confrontation would be while we were going to the Chinese restaurant."

"That explains a lot," Roedl mused. "My apologies. You both did well and it appears you are both on your best game. I should learn to trust your whole team better. It's just that I've never had a team that works as seamlessly as you all do. Thanks for the explanation as it helps me a lot. Now I need to tell you about the text. The IDs of the men that were after you were official IDs from the Defense Intelligence Agency. The only problem was the IDs were registered in the logs but the people carrying them were not in the active personnel database. That's the reason they came up as nonexistent. I figure someone in the DIA pass office is working with this group, whoever they are."

"Where does that put us, Sir?" Norman inquired.

"You all keep doing what you were tasked to do," Roedl answered. "Keep your weapons on you and, when you are outside, operate in teams of two and keep your primary calling number for emergencies set for the Rapid Response Team. The team doesn't need to know where you're at as long as your phones are on. They'll find you. I'll instruct the others. Now, go home and get some sleep. We need your answers to the codes."

"One clarification, Sir," Lawson added. "We were distracted. We didn't notice the guy following us until we crossed from Independence Avenue to Pennsylvania Avenue. Your concerns were not without merit."

"Thanks for your honesty, Lawson," Roedl acknowledged. "I know what it's like to develop a relationship under these conditions. If you do decide to get married, we'll have to reassign one of you to a different team. We have rules against husband and wife working on the same team as we can't have family issues and events at home being carried into the job. I know this as my wife and I met on a mission twelve years ago and we had to be reassigned once we got married so I tend to be lenient on interoffice relationships as long as they don't interfere with the work. Now get out of here and get some sleep."

Everyone left, careful not to converse in the hallway as they headed out to their cars. Following the order by Roedl to operate in teams of two, Lawson agreed to take Norman to her apartment and head for home. As he opened the door to the car, he raised a question to Norman, "Think the car is bugged?"

"I'd be more concerned about a bomb," She replied. With that comment, Lawson looked under the car which resulted in Norman laughing.

"Very funny," Lawson remarked.

"Well, now that this evening is over with, why don't you drop me off at my apartment and go home and get some sleep and don't forget to pick me up in the morning," suggested a tired and hungry Norman. Lawson put the car in gear as he drove out of the parking lot, doing a quick check of Norman's car as they passed by it.

Chapter 7

Meeting of the Minds – Day 3

"Identify, Improvise, Adapt and Overcome"
- Marine Corps Mantra

It was 7:30 AM when Gunny arrived at the statue of Theodore Roosevelt on Theodore Roosevelt Island on the Potomac River. Dressed in a suit and tie, he moved to the figure standing next to the statue. "Hello, Josh," Gunny said while looking around to see if anyone else was in the area.

"Hi, Gunny," Josh Henry said. "It's been a long time since we've seen each other. How's the Admiral doing?"

"He's doing fine," Gunny replied. "Beth Norman also says to tell you 'hi'."

"Ah, Beth," Josh reminisced while he motioned Gunny to walk with him. "She's a jewel and one smart lady. Let's walk to a bench that's just up the trail." There was a park bench about one-hundred yards from the trail entrance. They both went to the bench and sat down.

Josh Henry was a short man in his early sixties that looked more like an accountant than an intelligence agent working for the U. S. government. He started early in his career with the NSA in 1975 after graduating from college, then followed that stint by working with the Defense Intelligence Agency from September 2001 to the present. He was well known for his catching small details that brought a puzzle of facts together to an answer. Gunny thought that he was an older version of Lawson, same skills and same demeanor. Josh warned the government about the dark web ten years before it developed into the behemoth that it had become. He also warned his superiors that the dark web would be the market place for selling classified information as a black market commodity. Both predictions proved true.

"So, what is so sensitive that we had to come out here to talk?" Gunny posed.

Josh contemplated Gunny's question for a moment, "You guys are a hot potato right now in the dark net arena and I can't afford to be found talking with you or any of your team members. The users of the dark web think that you guys are after them. I know that's not true but I can't risk exposing that knowledge and losing the trust of those in the cafes and sites I visit. Besides, what I have to tell you cannot be trusted to be talked about anywhere in the Washington structure. It's far too lethal."

Gunny pulled his suit coat closer around his body as the air was cold. The forest around them had a heavy fog drifting through the area with the vista becoming lighter and darker at times due to the change in density of the fog. A typical February day on the Potomac where the moist air made it seem a lot colder than it was. "So what is this 'lethal' thing you're talking about?"

Josh adjusted himself on the bench. "I keep hearing a series of comments being stated on the dark web concerning a user by the name of 'Hotrod Lincoln' and the ability to launch a U. S. nuke missile by bypassing the normal code restrictions. Now normally, I would let something like this pass as part of the rumor mill but the date of February 7 was passed along with the info. It seems that Hotrod is planning to do a demonstration on that date to show the world the missiles can be launched by anyone with enough information. What makes this more disconcerting is the level of inside information coming out on the potential of this event happening."

"What type of information," Gunny requested as movement in the trees caught his attention, that being followed a moment later by a squirrel dashing between two trees. Gunny swung his attention back to Josh.

"Statements on the EAS alert handling on a submarine, launch code change dates, which I checked and found they were accurate and targeting vectors using GPS," Josh said as his appearance seem to indicate heightened anxiety. "Any one of these wouldn't mean much but put it all together and it brings it closer to reality. Now as to the identity of who the person might be, I can't be sure but there are three names that ..."

Gunny saw Josh lurch backward then slump forward. At the same moment, Gunny spun from the park bench to its side as a bullet slammed into the back of the bench where he was sitting, throwing splinters of wood out the back of the bench into a tree behind it. Gunny leaped to the tree, putting the tree between himself and the shooter. By this time, Gunny had the .38 caliber pistol in his hand. Seeing a figure run from behind a tree about seventy-five yards away from him, Gunny sighted in on the figure and pulled the trigger. His shot appeared to hit the individual as their forward motion was stopped for a moment then continued. "Got him in the shoulder," Gunny said while moving to close in on the person. At that moment Gunny stopped as he realized that the shooter could disappear quickly in the fog and Josh needed immediate medical attention.

As Gunny turned to Josh he got on his cellphone and dialed '911'. Laying Josh down on the bench Gunny checked for a pulse. It was still strong. He ripped open Josh's shirt to see a hole in Josh's chest and determined that the bullet should have missed the heart, lungs and major arteries. It was low enough however to have penetrated his stomach. At that moment, the phone came alive, "911, what is your emergency?" Gunny looked around to be sure the shooter wasn't making a return trip.

"I have a man that's been shot in Roosevelt Park about one-hundred yards north of the statue. He needs a Medevac chopper."

"Sir, I'm contacting Lifeflight now."

"Great," Gunny shouted as he put pressure on Josh's wound. "Also notify the park police that we have an active shooter in the park."

"I will," said the 911 operator. "Please stay on the line until the park police get there."

"Will do," said Gunny as he set the phone down and attended to Josh's wound.

A few minutes later a park policeman arrived on the trail with weapon drawn. At the same time, Gunny could hear the sound of the approaching helicopter. "Sir, step away from the body," the officer said while seeing that Gunny's pistol sat on the bench near Josh's head.

"I can't," Gunny responded. "I'm putting pressure on the wound to keep him from bleeding to death."

The officer stepped forward with his weapon about three feet from Gunny's head, "I said, step away from the body."

"This is a live man, not a body," Gunny shouted back to the man Gunny determined was a rookie cop. "Give me some help here."

The rookie was getting agitated and stepped closer. Gunny had no time for it. Swinging his hand in a motion resembling a swimmer's backstroke, Gunny ended up with the officer's weapon in his hand and the perplexed officer wondering what just happened. "Now, do something useful. Put your hand here to keep pressure on this wound while I show the medical people where we are." With that, Gunny slammed the rookie's weapon back into the officer's holster and walked toward the trailhead. As he did so, two emergency responders came running up the trail with their medical kits. They moved the rookie to the side as they started working on Josh. A more senior park policeman of the rank of lieutenant was coming down the trail, meeting Gunny about halfway to the entrance.

"What happened here?" the lieutenant asked as Gunny stopped to talk to him. Gunny proceeded to explain all that happened including the fact that Gunny appeared to have wounded the assailant and an active shooter was in the park. Gunny and the lieutenant walked to the bench where the medical people were working on Josh while the Lieutenant got on his radio and called for backup.

"Here's that guy's weapon, sir," the rookie said while handing Gunny's weapon to the newly arrived lieutenant.

"You have a permit for this weapon," was the lieutenant's question to Gunny. Gunny pulled out his ONI ID badge and military ID card. "These don't provide you with permission to carry a weapon." Gunny then pulled out his military courier card. The lieutenant looked it over then handed Gunny's military ID card to the rookie. "Run a check on this guy." The rookie pulled a card scanner off of his belt and proceeded to scan the card.

While they were waiting, the lieutenant asked Gunny, "What's this all about? And don't tell me you can't tell me because of national security. That one is getting old."

Gunny smiled and replied, "I can't tell you due to national security and you're not cleared to know."

The lieutenant, now totally aggravated by Gunny's response, turned to the rookie. "What have you got," he shouted.

"I'm not sure, Sir," the rookie officer said while looking at the screen of the scanner. "It says here in bold words, 'Do Not Detain'. All his information, except for his name and military ID number, is blacked out."

"Let me see that," came the lieutenant's response. About that time, another park police officer stepped into the scene walking past the medical people moving Josh on a stretcher toward the helicopter.

"What's going on here?" the new police officer with the rank of captain said while looking at Gunny. "Oh, hi Gunny. You doing cloak and dagger stuff again?"

"Hi Ben," Gunny responded. "Yup, still working for Roedl. Never a dull day."

"You know this guy?" the lieutenant asked the captain while holding Gunny's pistol.

"I take it that is Gunny's weapon," the captain replied.

"Yes, Sir, it is," came the Lieutenant's terse response.

The captain looked at Gunny then the lieutenant. "Give his weapon back to him and don't you ever let your people get so close to a suspect that they can have their weapon taken away from them. Gunny is average compared to some of the operatives I've seen."

The lieutenant handed Gunny his weapon as the rookie looked around trying to determine how the captain knew what went on. The lieutenant was perplexed as well. "Well, Gunny, just like old times, huh?" the captain said while handing Gunny his cellphone and checking his own phone. "By the way Gunny, I was just texted by Kelly, the paramedic, that your friend is going to be ok. What were you doing out here talking with Josh Henry in the first place. They have secure rooms in a number of facilities where you can talk without being shot at." Gunny just smiled as he pocketed his phone and headed for his car.

About halfway down the trail, Gunny looked back and shouted, "Ben, as always, treat this incident as routine."

The Captain waved to Gunny then shouted, "Gunny, strange but routine, I get it. You're still a scoundrel." All the Captain heard from Gunny was laughter as Gunny faded into the distance.

Chapter 8

Exposed

"There's a world of difference between truth and facts. Facts can obscure truth." - Maya Angelou

Myers sat looking at the screen of the computer as he contemplated his options concerning the code on the sheet. He had been going through possibilities on how the code would present itself when he heard the familiar 'beep', telling him someone was about to open the door. Having been instructed by Admiral Roedl about the reasons for Norman's and Lawson's actions the day before, he put the 'panic button' in his hand and pulled his .38 caliber pistol from its holster as he waited to see who was getting access to the room. Commander Norman stepped in as Myers put the weapon back into its holster and the panic button back on the desk.

"Good morning, Myers," she said while handing him one of the two cups of coffee she carried in with her.

"Good morning and thanks," Myers exchanged as he took the cup from Norman's hand.

Norman looked at the computer screen then the whiteboard, "What progress are we making this morning?"

Myers looked at the time at the bottom of the computer and saw that it was 9:30 AM. "I just got here just a little over a half hour ago. I've been looking at the code page and still haven't come to any conclusions as to where to start using this book," he said while holding up a new copy of the book, 'The Huns'. "I got it this morning as soon as the bookstore opened." He handed the book to Norman as he continued talking. "Henderson was supposed to be here at 9:00 this morning but he never showed up."

Norman saw the Bible sitting on the desk and noted the words 'NIV Bible' on the front cover. "I am curious," she said while setting down the book Myers gave her while picking up the Bible from the desk. "You're a well-educated man that, by anyone's measure, you're a true scientist. You've got knowledge that most companies would kill to get so they could have you head up their research facilities. An advanced degree from MIT, a proven computer hacker in your own right and far more technologically advanced than any of the rest of us. Yet I understand that, according to Gunny, you believe in God and were going to be a minister at one time. How is it that you have so much education under your belt and yet you believe this stuff?"

As she handed the Bible back to Myers, he responded, "Don't think that getting deeper into education counters the beliefs in a supreme being. That's a false stereotype that a lot of educators and the media use. Quite the opposite is true. A lot of my friends at MIT also believe there is a God. Many of us got to that point as we increased our knowledge in the sciences. We saw patterns and mathematical equations that exhibited order and design. Things that only could be explained by an intent to making something, not something occurring by accident."

"So what makes you think that God and science can coexist in the same sphere?" Norman asked as her curiosity increased.

Myers took the book 'The Huns', placed it in his briefcase and locked it. Turning back to her he said, "The formula we're using right now to help solve this puzzle is a good place to start."

"You mean the Fibonacci Sequence," she replied.

"Yes," Myers continued. "You yourself said that the Fibonacci sequence is seen throughout nature, a basic design that can be seen in so many things. It seems practical to logically assume that this is design and not just accident. There's also microbiology, DNA and the formation of a baby in the womb. How is it that for several months of development in the womb, the baby's bones are cartilage then change to bone while other pieces of cartilage, like in the nose, remain cartilage? That requires some form of programming that can be replicated. Then there's the basic reconstruction of the DNA strand in the cell that requires the DNA to be separated into half a chain, read by a DNA reader with a new strand of DNA being constructed that matches the original DNA. This takes three functions or machines to carry out the process. This is programming, something that had to be designed. It just didn't happen by accident."

"I see what you're saying," Norman interrupted, "but life had millions, if not billions of years to do this."

Myers took a sip of coffee then continued, "The primary argument in the development of the basic cell says many accidents were needed to develop the chemical makeup to make a single cell. But they forget to say that there are going to be many accidents of nature that will tear that same combination down. It's like playing the lottery, you've got one chance to win out of several million chances. Now we're talking about the odds of a billion chances to one for the development to get one cell to form so you've got to win against far greater odds than that found in a lottery. On top of that, you have to win against those odds a great number of successive times just to get a protein molecule, the basis for all life. It also requires in the creation of that single molecule to replicate itself within a very limited amount of time. It has to reproduce the DNA and how is that going to happen if it also requires the creation of the machines and programs to do that?. That takes a lot of faith to believe that. As for whether we are advancing beyond past cultures, in my last year at MIT working on my Masters, we found out about thousands of clay tablets that were believed to be earlier than Sumer era of 4,500 BC. These tablets had trigonometric calculations based upon a sixty-based numbering system that was much more accurate than what we have today. We see indications, going far back in our history that we may actually be less accurate in our sciences than they may have been, so my theory is that we are slowly losing our intellectual edge, not increasing it. Yes, we are making advances in certain areas but there are so many contradictions in the stuff we know as the sciences that, in my opinion, the process has been corrupted and the whole arena has become a religion in itself. After all, what is religion? Something we believe but can't prove with the tools we've got. We model things with partial information and then tout it as fact when the missing pieces, most likely, will tell a different story. I've had many experiences in my life that exhibit greater proof to me that there is a God than what I think the sciences supposedly prove on what we understand based upon snippets of information and supposition. Whether it is God or science, much of what we know is based upon faith and, many times, my faith in science is challenged by those that modify their findings to come to a predetermined outcome. Areas like drug research, climate change, social engineering and psychological sciences appear to be strongly influenced by politics at the cost of scientific analysis. Grant money overrules critical thinking. When the foundation of what we are led to believe comes into question through the manipulation of data then where's our reference point for the truth? Yes, I believe there is a God but I'm not here to convince you of that. I'm just answering your question as to why I believe what I believe. If you want to know if he's real, ask him yourself and see how he answers."

As Myers had finished, he looked up to see Gunny standing next to the bookcase. "I didn't even see you come in," Myers said while Norman turned to see who Myers was talking to. Both of them realized that they were so deep in the discussion that they didn't hear the door beep or see Gunny come in.

"Gunny, when did you get here?" Norman asked while Gunny smiled.

"About five minutes ago," was his response. "I see you been trying to pin Myers down on why he believes there's a God. He and I have had this conversation numerous times. He doesn't debate it, he just lays out what he believes. He's not going to say whether you're right or wrong in your beliefs. He bases a lot of his opinions upon calculating statistical possibilities given the information he has. If you want to know how real it is to him, watch how he lives it out. There's your proof."

"You believe what Myers said about his religion?" Norman queried.

"It's not what I believe that's the question, it's what he believes," Gunny blurted. "What I mean is that my beliefs have nothing to do on whether he is right or wrong. He supports his beliefs with facts better than what I can do. He says that what he has is not a religion but rather a relationship with God. Big difference. Besides, you might want to see how what he believes applies to what we are doing. He has that Bible here for a reason." Norman was confused by Gunny's last comment. What does the presence of a Bible on his desk have to do with what they are doing?

Myers was quick to answer. "This book tells me a lot about human nature. Most importantly, it tells me that people, any people, will change their minds or justify an action if their worldview is threatened. The actions involved in group-think is different than a person acting as an individual. A group reacts differently to a situation than an individual does. A group can get caught up in actions they would never think of doing as individuals. Individuals came to Jesus Christ for answers yet, I grant you, some of those same people were probably in the group that demanded Christ's crucifixion. They got caught up as a part of the group and the religious leaders of that time were experts on how to stir up and use a group. They had done it on many different occasions, which gave the Roman soldiers fits. I've been looking at this code, the opposition we're getting and the events happening to determine if we are dealing with individual decisions or group pressure. Lawson definitely understands the dynamics. I'm trying to understand them as well."

Norman smiled at Gunny's comment and Myers' answer then went to the whiteboard. Picking up the whiteboard marker, she rolled it around in her hand as she gathered her thoughts. "How'd the meeting go with Josh Henry?"

"Well," Gunny started, "He's in the hospital with a bullet in his chest and the guy who shot him is wandering around Washington carrying one of my .38 caliber bullets in his shoulder." Both Myers and Norman stopped what they were doing and focused their attention on Gunny.

"Did you report this to Roedl?" Norman demanded as she realized they may all be targets after the experience of the previous evening.

"No," Gunny replied. "I came here to report it to you since you are next in the chain of command. Henry said that the dark web conversations indicate that Hotrod Lincoln plans to demonstrate something to the world on February 7th, maybe that he can control the launch of a U.S. nuke missile by bypassing the normal EAS channels needed to authorize the launch. Josh felt it was a real threat."

"How confident are you that his info will result in an actual event?" Myers asked.

Gunny thought for a moment as he didn't want to give up any classified information in his answer. "I worked with Josh years ago when Admiral Roedl had just come on board the intelligence group for the Fifth Fleet in the Mediterranean. We worked on a project that was meant to keep the Iraqi opposition from determining our planning after the Iraqi rebuilding effort started. I had the responsibility for determining the weapons needs for the teams needed to carry out our plans, much more than that I can't tell you. Josh is very much like Lawson. Give him a bunch of disconnected facts and he can piece them together into a viable conclusion. If Josh felt that this threat was significant enough to give credence then I would believe him. By the way, where's Lawson?"

"He's checking on a piece of information for me," Norman answered. "He should be here any time. Now, Myers, what have you got so far?"

"Well," Myers responded while looking at the code sheet on his screen, "I'm not sure that the code we found using the Fibonacci sequence is real. We have nothing, outside of a number we came up with last night, to say that the number references a book. I've tried using the number as references to map coordinates which turned up nothing. I've also tried it as a reference to a part number or a process number. No luck. I thought that maybe the minute hand on Big Ben would be the starting place for the message but again, no luck, it was just gibberish but has some pattern similarities to line four. Everything I've searched for keeps pointing back to this book. If the number does reference this book, then where do we start and what technique do we use?"

They talked for a couple of minutes more when they heard a beep and the door opened. Lawson came in with a number of documents in his arms. Norman walked over to the table with the coffee maker on it, set the coffee maker on the floor and motioned for Lawson to come over. Lawson sat the documents on the table, pulled a chair over to the table and sat down.

"So what did you find?" Norman queried.

Lawson pulled the top document from the pile and handed it to Norman. "Your suspicions appear to be correct," he said while grabbing the second document in the pile. "The pictures were taken from the archives at the Library of Congress. This means that the code was generated using the pictures to dictate where the information would go on the code sheet not the other way around where they would have to take pictures to match previous code. Another way of saying that is that the pictures came first, then the code. That being said, no one had to go to London or Paris or New York to take the pictures. So the planning and set up of the pictures and messages could have been done anywhere."

"Good work," Norman said.

"One more thing," Lawson continued. "All three pictures came from the same book which indicates to me that the pictures are not related to the locations being targets. The book is not that well circulated and has not left the Library of Congress to go to any of the other libraries in the past year. So my guess is that the pictures taken from the book were copied here in Washington. I also checked to see who might have checked out the book. It's been checked out four times in the past year but Kinder Amquist, the historical section lead librarian, said they don't have to check it out to look at the book if it stays in the historical section, only if it leaves the section to go to the reading area. She says that a lot of people use their cellphones in the section to take pictures of the pages they are interested in rather than paying for copies of the pages. So, many times, the book never leaves the section but the pictures are captured. Whoever got these pictures was someone experienced in covering their trail. By the way, if the picture was taken using a phone, how did they get the color layers set up. More likely the pictures were taken using a high-quality camera that could separate the colors or they used a software program that separated the colors."

Lawson handed Norman the second document. "This document is a set of investigative reports by the Capitol Police on incidences concerning the bugging of offices relating to the House and Senate facilities. There were fourteen incidents in the past year up to the end of the reporting period which was December of last year. What is interesting is that all of the incidents happened up to August of last year then, no more reported incidents. We are the first incident of bugging to be reported in this facility since that time. It is my observation that the reason the bugging appeared to stop is because those bugging the facilities changed from active bugs to passive ones. The passive bugs are the type that transmit their messages in burst mode through cell phone towers, like the one we found yesterday. The rooms are swept for active bugs but, because the technology for these passive bugs is so new, no one has thought to sweep for them. So why is this important for us? Because, if sensitive information is the vehicle of transaction for the dark web, the passive bug becomes a huge asset in getting that information. What I am saying is that each member of this team is in jeopardy because the conversations going on throughout this facility will reference us at one time or another and those interested in what we are doing will find out who we are and where we're going. That information ends up on the dark web where the key players we are up against may be following our every move. May sound paranoid but those are the facts."

"In other words, they are always one step ahead of us," Gunny opined.

"Exactly," Lawson acknowledged. "Now that being said, let's get back to determining the coding we need to break." They all proceeded to talk about the different options.

"With the attempts on us last night and Gunny and Henry being attacked this morning, I think it smart we travel in pairs as much as possible as Roedl advised," Norman told the team. "Whoever they are, they appear to be getting more aggressive."

"Listen," Gunny interrupted, "I just got a text that Josh Henry is out of surgery and is talking. I'm going over to the hospital to talk to him." With that, he sat his military holster and weapon on the desk. "They frown on weapons at the hospital," he said as he prepared to leave the room.

Lawson was surprised by the comments from Norman and Gunny as he had not heard about Gunny's actions that morning in the park. Gunny filled him in before he left. Norman left at the same time as Gunny to get her clothes from the drycleaners. It was obvious to Gunny that the advice to travel in pairs was not yet an achievable goal.

It was an hour later when Admiral Roedl came through the door as Lawson and Myers were still debating where the message could be on the sheet. Roedl sat down in a chair and pulled a book from the bookcase and began thumbing through it. "I'm just here observing," He said.

"One thing bothers me," Lawson stated. "Why did they start the book number on the code sheet at the second five-digit number and not the first. The number '1' is part of the Fibonacci sequence so why didn't they start with that position on the line?"

Myers looked at the number in the first position Lawson was referring to. "The number is '22106'," Myers observed.

"Maybe it refers to a line number in the code page." Lawson said as Myers looked at the code page.

"There's only forty-nine lines in the code page and the last two digits of our number in question gives us an '06' as a number but that is part of the line of code giving us the ISBN number," Lawson said while looking at the screen. "I doubt that they would use the same lines for the message, though it wouldn't be impossible. Most likely, they used a method similar to Ben Franklin's running-key cipher but modified it to use a book for deciphering the code rather than a single page of writing. In the modified version, the page number would typically be first followed by the line number on the page then the position of the character on the line to make up the five digits of the number. They would have to use all five digits in each number on the code page to code the message from the book. First, we have to find out what line on the code sheet the message starts with. What about the first two numbers, twenty-two in that first five-digit number in line four of the code sheet? Could that be a line number?" Myers counted down the rows until he hit the twenty-second line.

Lawson took the book Roedl was holding and handed it to Myers. Myers looked at Lawson, then at the book in his hand then his briefcase. The book he was holding was 'The Huns'. Myers was confused.

"Who got into my briefcase?" Myers exclaimed, knowing that he had locked the up the book in the case yet here was the book.

"I got that from Admiral Roedl," Lawson replied.

"I got the book from the bookcase," Roedl answered while Myers opened his briefcase to see his copy of the book still laying there.

Lawson looked once more at the book Myers had in his hand and made sure the book Myers was holding was not the book in the briefcase. Taking the book from Myers hand, he looked at the first five-digit number on line twenty-two of the code sheet. Doing some quick thinking he said, "It has to be page fifty-one," after looking at the number '51342' on the screen. Next he looked at the next three digits in the five-digit number, assuming the third digit had to be a line number and the last two digits had to be the position of the character in the line. He figured that doing it any other way would greatly limit the number of characters a person had to choose from to create the code. He opened the book to page fifty-one and looked at line three. There was the evidence he was looking for. Underneath each of the characters in line three of page fifty-one in the book were very slight marks made from an ink pen. One mark under each character until it stopped under a 'U', the forty-second character in the line.

Lawson looked at the bookcase then rushed to the door. Moments later he came back in while everyone was wondering what got his attention. Meanwhile, Gunny had finished his visit with Josh and, seeing Lawson had the door open, followed him into the room.

Everyone watched as Lawson started to determine the next character of the message, all of them except Gunny still curious as to why he went out of the room. Lawson tried the next number on the code sheet, '31908'. Once more Lawson followed the number sequence to page thirty-one, line nine, the eighth character in the line to see that the next character was an 'S' with ink markings under each of the letters going to the 'S'". He continued with each five-digit number until he felt he had enough information to assure himself that the sequence on line twenty-two was the start of the message. By the time he had gone through the ninth number on line twenty-two, he had 'US NAVY' showing from the analysis. All but two of the pages he looked at had ink marks underneath the characters in the book. Whoever used the book had counted the characters from the beginning of the line to the position of the character in the code using an ink pen as a pointer. The book had been used to make the code.

"Myers," Lawson said as he looked at the others in the room, "the coding seems to show that if the third digit is a one through a nine, then we use that five-digit number to decode the message. If the third digit in the five-digit number is a zero, we ignore that five-digit number because there is no line zero on any page. The more important thing I've noticed is that we have the code and it was made by the person who occupies this room." Everyone looked at Lawson wondering how he came to that conclusion.

"Go tell," Roedl ordered. "This had better be good."

Lawson grinned and replied, "Admiral, you got the book from the bookcase, his bookcase, and it appears the message was created using this book from the fact that there are marks under each character to the character in question. That's item number one. Second item, the first message we found on the code sheet was the message 'OUT FEB 1'. If I recall correctly, Rod Lavlery went on vacation on the 1st." Roedl nodded 'yes'. "Then there is the situation that Gunny found where Congressman Latershan's phone card was left in the phone when the congressman left his office. That leaves Latershan's phone and computer available for someone to send emails. Lavlery is on Latershan's staff so Rod using Latershan's computer would not raise any suspicions. Gunny also said that Latershan most often would leave his computer logged on when he went out to get a cup of coffee, use the restroom or meet someone else in the corridor. Lavlery would know this pattern and, I assume, would take advantage of it."

"Well," Roedl interjected, "that all makes sense and the evidence is there. Is it enough to bring up charges?"

"Don't know," Lawson replied. "That's something for the feds to figure out. I have one more supposition that would interest all of you. The reason I went out in the hall was to see the nameplate on the wall next to the door, 'Rod Lavlery'. Lavlery's first name is 'Rod'. It seems coincidental that we are investigating a potential terrorist with the pseudonym of 'Hotrod Lincoln'. Again, coincidence or a relationship?"

"Josh Henry came to the same conclusion," Gunny stated. "I just got back from seeing him and he says that he thought that one of the people that could be Hotrod Lincoln is Rod Lavlery. He said that about a month ago, the name 'Lavlery' came up in a Chinese communique between a Chinese Colonel in charge of foreign espionage whose name was Colonel Qiang Zhu and a Chinese student at Lawrence Livermore Labs that we picked up just after the message was intercepted. Our intel people thought the name 'Lavlery' was a misspelling of a different name."

Roedl looked around the room at the team. The importance of Lawson's conjecture and Gunny's comments just hit him. It was not just a question of a person being a spy and potential terrorist but the possibility that that person holds the very room the team was working in. He realized he must get answers quickly.

"I wonder if this is the same Chinese Colonel that was mentioned during the inquiry about the persons believed to have received the pictures that you guys are analyzing?" Roedl inquired with the query being more of an observation than a question. Everyone thought about Roedl's comment for a moment then turned to the conclusions Lawson came up with.

"So, we have a good idea of who sent the messages to the North Koreans from Latershan's office," Roedl said while he looked at each of the team members. "One other question," he continued, "has anyone seen Captain Henderson?" Everyone nodded 'no'. "Also, I want a BOLO put out on Lavlery immediately!"

"I'll take care of that," Gunny replied. At that point, Roedl exited the room.

Norman came into the room as Myers and Lawson began to go through the book, putting the message together from the code sheet. After numerous interruptions and discussions on Lawson's analysis of Lavlery's connection which also involved bringing Norman up to speed on what had taken place, they finally got the coded message interpreted.

"It appears that the first number in the message has meaning," Lawson reported. "As you know the first two digits of the five-digit number is the line number. From what I can see, the last three digits are the number of characters in the message. If I count all characters including spaces, special characters and end of sentence punctuation, I come out to one-hundred and six characters for the message. The last three digits in the first number on the ISBN number line that we used the Fibonacci sequence on is '106'. It matches."

"That's great," Norman said, "What does the message say?"

Myers looked at the screen and read back the results, "'US NAVY WILL HAVE ALL SHIPS OUT OF YOUR AREA BETWEEN FEB 1 AND FEB 8. BEST TIME FOR LAUNCH TESTS IS FEB 4. DEPOSIT PAYMENT IN GRAND CAYMAN ACCOUNT', so it appears that North Korea plans some sort of missile launch for February 4th."

Norman looked at the screen, wincing as she thought through the potential of what the message meant. "I want you guys to continue analyzing the code sheet," she ordered while continuing to process the information. "There's an awful lot of code on that code sheet for just this message. There may be more information buried in the sheet." Lawson and Myers looked at each other, both realizing that she was right.

"On it," Lawson said while Myers closed the screen with the message and brought the code page back up.

"Look guys," She continued, "It's getting late and we have a full day tomorrow. With this Lavlery thing coming to the forefront and the search for Gunny's shooter still active, we need to be alert and not lose our sharpness because of fatigue."

"What about the urgency and limited time frame?" Lawson inquired. "The message says February 4th and today is February 3rd which means that it's already February 4th in North Korea."

Norman pondered Lawson's comment for a moment then replied, "I'll contact Fort Gordon to check on any communications coming out of North Korea and I'll get the West Pacific radar trackers to focus on the North Korea area. Anything else?"

"Satellites?" Lawson responded.

"Thanks, Jim. Good point," Norman agreed. "That would help us a lot. I need to go so that I can get these requests going. Anything else?" They all nodded 'no' as they proceeded to put their items in the safe.

Chapter 9

Escape

"Every man builds his world in his own image. He has the power to choose, but no power to escape the necessity of choice." - Ayn Rand

It was 1:20 PM Pacific Time on February 3rd as Rod Lavlery arrived at the shipping complex after flying to Los Angeles then taking a taxi to the Port of Los Angeles at San Pedro. The shipping complex was where numerous ships a day would come into the port to offload their cargos. Most ships were container ships carrying hundreds of large metal containers that would be offloaded by large cranes once they docked at the piers. Due to the heavy traffic in the port, the ships had a tight schedule, as the transfer of containers from the ship to the docks was fast and very efficient. The port had forty-three miles of waterfront with twenty-seven cargo and passenger terminals that supported container, automobile, dry and liquid bulk with supporting warehouse facilities.

Lavlery had the taxi take him to terminal 100, the China Shipping Terminal, after he cleared security at the gate on Pacific Avenue to enter the port. With his letter of access to the port and his luggage case, Lavlery got out of the taxi, paid his fare and walked toward berth 100 where the container ship, 'Pacific Jade', was nearing completion of its offloading process.

He walked down the causeway to berth 100 and handed the letter of access to the security officer at the bottom of the gangway going up to the first deck of the ship. Once the security guard looked at his letter and verified his access authority to board the ship, he waved Lavlery to proceed. Rod Lavlery walked up the gangway to a waiting Chinese man dressed in a three-piece suit and tie standing at the top of the gangway.

"You're late," The man said in a heavy Chinese accent.

"Sorry, Colonel," Lavlery replied, "I got here as quick as the airline schedules allowed."

"Well, you cut it close," the Colonel observed. "We leave the port in ten minutes. I'll show you to your stateroom and once there, we can discuss your progress with our plan." With that, they went to the rear of the ship and up a ladder to the next level. Walking down a passageway, they came to door 214 and entered the stateroom.

The stateroom was small, barely enough room for a bed and a place to put the luggage. It had one porthole looking out on the channel where the ships came into port. There was one overhead light with a pull chain attached to it used to turn the light on and off. The room was painted white with streams of rust at various points in the walls. The door to the stateroom had seen its better days as it was rusty with dents in it declaring a history of some violence that occurred in the distant past. The room was musty and humid. Lavlery thought about how this room would get to him during the sixteen day trip to Manila, Philippines. He sat down on the bed as the Colonel followed in behind him and closed the door.

"We didn't get any in-depth information on your progress from your last message," the Colonel said while leaning against the wall.

Chinese Colonel Qiang Zhu was five feet, ten inches tall with an athletic build. He got his Masters degree from Ecole Polytechnique, a university in the southern suburbs of Paris, France. Majoring in digital technology and human motion engineering, he spent another six months in Canada with clandestine visits to the U.S. before returning to Bejing, China. Once back in China, he tested for a leadership position in the Chinese Army and rapidly rose in rank to his present rank of Colonel. As a member of the Ministry of State Security, his primary function in the Chinese intelligence apparatus was in the foreign intelligence arena, turning citizens of other nations into spies. Sometimes he accomplished this with radicals that had a problem with their government, sometimes it was with people that had a question of conscience but the majority were people that wanted money in exchange for information. Money was Lavlery's incentive, five-million dollars worth.

"You didn't get any detailed information on the latest movements of US naval forces in the western Pacific because, up till now, I haven't received any payments for prior information I gave you," Lavlery replied while measuring Zhu's facial response.

"Whatever," Zhu lamented. "The transition of monies is always slow. What have you got?"

"The North Koreans are planning for a launch of an ICBM missile on the seventh of this month."

"ICBM?" Zhu exclaimed. "How long have you known this? This may complicate our plans."

Lavlery shifted on the bed while he realized that the Chinese government had no idea what North Korea was up to or at least the intel community was closed out of the information. "The US intel community knew about this on January 27th. I sent you info about it in the Paris picture. You got that picture, didn't you?"

Zhu nodded 'yes' and proceeded with his concerns. "I realize now that the message sent in the Paris picture and the message sent in the London picture have to be used together to make sense. That violates our rules and agreement on how you were to send the messages. It was one topic, one picture."

"I know," Lavlery answered. "There were rumors, credible rumors, that Admiral Roedl of the ONI's Special Operations Goup has a team of people that were being considered to use to break our code. As you know, Captain Henderson was to lead that group if ONI determined that CAT205 was to be the team. The CAT205 team appeared to be very effective, so I couldn't chance the whole message being on one picture."

"CAT205," the Colonel pondered. "I read a Russian intel report intercepted by our communications people that identified a CAT205 unit as radically changing the methods and protocol on the way information is gathered and how threats are removed. This group was very effective in Iran, though we don't know what the Russians lost or what this group got."

"I'll tell you what they got," Lavlery exclaimed. "This is bonus information to you at no additional cost. They got the plans for a five-hundred kilowatt laser system that can work in almost any weather."

"And how do you know this?"

"I know it because I work, or shall I say, worked in the office of Congressman Latershan. He's on the House Intelligence

Committee. The information went through his office. Your people are coming up short…"

"OK," Zhu interrupted as his expression changed to one of concern. "We will meet at 15:00 Zulu tomorrow night for the money exchange on the aft section of the ship. Anyone finding out that you have that money on you will make you a target on this ship. So we'll try to keep this as quiet as possible."

"So, 15:00 Zulu. That makes it 11:00 PM in the present Pacific time zone, That's, uh, thirty-three hours from now. That works," Lavlery said while he looked at his watch.

Colonel Zhu left the stateroom and went to the radio room on the ship and set his code in to scramble the message so he would have a secure link. He sent a message to his command in China about the CAT205 team, the laser weapon and the information about North Korea potentially sending up an ICBM missile on February 7th. His thinking is how this would make points for him at the highest levels of government.

As Lavlery walked about the ship during the afternoon, he began to realize that the crew was not what he expected. They were not your usual crew members, hired for their strength but not their mental acuity. These men appeared to all be well trained and disciplined. They carried themselves around as ones that were focused on a single goal. Once the ship had cleared the twelve mile limit, all of the crew members suddenly appeared with side arms. It was also apparent that there were many more personnel on the ship than is normally needed, all armed.

Lavlery wondered why the heavy presence of armed personnel. As he stood watching the crew members move around, Colonel Zhu stepped to his side.

"I see you're noting the number of crew and their weapons," he said while putting on his own sidearm.

Lavlery turned to look at Zhu, surprised that that he had changed to his military uniform. He looked back down at the container area to see large caliber weapons being set up on permanent mounts. It also appeared that more people were coming up on deck in uniforms and carrying AK-47 automatic rifles. Lavlery turned to Zhu.

"I've noticed that this appears to be setting up as an armed vessel," Lavlery mused. "Is there something out there that is that much of a threat to this ship?"

"This is between you and me," Zhu said while he looked around to see if anyone was nearby. "We have ten-thousand PF-98 120mm Anti-Tank missiles and over a thousand launchers down in the lower hold. We'll be delivering them to the New People's Army in the Philippines. The troops you see on this ship are to ensure that we can make the delivery without being overwhelmed by a surprise visit by the Philippine Army or an attempted takeover of these weapons by pirates in the South Philippine area."

"Now, you wanted details of what has been done," Lavlery stated.

"This is as good a time as any," Zhu responded.

"The Big Ben picture is the one they'll analyze first since it was the last sent. As such, I doubt that they will get anywhere to the next level of decoding under that picture so what we have hidden is safe." Lavlery explained. "All they have to do is click on the picture while they are on the internet. That will happen when the Fort Bevoir team presents their report to the Joint Staff, which I have arranged for timing purposes. The US will be accused of instigating an attack without provocation and the rest is history. Now a question, why are you paying me here instead of depositing five million into my Grand Cayman account?"

Zhu looked around the decks then answered, "It was necessary as our Chinese internal security is monitoring all large electronic transactions and we can't leave any trail that would tell any other country, by either accident or on purpose, what we are doing."

Lavlery took in and analyzed Colonel Zhu's comments as he went to the galley area to get dinner. He felt naked, being the only person in the galley seating area not wearing or carrying a weapon. Finishing his dinner, he went back to his stateroom and dropped off to a very apprehensive sleep. "We are preparing for war and I'm to start it" were the last thoughts he had as he faded off.

The alarms were loud and the language undiscernible. He knew it was general quarters being called out in Chinese. Jumping out of his rack, he looked at his watch, 6:35 AM. Putting on his shoes, he opened the door to his stateroom to see person after person running down the passageway. Finally, when there was a break in the traffic, he stepped out and ran to the ladder taking him to the bridge. He went up several decks until he came to the bridge then opened the hatch that allowed him entry onto the bridge control center.

The bridge had two rows of control stations going the full length of the bridge area. Each of the stations had screens built into the cabinets of the stations set at a sixty degree angle from the person sitting at the station so the person could see the screen information while being able to look out the windows. Below each screen were dials, lights, switches and buttons arranged in special positions based upon the function of the station. Lavlery was surprised that there appeared to be no steering wheel, called the helm, used to change the ship's direction as there were in older ships. After looking at each station, he found a center console between two captain's chairs that had a helm built in almost flush with the surface it was attached to. It was obvious that the helm was seldom used as most of the steering was done from touch display entries in front of the captain's chairs. Looking forward toward the front of the bridge were large windows that extended the whole length of the bridge and to the sides up to the side hatch used to enter the bridge. The windows allowed for the personnel on the bridge to see what was in front and to the sides of the ship. It also allowed them to see a majority of the cargo sitting above the main deck, which was essential, particularly in heavy weather. The shifting of cargo could lead to serious damage and, if the weight distribution was too extreme, could cause the ship to roll, dumping much of the cargo into the sea.

As Lavlery looked around he could sense the panic of those on the bridge. Everyone, except the radar person, was focused on an object on the horizon. Looking at the map on one console, Lavlery could see that they were one-hundred twenty five miles away from Los Angeles. That meant that they were traveling about twenty-five knots. As he looked closer at the consoles, on one, he saw markers displayed on the screen that indicated the object on the horizon was a ship. It was moving toward them and closing fast. Looking from station to station at the line of consoles, he realized that these were not ordinary bridge controls. One station showed identifiers for the ship approaching while another showed the condition for weapons systems. He realized that this was an active military vessel camouflaged to be a commercial ship. As he realized the situation a familiar voice resonated next to him.

"So you've figured out who we are," Colonel Zhu observed. "I figured it wouldn't take long for you to do so. We could be on parity with the U.S. Navy ship but we will concede to a boarding and inspection. They can't get to the weapons stored on board without moving the containers and they don't know of our hidden passageways to those areas. So we are having our people move the above-board weapons systems back into their hiding places. Once more we will look strictly commercial."

"But what about all these people?" Lavlery asked as he looked around. "How do you explain this number of crewmembers to the inspectors and, remember, we're about one-hundred twenty miles from the coast which still puts us in the US economic zone, so they can legally board this ship without any diplomatic repercussions."

Zhu thought over Lavlery's comments. He was right. They were in a position where the Navy destroyer could stop them in their tracks and delay them for days, if they wanted to. Zhu shouted something in Chinese to the others on the bridge. Seconds later an announcement was made in Chinese to the crew throughout the ship. As soon as the announcement went out, everyone took off their weapons and military clothing, putting on their working clothes normal for a ship's crew. The side arms and rifles quickly moved down the ladders to the main deck and disappeared from view. Weapons mounted on the main deck disappeared as well. Everything went back to the scene Lavlery first saw when he came on board.

"How are you going to explain the additional people?" He asked as he looked at Zhu.

"They all have this notebook," Zhu said as he handed the notebook to Lavlery. It was written in Chinese but, based upon the pictures, was obviously some sort of training manual. "They are now trainees, learning how the ship operates as they are future crewmembers for the new container ships." Lavlery was struck by the planning and orderly nature of the people on the ship. "The mysterious, inscrutable Chinese," he thought. "Always one step ahead." A stereotype that had a lot of history behind it and now he was seeing it first hand as the Navy ship approached.

"Standby for boarding," came the call as the Pacific Jade had come to a complete stop after reversing the engines ten minutes before when the destroyer had radioed for the container ship to stop. It takes some time for a ship of this size to stop and the destroyer commander had anticipated that and slowed down long before launching his boat team to do the inspection.

"You are on the manifest as a passenger," Zhu explained. "Do you have your passport ready for them to see? You also need your access letter you used to get into the port. That will identify your authority to travel on this ship since you are American and this is a Chinese ship."

Zhu said something in Chinese to the ship's captain then went back to Lavlery. "I told the captain that he has to have his logs and manifests ready for inspection. He's just given orders to the first mate to get the documents together while he goes down to meet the boarding party. When they ask you what's your destination, tell them. Now, we'll all have to go down to the main deck for document verification. I need to leave you to see to the other people and their documents." With that, Colonel Zhu left the bridge and headed to the aft section of the ship. Lavlery went back to his stateroom, retrieved his passport and access letter and headed for the main deck assembly area.

He waited for a couple of hours while the papers of each person were checked then he heard his name called. Going to the cabin where the naval officers were checking papers, he entered the door and stepped inside. Handing his passport to the naval officer sitting at a desk, he looked at the two armed naval petty officers holding M4 machineguns. "Access authority papers," came the request. Lavlery pulled the paper from his pocket and handed it to the officer sitting at the desk. The paper was previously stamped with a US State Department authorization to travel on the ship. The officer looked at the paper and nodded to the armed sailors. They exited the cabin and closed the door behind them.

"Captain Henderson said that you are to meet a man wearing a gray fedora hat at the Regency Hotel in Manila," the officer said while pulling some items from a courier pouch. "He said that the man will give you instructions on what to do next. He'll identify himself as Robert McNamara." Lavlery thought it funny that a guy's code name would be that of a former Secretary of Defense.

"What about the money," Lavlery asked.

"Henderson said that you can keep the money and you are to disappear. Here is your new identity," the officer said as he handed Lavlery a new passport and authorization paper taken from the courier pouch. You'll be Sam Ginty. When you see the man in Manila that is what you'll identify yourself as."

Lavlery took the new passport and paper as the officer took his old passport and paper, putting them in the pouch. "We're done here," the officer said while he put the pouch in his briefcase and closed it. They both went out the door of the cabin together and, as the officer exited, he motioned for the US naval personnel to go back to the boat. Once they departed, Lavlery went back to his stateroom. The rest of the day was quiet as Lavlery remained in his stateroom and Colonel Zhu was nowhere to be seen.

After eating dinner in the galley area, he went back to his stateroom to get some sleep. It was 10:45 PM when the alarm on his wristwatch sounded. Getting up, he put his shoes on and headed for the aft section of the ship. Passing by the galley sitting area, he saw that the crew was watching a movie he recognized as the western movie 'Silverado' with Chinese subtitles. Smiling about that observation, he went to the very back of the ship where he could look over the rear railing to see the turbulence generated from the screws driving the ship forward. He was impressed by how much power was being produced.

"I see you're on time," the voice from behind him proclaimed.

Lavlery turned to see Colonel Zhu setting down a large gym bag and unzipping it. "Five million dollars," Zhu said while Lavlery reached down and pulled out a couple of bundles of one-hundred dollar bills.

"So, this is what five-million dollars looks like," Lavlery exclaimed as he thumbed through one of the stacks of money.

"Yes, it is and I wanted you to get the joy of seeing it, after all we are not vicious people," Zhu responded. Curious as to what Zhu meant, Lavlery looked up to see a Chinese pistol with a silencer pointed at him. Joy turned to panic as Lavlery realized what was happening.

"Why the weapon?" he questioned. "Didn't I do everything asked of me?"

"You did," was Zhu's response. "However, we can't leave any loose ends for someone to discover what really happened after all your coding comes to fruition. Besides, we Chinese hate traitors." Lavlery lunged forward toward Zhu as Zhu fired one shot. The bullet kicked Lavlery back as Zhu put a second shot into his head. Lavlery fell back against the railing with the force of his movement backward causing him to flip over the rail and off the back of the ship. Zhu watched as Lavlery's body was caught in the turbulence of the water below and disappear.

Finishing his task, Zhu zipped up the gym bag, picked it up and carried it back to his stateroom. Depositing the money in the room, he went up to the radio room and sent a message. Once the message was completed, he went to the bridge control room and signaled the ship's Officer of the Deck (OOD) to come to him.

"Turn off our ship location identifier then change course to two-nine-zero degrees," Zhu ordered. "We're going to Singapore."

"But, Sir, what about the weapons we are supposed to deliver to the Philippines?" The OOD questioned.

"Those weapons are going to go to our southern border for our troops facing North Korea. They'll be needed there," Zhu replied as the OOD input the new coordinates into the ship's navigation computer for travel to Singapore.

"Don't navigate by computer for the present," Zhu instructed, seeing the OOD enter the coordinates. "A course of two-nine-zero will keep us out of the normal traffic paths and we need to be as invisible as possible."

The OOD confirmed the order and set the new course as he wondered why they were going to Singapore and not Shanghai.

Next, Zhu went to the galley where the movie was being shown and pulled the troop commander for the military personnel on board the ship and instructed him. "We are outside any U.S. controlled waters. As we are in international waters, I want you to go to wartime standard procedures. All weapons to be up on deck and ready to fire. Any ship challenging us will be sunk and we are to maintain radio silence. Our ship identifier has been turned off so that we cannot be tracked. We'll be going to double-teamed four hour watches. Is that understood?"

"Yes Colonel," came the response as the troop commander communicated the orders to his personnel. Moments later, an order was issued through the PA system, which resulted in a significant increase in activity on the main deck.

"Now," the troop commander queried, "we changed out the manifest that had Lavlery as a passenger and changed it to having Ginty as a passenger but doesn't the master manifest in Los Angeles have Lavlery as still the passenger?"

Zhu turned to walk down the passageway. "The list that was used to check everyone on board at the wharf in Los Angeles had Lavlery's name but the master list does not. I paid the Wharf Master 50,000 U.S. dollars to check off everyone coming on board on both the master list and the fake list. He was to use the fake list to see who was really coming on board and turn in the master list as the list he checked. You see, the master list has neither Lavlery or Ginty."

"That's not true, sir," the troop commander disagreed. "He turned in the checklist with Lavlery's name on it. I know this because the ship's captain got the final transmitted list for confirmation once we were out to sea. Lavlery's name was on it."

"Well, it won't matter," Zhu responded. "We aren't going to the Philippines so we haven't any need to verify the manifest to anyone. Besides, neither Lavlery or Ginty are on board, so the master list in Los Angeles won't matter. See, no problem." With that comment, Zhu headed out on deck to check the ship as the troop commander wondered what happened to Ginty though he wasn't curious enough to find out. That might be a fatal mistake.

Chapter 10

Revelations – Day 4

"Men occasionally stumble over the truth, but most of them pick themselves up and hurry off as if nothing ever happened." - Winston S. Churchill

It was the afternoon of February 4th as Lawson paced back and forth in room 2337. Myers was at the computer looking at the code sheet. They had been looking at the code sheet for over five hours and argued during lunch about where to go next.

"I don't see any other viable code in here," Myers said as he continued to look at the sheet.

"The first time we did an ASCII scan of the sheet, you said something about some line having similarities to the line where we found the ISBN number," Lawson stated.

"I remember that, but I don't remember why it stuck out. What line was it?" Myers asked as he searched the directories on the computer for his notes.

"It had something to do with the picture," Lawson remembered. "Go back to the picture." As Myers did so, Lawson looked at the clock in the picture. Looking around at the scenery and the clock, he backed away from the screen.

"Got to look at the big picture, so what stands out that we haven't used. That's it! The minute hand on Big Ben, it's line forty-three!" Lawson exclaimed.

As they started to look at line forty-three of the code sheet, Gunny came in as they heard the familiar 'beep' that indicated someone had accessed the room.

"Compliments of Admiral Roedl," Gunny said while setting a cardboard box on the table that contained sub sandwiches, chips and drinks.

"Ah," Myers observed, "a programmer's meal." They laughed as they unwrapped the sandwiches and set them out in their personal spaces,"

"This place is a mess," Gunny observed as he picked up coffee cups, paper bags and empty pizza boxes. "I feel sometimes like you guys need a mother." Lawson and Myers looked at each other and laughed. "All right, guys," Gunny continued, "you don't have to help but at least use the trashcan."

"They think that the trashcan is just a piece of artwork. After all, they're engineers," came the voice from the corner of the room next to the books.

"By the way, you've got a visitor," Lawson remarked.

Gunny looked to see a man sitting in the corner. "Josh Henry, what are you doing here?" Gunny questioned. "You are supposed to be in the hospital."

"I know, Gunny," Josh whispered as talking hurt with the bruising the bullet had caused to his chest. "It was important for me to talk to you in a secure place and the hospital has too many ears."

"Understood," Gunny retorted. "As soon as we're finished here, I'm taking you back to the hospital."

Josh just nodded and proceeded, "What do you know about Captain Henderson?"

Gunny sat on the edge of the desk while Lawson and Myers turned to hear the conversation.

"I know he's a JAG officer that's also a deep agent in the Pentagon, working for the Defense Intelligence Agency," came Gunny's explanation.

Josh stretched out as he tried to relieve the pain in his chest, "A deep agent for whom?"

Gunny was taken back by Josh Henry's comment. Lawson stood up and began to pace again as Myers leaned back in his chair. The question caught them all off guard. Lawson knew of Josh's reputation. This question would not have been raised if Josh didn't have some pertinent information backing up the comment. Over the past two days, Lawson took some time to check out Josh Henry after he found out about Gunny's meeting with him. Checking some records and talking to several people at the DIA, Lawson found out that Josh Henry's record for ascertaining the activities and relationships in Washington, DC was impeccable. He was a guy worth listening to.

"So, what have you got, Josh," Gunny probed.

Josh took a couple of slow deep breaths. Gunny was about to help Josh up and get him back to the hospital when Josh spoke, "As you know, I frequent a cyber café in Reston, Virginia. It's there where I find out a lot of classified information I might not normally be privy to. In my wanderings among the purveyors of information in that place, I came across a comment about Hotrod Lincoln and another person whose pseudonym was Captain

Crunch. It didn't mean much to me until I decided to follow the exchange which concerned an exchange of money for a programming skill. That's not unusual within the café. What was unusual was the offer of five-million dollars for a program. The person was acting as an intermediary between Hotrod Lincoln and another person with the pseudonym of 'Prism'. I had to go back several years to remember that person and, while lying in the hospital, it suddenly came to me. I am almost sure that 'Prism' is the pseudonym of a Chinese Colonel by the name of Qiang Zhu?"

"I remember you mentioning him a couple of days ago," Gunny reminded him.

"Ah, I did tell you about him," Josh remembered. "However, I had time to get on the computer and check out some information while I've been at the hospital."

"You don't have access to classified information at the hospital," Gunny observed.

"Right you are, Gunny," Josh agreed, "but I do have access to the dark web and, in searching it for Zhu's messages, I found one that was particularly interesting. It states the pickup point as being the 'Pacific Jade', the contact as being Sam Ginty and the message to be carried by the U.S. Navy Destroyer Warren Magnuson. First, Sam Ginty was the real name of a hacker that was thrown out of the Defense Intelligence Agency two years ago for attempting to hack a Chinese missile site without authorization. He seemed to have fallen off the face of the earth until this message showed up. Next, the manifest for the ship 'Pacific Jade' shows their February 3rd manifest of having another person on board of great interest, Colonel Qiang Zhu.

The message to the Destroyer Commander was to give Sam Ginty his passport and access papers. The question was, how did Sam Ginty get on a formal manifest without a passport?"

Lawson, Gunny and Myers were wondering where Josh was going with this. Gunny looked at the other two and pointed at his head. They both understood Gunny was thinking that Josh was not thinking clearly from the pain and drugs he had been given.

"Don't do that, Gunny," Josh remarked. "I'm in full use of my senses. Just let me get through the details and to the end."

"Sorry, Josh," Gunny replied. "We just don't see the picture yet as to what the Pacific Jade and this Sam Ginty has to do with our operation."

Josh took a couple more deep breaths and continued, "It will all be clear in a couple of moments. Now where was I?" Josh looked at Lawson, "Lavlery disappears and Ginty shows up. Kind of coincidental, don't you think. I know you're already putting this together, Lawson."

"I see the parts, just not how this applies to Henderson," Lawson answered.

"What do you see in this, Lawson?" Gunny posed.

"Well, it's like this," Lawson started. "Lavlery had to leave the country pretty quick as these messages were discovered sooner than he thought once the pictures were picked up by Fort Gordon. A Chinese vessel is one way to get out and I think Sam Ginty is actually Rod Lavlery. The reason I think this is the case is that Sam Ginty would not be able to get on the Pacific Jade without his passport but Rod Lavlery would with his own passport and a letter of access. Then by being provided Sam

Ginty's passport and access papers later, the manifest matches the personnel on board and Rod Lavlery disappears into thin air. The question I have is who gave the orders for the Captain of the destroyer to deliver the Sam Ginty passport to Lavlery. It would take a State Department action to give a Navy destroyer crew orders to provide a different passport to an individual outside of the U.S. territorial waters, as I assume this happened more than twelve miles out."

"Right so far," Josh commended.

"Let me answer another question Gunny's about to ask," Lawson continued. "Why would Lavlery take back an old name that was already attached to a tarnished reputation. The answer is simple, Lavlery was not anticipating having to leave so quickly but someone probably informed him that we were getting close to determining the message. Something he didn't expect to happen until after his actions became reality. Since he had to leave and he had not yet received another passport under a different name and he couldn't use his present one as he would be tracked, he had to fall back to his previous but still active passport. That's what was being delivered to him."

"Outstanding," Josh said. "You're right, Gunny. This guy knows how to put a puzzle together and..."

"OK," Gunny interrupted, "Josh, you implied that Henderson had some doing in this escapade."

"Wow," Josh reacted, "Your English is improving. Lawson is rubbing off on you." Gunny just gave a wince as Josh continued, "Someone had to send the orders to the destroyer along with the documents to intercept the Pacific Jade. The Pacific Jade came from San Pedro harbor while the destroyer came from San Diego harbor. I checked the courier listings to see what went from Washington, DC to San Diego Naval Station. A number of messages but nothing stood out. I was about to give up when I saw a delivery by a civilian courier service. The pdf of the delivery document showed it came from Washington, DC, delivered to the Point Loma Naval Station and had, in the sender section, 'Captain Crunch', with the sending address being the Pentagon general address. The Warren Magnuson had just finished degaussing at Point Loma when the delivery was made. It's rational to say that the delivery at Point Loma and the delivery on the Pacific Jade are one and the same. Everyone with me so far," Josh asked as he looked around.

"What about Henderson?" Gunny probed.

"Henderson is Captain Crunch," Josh added. "I know this because I checked the date and time logs when I saw Henderson in the cyber café with the information exchanges going on in the café and the occurrence of the name 'Captain Crunch' showing up. They match time and date exactly. Furthermore, the order to the destroyer had to come from someone authorized to issue that order without having to go through the normal chain of command or working through the State Department. Something an intel officer in an active operation can do. Catch my drift."

"So what if Henderson is doing this legitimately as a part of our operation?" Gunny asked. "After all, there are sub-plots going on all the time in these types of operations."

"That's a good point, Gunny," Josh answered. "That's one reason I haven't run this up the flagpole. It might be that he is operating his part of the operation and raising a question would endanger his mission and his team. I'm just laying out what I see and what I think. Now, Gunny, if you don't mind, I could use some help up. I'm ready to go back to the hospital."

Gunny lifted Josh from the floor and helped him out the door and down the corridor. Lawson and Myers went back to their work while thinking about what Josh had told them. Having just found the line number for the next message among all the interruptions, Lawson and Myers felt burned out and decided to call it a day. They left the room and ran into Gunny and Josh in the parking lot as Gunny loaded Josh into his car.

"Where are you guys going?" Gunny inquired.

"We've hit our limit. We're out of here," Lawson explained.

"But it's barely after 17:00 hours and you're in a time crunch!" Gunny exclaimed. "What'll I tell Norman when she comes in?"

Myers looked at Lawson then responded, "Tell her that we've hit a mental block and can't concentrate. We need sleep. After the events of last night being a late night for all of us and the constant interruptions of the day, we need to get rest and a fresh mind. We know where we are going in the code, we just don't know if we can evaluate the impact of the messages without getting a fresh start. Tell her that, she'll understand." Gunny agreed as he left with Henry.

Seeing he forgot his weapon, Gunny left Josh in the car as he ran back to get his weapon from the room. As he entered the room, he saw the forgetfulness of his team mates.

"Wow, they must be tired," Gunny mused as he saw all of the paperwork and computer still on the desk. Opening the safe, he placed everything inside and locked it. He saw formulas on the whiteboard that looked rather complex to him causing him to resist erasing the board. "Should I leave the formulas or erase them?" he said to himself. "I don't want to destroy something that they may not be able to reproduce. No problem." Taking his camera out of his pocket, he took pictures of what was on the whiteboard then erased the board after verifying that he could read the information in the photos he took.

Checking the room out once more, he checked to see that his weapon was in his holster, turned out the light and left after making sure the door had closed and latched. As he was walking down the hallway, he ran into Norman. Motioning for her to follow him outside, he went out to the sidewalk and explained in a low voice what had transpired. She exhibited a sigh of tired relief as they both walked together to their cars with Norman leaving to her apartment and Gunny taking Josh back to the hospital. Gunny realized that he was also very tired but he still had a lot of work to do before the end of the day. He looked at Josh as Josh had fallen asleep. "I guess he'll be OK," Gunny thought to himself as he proceeded onto Independence Avenue on his way to the hospital. He began to realize that Josh's visit had just changed the whole landscape and it was very disturbing.

Chapter 11

More Code and Confrontation – Day 5

"Be leery of silence. It doesn't mean you won the argument. Often, people are just busy reloading their guns." - Shannon L. Alder

Lawson and Myers got back to their work on the code sheet the next morning. It was February 5th and Lawson's suggestion about looking at line forty-three paid off. Myers went through the same process, using the Fibonacci sequence to determine the sequence of numbers to identify the book used for the code. Once they got the numbers set up in proper order they searched for the book name.

"So, number '0471056294' is what we've got and, doing a search, brings up the book 'Physical Geography'," Myers said as he turned to look at the bookcase, "and here it is." Pulling out the book, he handed it to Lawson.

"What does the first five-digit number in the code sheet for the ISBN show for the line number?" Lawson asked.

"It shows '27165',"Myers called.

"So, we are going to go to line twenty-seven to find the page number, line number and character position for each of one-hundred sixty-five characters, Correct?"

Myers nodded as he called out the first five-digit number to Lawson. Lawson searched for the point in the book and came up with a 'B'. Going through the process again, he came up with an 'E', then an 'S'. By the time they finished the sequence, they came up with the message 'BEST LAUNCH DATE IS FEB 7,

WASHINGTON TIME. THEY SHOULD HAVE LOWERED THEIR ALERTNESS FROM FEB 4 DATE IF THEY BROKE THE FIRST CODE WHICH IS ALMOST IMPOSSIBLE.'.

"This thing is loaded with red herrings," Myers said as he looked at the message. "How do we know this one is real?"

"Right now, we have to assume it is," Lawson stated. "We're long past February 4th in North Korea so this message has a greater possibility of being right."

"So, seeing these messages, how do we approach a recommendation?" Myers probed.

"Ok, let's look at this," Lawson began. "We have three different threats we are dealing with. We have this apparent missile launch that I suspect is an ICBM missile. That belief is based upon the amount of effort being put into trying to hide the information. Second, we've got a mole or an opposing operation somewhere here in Washington that is trying to keep us from finding the truth and, maybe, trying to create some other incident. And, third, we have opposition from those that don't like Admiral Roedl's methods for running things."

Once they got the message documented, they looked at the picture once again to see if there were any other number references. They checked the number of windows in each floor of the Parliament, the number of supports for the bridge, cars, spires and even birds. Nothing else came up.

Lawson looked at his watch. "I've got to go to the Warfare Center. Admiral Roedl wants me there to meet him at 2:00 PM."

"That works," Myers replied. "I've got to get something to eat and I have to get to the cafeteria downstairs before they close."

"Don't forget to lock everything up," Lawson directed. "If you leave, the room will be unattended." Myers nodded his head affirmative as Lawson walked out the door.

As Lawson entered the Admiral's office, he could tell that everything was the same as the last time he had been in the office seven months previous. There was a desk in the center of the room that was heavy oak and very organized. There was the obligatory phone, desk pad, a set of rubber stamps on a stand used for stamping documents and a nameplate reading 'E. Roedl, RADM' with a pen holder on one side with a gold pen in it. A computer monitor sat on his desk to the right side with the keyboard just in front of it. Behind the desk was still that picture of a sea battle from World War II. To his left was a wall with certificates, awards and trophies with a door at the end of the wall. On the right, another wall exhibited pictures of a guy that liked to play golf, go fishing and liked football. Below the pictures were a set of cabinets running the length of the wall. Behind him, above the door he just entered and to the sides of the door was the clock that was still two minutes fast, a calendar (the typical three-month government calendar with last month at the top, the present month in the center and next month at the bottom).

Lawson was caught by surprise as the picture behind the desk of the World War II sea battle suddenly disappeared and a live screen came up with audio included. There were four people sitting at the end of a table in a room, all apparently waiting for a meeting to start. As Lawson looked at the picture, now a live feed, Admiral Roedl came in through the side door to the left, nodded to Lawson and motioned for him to sit down in one of the chairs while Roedl moved to his desk chair. It was at that moment Lawson saw the camera built into the World War II sea battle picture frame that was actually surrounding a large screen monitor.

"Good afternoon, everyone," Roedl said as he garnered the attention of those on the screen.

"Good afternoon, Admiral," came a joint response.

"I would like everyone to meet Lieutenant Jim Lawson," the Admiral said while pointing to Lawson. Lawson was surprised by the meeting as he thought it was to be just him and the Admiral. It became immediately clear to him that things were changing and he was being brought up to speed. Even so, he had information he thought the Admiral should hear first before he presented it to people he didn't know. That expectation just left the building.

"Admiral, we were alarmed by your last memo," a Navy Captain stated as he started the exchange.

"What bothers you about it, Tom?" Roedl questioned.

"Well, you're giving full authority for your Lieutenant to act in areas we have not agreed to or been informed of," he responded. Everyone in the other room on the screen nodded agreement.

Roedl looked at his desk for a moment as he gathered his thoughts. "Mr. Lawson, here, has extensive skills in ascertaining the truth behind activities being carried out by both foreign powers and those within our own government. As mentioned in the memo, he and his team are working on a North Korean connected set of pictures that appears to have significant importance in our understanding of what the North Koreans plan to do. We can't go through the normal channels as that would take too long and time is of the essence. We've also been blocked on a number of occasions by those trying to go by the book. The threat he is analyzing appears more real day by day. I know you don't like being on the outside looking in, but it is essential for you to be so at this time. Mr. Lawson will update you at this time which is why I called this meeting."

"Good afternoon, Lieutenant Lawson," the Navy Captain known as Tom began.

"Lieutenant Lawson," the Admiral interrupted. "At the front of the table is Captain Tom Nyquist, head of our ONI operations in San Diego. Now, going clockwise, the next person is Colonel Jack Kelvin, Marine Fast Response Commander from Camp Pendleton. The next person is Captain Barbara Aviela, Joint Operations Commander for Pacific Intelligence Operations and the last person is Miss Joanne Benson, advisor to the Joint Staff on Eastern Asian affairs."

"Good afternoon to you all," Lawson interjected.

"Since the Admiral likes to use first names, I would like to use that protocol to remove any confusion in our conversation," Tom began. "Anyone have a problem with that?" As they looked around at each other, they all appeared to agree.

"So, Jim," Tom started as he directed his attention to Lawson, "why don't you update us on what you've got."

Lawson cleared his throat and began, "Well, Tom, the London picture exhibited a message behind the picture in code that indicated that the North Koreans plan some sort of missile launch on the seventh of this month. That's two days from now. I think it may be an ICBM missile."

That comment brought an immediate reaction from those on the screen. Roedl just sat and watched their reaction.

"Evan," Captain Aviela responded, "why were we not told about this?" she said as her question was directed toward Admiral Roedl.

"You are being informed now," was his response.

"Go on, Jim," Tom commanded.

Lawson looked down at this notes, "Well, we are sure that the message buried in the code is real. However, I am convinced that the message is only part of the use that the picture provides. I don't have anything yet to point to that assumption but, based upon what I've seen so far, that message could have easily been sent without going through all the effort of coding the message. I'm digging to find out if any other components are left in the picture."

"And have you found any?" Colonel Kelvin asked.

Roedl looked at Lawson while Lawson put his thoughts together. Roedl didn't realize that Lawson was going to present this theory because Lawson had not told him about this part of his concern yet. Roedl now wished that he had talked to Lawson before the information was presented to the joint commands. Lawson looked at Roedl then back to the screen.

"I haven't, as yet," Lawson answered. "Whatever I find will only be given to Admiral Roedl to deal with. I'm doing this separate from my other team members. They won't even know if I find something because we already found a bug in the office we are working in and I don't want this information coming out if there is something else there. Like I said, this is just theory and may be nothing, but my gut tells me that there is something there."

"Evan," Tom interrupted, "you have faith in this guy and his intuitions? This sounds to me like a lot of wishful thinking and I don't like the idea of him going on his own, with no accountability, on a fishing expedition."

"Tom, what have we got to lose by Lawson doing this check," Roedl responded. "If he finds nothing, at least he's doing due diligence in checking every corner and if he's right, the less people to know the more options we have on how to deal with it."

"Well," Joanne Benson chimed in, "you have a history of going rogue, Admiral, and this should be no surprise to us. I don't know if the Joint Chiefs would agree with you but I'm all for giving you room to figure this out. However, you just might hang yourself on this one. The reason we have reporting channels is that it keeps someone from going off the reservation and setting their own policy. Mr. Lawson seems to have tried to set policy during your last escapade in Iran and that appears to be his MO."

Lawson became agitated by Benson's remark and Roedl could see that if he didn't answer immediately, Lawson would give Benson a lesson in history that would make it to the Joint

Staff. "Joanne," Roedl began, "Lawson was highly successful in his mission in Iran. Now, some of the Joint Staff might disagree with his methods but they were ecstatic with the results. To paint him in the fashion you did was, in my opinion, unprofessional and unwarranted. We're here to solve problems. I have half a notion to allow Lieutenant Lawson to address your concerns."

"Bring it on," Benson tersely responded. Admiral Roedl looked at Lawson as Lawson smiled at him. Seeing that Lawson was ready for a fight, Roedl unleashed him.

"I would normally start with the typical line 'with all due respect to you'," Lawson started, "but, Joanne, I have learned that every time someone started off with 'all due respect', respect is the last thing they have on their mind. So I'm just going to address your comment. I got results. They were costly in loss of life but that was unavoidable. Had the Russians been able to produce the laser weapon that Doctor Polevsky created, we would be in a world of hurt, while also considering that the Iranians would have had the same weapon and the Middle East would become a much greater quagmire. So your criticisms may ring true for you desk jockeys but I live in the real world made up of life and death. You can read about it all day but I have to live it. As far as making policy is concerned, you probably make more policy in one day than I'll make in a lifetime, even though that is not your role. You're an advisor, you advise but, from what I've seen on several documents coming from the Joint Staff, your name is on them approving policy. When did you get that authority? Stop your hypocrisy before you turn the very people you rely on against you. And that's a real warning. Any comments?"

Before she could comment, Captain Nyquist intervened, "Good going, Evan. I've heard about Lawson's ability to take a person apart but, until this moment, I thought it was all myth and legend. I've got to say, Lieutenant, you've eloquently held your ground. I can't say whether you've won this round, but you've got our attention. You must remember that you need us as much as we need you."

Roedl turned to Lawson allowing for Lawson to reply. "Captain, thanks for your comments. I wasn't trying to win or lose anything. I'm just tired of people that read and make reports somehow think that authorizes them to be critical of those doing the work in the field. I have a suggestion. I am requesting that Joanne be assigned to our team for our next operation. After all, some first-hand knowledge would make her a more effective advisor."

Nyquist laughed as Lawson made his comment then stopped and looked at Joanne, "You know, Ms. Benson, that might be the best suggestion I've heard in this meeting."

Benson's face exhibited panic as she responded, "Only the Joint Staff can order something like that. You can't be serious!"

"I'll take it up with them," Nyquist said. "We've been talking about intermingling people and their roles to get them more familiar with the difficulties of each other's job and, if I remember correctly, Joanne, you were the one pushing that idea."

"That was for people working in the Pentagon not for something like this!" she exclaimed. "Thanks, Lawson! I don't find this very amusing." Lawson just smiled and nodded to the Admiral.

"Thanks, everyone for your attention to these matters," Roedl said as he pressed a button on his desk to disconnect the screen. Once the meeting scene went off, the picture of the World War II sea battle came back on.

"I've wanted to do that for over a year with her," Roedl said as he turned to face Lawson. "I would like to be in that room now to see what comments are being made. I knew that you'd come up with something that would reduce the amount of criticism we get from the staff people at the Pentagon. I can grant you, inside of a week, most of the staff within the Joint Chiefs of Staff will have heard the results of your exchange with Benson and that will definitely calm them. None of them wants to end up in a third-world country having to do what we do. They only like to write about it in their reports. Now to that gut feeling you have, explain it to me."

"Well," Lawson started as he thought about his theory, "the messages we found are pretty routine for needing to be hidden in code. These messages have times and dates, which are something to hide, but they don't give credence to the importance that matches to the level of code efforts that were used. We've already seen that they went to two levels of coding to send the message. The first message, 'OUT FEB 1', was a red herring even though the message was true. I think it was created to stop us from looking deeper which appeared to give support to the supposition that the messages buried deeper had significance."

"So you knew not to stop there," Roedl observed.

"Yes, it was too easy to find," Lawson said then continued. "The next message, 'US NAVY WILL HAVE ALL SHIPS OUT OF YOUR AREA BETWEEN FEB 1 AND FEB 8. BEST TIME

FOR LAUNCH TESTS IS FEB 4. DEPOSIT PAYMENT IN GRAND CAYMAN ACCOUNT', was found using the book 'The Huns', discovered as the code template by using the Fibonacci Sequence. The hour hand of Big Ben gave us line number four, which allowed to find the book's ID number," Lawson said as he looked at his notes. "The first number in the Fibonacci Sequence gave us the line number and the number of characters in the message."

"This is detail Norman didn't give to me," Roedl exclaimed.

Lawson looked at Roedl then at his notes. "There's more, Sir. There was the next message 'BEST LAUNCH DATE IS FEB 7, WASHINGTON TIME. THEY SHOULD HAVE LOWERED THEIR ALERTNESS FROM FEB 4 DATE IF THEY BROKE THE FIRST CODE WHICH IS ALMOST IMPOSSIBLE.' That was decoded using the book 'Physical Geography' which was identified by line number forty-three, specified by the position of the minute hand on Big Ben in the picture. However, the messages themselves didn't carry much impact. The pattern of what the messages represented and the extensive level of effort doesn't match with their importance. I figure that there is more to the coding beneath the pictures than we are seeing."

"I see some significant impact with the messages," Roedl said while taking Lawson's notepad and looking at the information. "However, you are right. The messages may carry an impact but the overall importance of the message is not there. We know they will do test launches. Paying money for finding out a best window to launch isn't typical based upon their previous operations. What other type of messaging techniques could they be using if your theory is true?"

Lawson pulled the Admiral's pen out of its holder and contemplated its function. "It's like this pen. Its function is to write but the true value is that it is part of a bigger picture made up by the nameplate and title it's associated with. I grant you that you have seldom, if ever, used this pen for writing. It's used to display a certain presence of authority. That may be the same with the coding we're looking at. The code we captured, I think, is part of a bigger display that carries a different, more impactful message or function. The function may not be a message at all but something totally different."

Roedl thought about Lawson's response and the timeframe for them to get answers. He couldn't afford his team losing focus when they were already deprived of the human resources needed to carry out the mission. These concerns brought his next response. "Is it possible that you're making too much of something that is a simple set of messages?"

"It's possible," Lawson responded. "But I feel an analysis is essential to ensure that we have not missed something important. After all, according to Josh Henry, someone was to be paid five million dollars to create a program. We have no idea what all that was about or if it has anything to do with this effort. However, there is substantial evidence that Lavlery was the potential receiver of the money."

"You have always seen things different than the rest of us," Roedl replied as he selected a course of action. "I can't afford for you to separate from the efforts of the team but your concerns have merit. I approve of you going after this theory with one restriction. You have to do this analysis on your own time. I'm sorry it has to be this way but things are moving too fast for us to take a break to go down rabbit holes. One other requirement, if you find something, you are to tell no one what you found except me. Captain Nyquist is right about one thing. With you branching out with this theory, the Joint Staff will hang us if they felt we had used resources to chase windmills. I want to manage the damage control if word gets out you are taking a different tack."

"Thank you, Sir," Lawson said as he got up to go out the door.

"If you find something, use the word 'penchant' in a sentence in an email and I will drop what I am doing to discuss your findings," Roedl said as Lawson opened the door.

"Will do, Sir," came Lawson's response.

Chapter 12

Discoveries – Day 6

"Seeing the obvious is often harder than seeing the hidden!"
- Mehmet Murat ildan

It was the morning of February 6th as Lawson sat looking over Myers final assessment of the messages they found on the code sheet. Almost two days of additional analysis of the sheet didn't provide anything else new. While Lawson was working on his own, he continued to see if there was anything else that was buried in the picture. As he promised the Admiral, he set aside his efforts on looking over the picture and its layers to help Myers and Norman go through the code possibilities on the code sheet.

They worked for hours, looking at different combinations and other different number sequences. Nothing stood out. Lawson spent time going through the books in the room looking for any marks or notes on the pages that would give additional clues. Several books had the same individual marks underneath characters in a line that indicated a particular book had been used in the coding process.

Lawson got an idea. Going page by page through one book, he took each letter identified and wrote it down. He figured that maybe he could rearrange the letters to identify a message. After about an hour of moving letters around, Myers threw in an observation, "Maybe he didn't count using an ink pen for every letter." Lawson realized that, with Myers' observation, the plan he had to reassemble the message was futile.

Lawson selected portions of the code on the sheet, copied the code and dropped it into another blank page using his word processor. Once he pasted the captured code onto the blank page, he worked through each of the five-digit numbers to see if there was any relationship between numbers. It was intense and time consuming.

Finally, he circled a section of code causing the page to change resulting in new information. His suspicions were verified. Pulling out his phone, he sent a text message to Roedl that said 'I have a penchant for a sandwich'. As he was doing so, the door beeped and Gunny came walking back in, his late afternoon rounds just being completed. Lawson and Myers looked at Gunny then went back to their tasks. Lawson cleared the screen of what he was looking at while Myers was looking at notes and pages of information on the floor, putting them in order to write his report.

The door beeped again as Norman came through the door. "Have you guys made any progress?" she asked while handing each of them a cup of coffee from a cardboard box. Both Lawson and Myers looked up at her, nodded 'no' and went back to their work. As they did so the door beeped again and Captain Henderson came into the room.

"Where have you been?" Norman inquired of the Captain.

He pulled up a chair and sat down. He looked exhausted and as though he had been sick. "I've been working long hours with the Joint Staff on legal issues associated with Lavlery. They are not happy that we have a mole that's deep within our government," he informed them as he adjusted himself in the chair.

Gunny sat looking at Henderson while drinking his coffee. While that was going on, Lawson got a text on his phone. As he read the text, he walked over to the computer and pulled the jump drive from the USB slot. Putting the jump drive in his pocket, he announced, "I've just got a text from the Admiral. I've got to go over to see him, might be important, might not."

As Lawson left the room, Gunny stepped over to Henderson and put his hand on Henderson's shoulder. Henderson winced in pain as Gunny did so. Norman questioned Gunny's move as a small spot of red appeared on Henderson's shirt. Gunny turned to the desk and, using his body to mask his moves, pressed the emergency button on the small remote device on the desk.

"What happened to your shoulder?" Norman asked as the red dot grew larger. "It appears you are bleeding."

"Yes," Henderson responded. "I had emergency surgery on my shoulder after tearing my rotator cuff. It appears the stiches didn't hold. Thanks, Gunny, for tearing them more."

Gunny turned and slammed his fist into Henderson's shoulder while pulling the .38 caliber pistol from the Captain's holster. Henderson moved backward and grabbed his shoulder in pain.

"I'll have you court martialed for that Gunny," he shouted. "An enlisted man striking an officer means prison time." About that time the door beeped again and three armed Marines rushed into the room.

"What were you thinking, Gunny?" Norman exclaimed as Gunny stood facing the armed Marines.

Henderson pointed to Gunny and shouted, "I want you to arrest this man for assaulting an officer!" The Marines looked at Captain Henderson's shirt and the blood on it. Moving forward, they pushed their weapons in Gunny's face while ordering him drop the weapon from his hand, which was Henderson's gun. Gunny dropped the weapon and moved immediately toward Henderson, leaving the Marines stunned as they moved to hold Gunny back. Fighting their efforts to stop him, he grabbed the Captain's shirt near the shoulder with both hands, tearing the shirt open and ripping off the bandage in one quick move.

"Don't shoot," he called out as he was forced back by the Marines.

Norman stepped forward and looked at Henderson's wound then put her hand on the barrel of the closest Marine's rifle and slowly pressed it down. "You guys been in combat?" she asked while looking at Henderson's shoulder.

"I have, Ma'am," the Marine closest her commented.

"Do you know what a bullet wound looks like after it's been treated?"

"Yes, Ma'am," came the response from the Marine.

She pressed the Marine further, "Does this look like surgery to the shoulder or a bullet wound?"

The Marine took a close look at the wound. "Ma'am, based upon the small tears around the stiches, that is definitely a bullet wound," came the Marine's response.

Looking back at Gunny then at Henderson, Norman ordered, "Captain Henderson, I am placing you under arrest on two counts of attempted murder and one count of espionage."

"I gave you an order to arrest Gunny, Marine," Henderson shouted. "You don't listen to her, she's a Commander and I am a Captain. You take your orders from me!"

The senior Marine in the response team looked each of them over and turned his weapon from pointing at Gunny to pointing at the Captain, "If you will stand up, Sir? You are under arrest. The evidence shows that you have a bullet wound that's been treated, though very poorly. We've also been informed about the shooting in the park a couple of days ago and that we were to give special attention to protecting Gunny Glendenning. I think there is a relationship about that shooting in the park and your wound so we'll put you in custody until we can sort things out. Ma'am, you'll need to come with us too."

"As the arresting officer, I would expect to go with you," Norman said as she motioned for Gunny to sit down.

Leaning over to Gunny, she whispered to him, "That was a dumb thing to do. I'm glad you found your shooter. Dumb Marine." Gunny smiled at her while he wiped the blood off of his hands with a paper towel. "Don't you go getting that blood on my freshly pressed white blouse," she said as Gunny went to shake her hand. She smiled at him then left the room.

Gunny leaned back and heard shuffling to his left. "Myers, I forgot you were even here. Why didn't you say anything?"

"Well," Myers replied, "I figured you two could work this whole thing out. As long as there was no gunplay, I was satisfied to stay out of the discussion. By the way, I just got a text from Lawson. He wants us at the Admiral's office."

"Then let's close up and go," Gunny advised as he picked up the computer and papers from the desk to put into the safe.

Gunny and Myers arrived at Admiral Roedl's office at the Kennedy Irregular Warfare Center to find Lawson waiting in the outer office for Roedl to call him in. Once Roedl called Lawson in, Myers and Gunny remained in the outer office. After entering Roedl's office and while the Admiral was watching, Lawson unplugged the Admiral's computer from the line to the network, checked to make sure his wifi and Bluetooth were off, isolating his computer from any outside connection. Next, Lawson plugged his jump drive into Roedl's computer and waited for it to come up. Once the jump drive was accessible, Lawson clicked on the picture of Big Ben and pulled the layers aside and demonstrated how the hidden code was accessible. Roedl felt panic at what he saw.

"I'll send this information to Fort Bevoir for them to analyze the code. You are to tell nothing to the other team members," Roedl ordered as he looked at the screen. "This is not what I expected as it will lead to war. You will all receive a memo by tomorrow afternoon at your room on what to do and the significance of the code. It will be delivered by courier. Do you understand?"

"Yes, Sir," Lawson exclaimed. "That's cutting it close, Sir, since tomorrow night appears to be when everything takes place if my calculations are correct."

"I know it's cutting it close but any earlier warning will leave us exposed which, potentially, will put us and some areas of the nation in immediate danger," Roedl replied. "You must be ready to present to the Joint Staff at the Pentagon at 21:15 tomorrow."

"9:15 PM, Yes Sir," Lawson said while shutting down the screen, removing the jump drive and rebooting the computer. "That's about the same time all of this North Korean missile launch stuff comes down as well but I think you already know that. Permission to leave, Sir."

"Permission granted," Roedl said as he stood and watched Lawson go out the door.

Myers and Gunny saw Lawson come into the outer office. "Well, what happened in there?" Gunny asked as Lawson sat down.

"I'm under orders not to say anything to anyone until we get a memo tomorrow," Lawson responded while he wished he could tell them everything.

Myers looked at Lawson's face while Gunny sat watching them both. The Yeoman typically on duty was not in the room. Lawson walked around to the chair at the desk and checked for anything that looked like a bug. None was found.

"Why do I feel like we're about to have Armageddon?" Myers said as Lawson gathered his composure. "I think you found something that is far more serious than a message."

Lawson nodded 'yes' then said, "I can't tell you anything about it now. We have to get things together to present to the Joint Staff tomorrow. I've got to be ready to present the findings at 9:15 tomorrow evening."

"That's interesting," Gunny interjected. "I was ordered by Roedl to act as one of the main entry security people at the Pentagon's Joint Chiefs of Staff conference room tomorrow. I'm to report at 21:00 hours, that's 9:00 PM to you Lawson. It looks like we're both going to be at the same place."

Lawson smiled at Gunny's comment. Myers sat back in the chair and wondered what he would be doing during that time. His question was answered immediately, even as the thought was forming. Roedl opened the door to the outer office and walked over to Myers.

"Myers, while the other two guys are at the Joint Staff meeting, I want you to finalize the report on this operation and have it ready for me at 0800 hours on the 8th, day after tomorrow."

"That's Sunday, Sir," Myers objected. "You know my convictions about working on Sunday if it's not critical."

"I know your faith and the strength of your convictions, Myers," Roedl responded. "I wouldn't ask you to do this on Sunday if it wasn't critical. We have some cleanup to do and it isn't just paperwork. Norman, Gunny and Lawson will be there as well. I need you and that report at that time because I'm about to put heat on some people to resign and I need you all there."

"Yes Sir," Myers acknowledged. "I guess that was a little selfish of me to respond that way without knowing the need. I serve you because I serve God, but I respect you not just out of respect to your authority but also because I know you to always be fair. You're as much a friend as you are a commander and I don't want to let you down."

"We all feel that way," Gunny confirmed. "We sense that something major is coming down the pike that only you and Lawson know about. We have learned to trust you enough to know that you have a plan that needs our trust. Let us know what we need to do."

"Thanks guys," Roedl welcomed. "You all and Norman have been my greatest advocates and friends. I wouldn't say this to you if I didn't also know that you would follow any order I gave you. That trust goes both ways. Now we have a job to do and you all have your piece in it."

"By the way, where is Norman," Lawson queried.

"Roedl smiled at Lawson's interest. "She's busy interrogating a traitor." Everyone but Lawson knew from that comment that she was busy questioning Captain Henderson. Somewhere along the sequence of activities, informing Lawson about Henderson had slipped through the cracks and everyone assumed he knew what was going on. Lawson gave it no thought as he knew Norman did other functions for the Admiral.

With that, Roedl walked out of the security vault room and into the hallway. Looking at his watch, he saw that it was nearly 8:00 PM. With what he knew about the Big Ben picture with its messages and code, the next twenty-five hours would be critical if they were to stop a war.

Chapter 13

Interrogation – Day 7

"Seeing the truth was never easy, especially when it revealed those closest to us could be monsters hidden in plain sight." - Kerri Maniscalco, Stalking Jack the Ripper

It was February 7th as Commander Norman sat in an interrogation room for a second day facing Captain Henderson across a table at the Naval Criminal Investigative Service Washington Field Office, Anacostia Annex in Washington, DC. The previous evening's discussion with him left her with little new information. She had to change her tack on how she approached his actions. As she did so, she sat looking at Henderson's personnel file while she collected her thoughts.

"You realize the attempt on the lives of both Mister Henry and Master Gunnery Sergeant Glendenning could get you life in prison?" she posed to Henderson while she looked at his personnel record.

"It doesn't matter," Henderson responded. "I failed at the key components for my mission. You may already consider me a dead man." Norman was taken back by his comment and now she wished she had Lawson in the room to thread his logic through the questioning. She began to realize that this may be bigger than anyone suspected.

"Who were you working for?" she asked, figuring it should be the first question in her new approach. Henderson remained silent. "You do realize that, if your statement is true, you're dead regardless of whether you tell me or not," she continued. "What have you got to lose by telling me unless, of course, you have bought completely into ideology that has pushed you to this point." Henderson just sat quietly looking at the clock. Norman looked up at the clock, 8:53 PM. She realized at that moment that the operation he was involved with was still active as this was the third time he had looked at the clock and each time, his face tensed up.

"So what's supposed to happen in seven minutes?" she asked as she played a hunch.

"What happens at 21:00 hours will answer all your questions," he answered as he leaned back in his chair. At that moment the door opened up with the Marine guard looking in.

"His attorney is here, Ma'am," the guard said as a man in a three-piece suit and tie walked in. Norman was surprised by the man's appearance. She was expecting a Navy JAG legal officer in a naval uniform to come through the door yet here was a civilian attorney she recognized as coming from a well-connected firm.

"Hi Miles," she said while standing up to shake his hand.

"Hi Beth," he greeted. "I read the charges and the incident report. What has he told you so far?" Norman picked up a glass of water and took a sip.

"He hasn't said much except that something is supposed to happen at 9:00 PM, so he is still active in whatever operation he was involved with."

Miles turned to Henderson, "You realize that if you're still in the active commission of a crime, my hands are tied in what I can do to help you."

"Whatever," Henderson announced as he smiled and once more looked at the clock .It was 8:56 PM.

"Miles," Norman interrupted, "he stated that he is already a dead man, so my guess is that the people he is answering to are either foreign nationals or a crime-related gang."

Miles put his briefcase on the table and sat in the chair next to Henderson. Norman watched his every move as she began to wonder if he had been searched for weapons before coming in. She looked at the clock. It was coming to about fifteen minutes before the Joint Chiefs of Staff briefing on Operation Scarborough where Lawson would be presenting the information on the operation before the Joint Staff. She desperately wished she had switched roles with Lawson as she was getting nowhere here. She had her cellphone in her hand under the table as she texted Admiral Roedl 'Something to happen at 21:00 hours. Not sure what.'

"Have you bought in to the program they have sold you concerning the CAT205 team," she queried as she had no path except to take a stab in the dark.

"The team is irresponsible and operates in an illegal format," Henderson said. She knew she hit a nerve with that question.

She continued down the path, "Don't you think that they have to break rules sometime with the time restrictions they have?"

"Yea, right," Henderson snapped back. "You're a part of it too. Back there at the inquiry, you as much admitted that you were willing to sidestep the law to get that computer out of the room. You're a hypocrite. You sit here judging me by the law when you don't follow the law yourself!"

Norman ignored his charge as she asked him, "Did you plant the bug in room 2337?"

"Yes," came Henderson's response. "I put it in a textbook and placed the textbook in the stack against the wall just before I left the room. We had to know what you were finding but it looks like you guys found the device before it did us any good. That was counted as a failure against me."

"By who," Norman shot back. Henderson didn't answer.

About that time, Norman's phone 'dinged' indicating a text had come in and it was from Roedl. She looked at the screen and read 'Let me know when you find something. Picking up Lawson at Rayburn building for Joint Staff briefing'.

"Well, if you must know," Henderson said while looking at the clock as it was 9:03 PM. "Your top technical guy, Myers, should be dead by now. They're going to take him out at the Rayburn building and your ability to stop our plan will go up in smoke when he's gone."

Norman immediately dialed a number on her phone and waited for someone to pick up. "Yeoman, get me Virginia!" she shouted into the phone. What seemed like an eternity went by as she waited, "Virginia, get over to the Rayburn Building, they're going to kill Myers! Take your weapon with you."

Realizing that she was supposed to be at the Joint Staff session at the Pentagon, she opened the door to the room and motioned to the Marine guard. "Take him back to his cell, I'll finish this later." The Marine nodded, put Henderson's hands behind his back, handcuffed him and led him out of the room. Norman had an uneasy feeling as she put her documents and papers in her briefcase as they left. Henderson and the Marine guard walked down the hall and turned toward the elevator. The guard looked around to see that no one was in the area.

"This is where you get off, Captain. You failed and we can't have you talking anymore," the guard said as he pulled a pistol with a silencer out from his jacket.

"I figured they'd have someone inside to finish the job," Henderson replied. "Get it over with."

At that moment, a gun barrel pressed against the back of the guard's neck. "I'll take that," Norman said as she took the pistol from his hand. Looking at Henderson, she said, "I figured you were not answering because someone was listening. Since you refused to answer before your attorney arrived, logic said it had to be the Marine guard which, my guess, is no Marine at all."

Henderson sighed a breath of relief as he leaned against the wall. "I couldn't tell you anything or they were going to kill my wife and daughter. It's obvious now to me that they will do so anyway just to tie up any loose ends. I'll tell you what you want."

Norman reached into her pocket, pulled a small remote button and pressed it. Thirty seconds later, four Marines raced into the corridor with the weapons drawn. "I called you," Norman said. Pointing to the Marine guard she ordered, "Put this man into custody, check him to be sure he doesn't have any other weapons or suicide pills on him and lock him up under a twenty-four hour watch. I'll need to talk to him."

"Yes, Ma'am," one of the Marines said while taking the arm of the guard and putting the handcuffs on him.

"And, Walt," Norman said to one of the Marines, "make him as uncomfortable as possible and get that uniform off of him. He's no Marine, he's a civilian!"

Turning to the Marine response team commander, she motioned for him to come with her while the other Marine continued to watch Henderson. "I've got to go over to the Pentagon," she said while watching the other Marines take the fake Marine away. "Get information from Henderson on where his wife and daughter are, send a rescue team to their location and get them to a secure location. Meanwhile, I want Henderson put under close security. There may be other attempts on him, now get going."

"Yes, Ma'am," came the response as the Marine smiled and started speaking into his microphone on his transceiver.

Norman left the building and headed to the Pentagon.

Chapter 14

A Contract Hit, a New Threat

"One need not destroy one's enemy. One need only destroy his willingness to engage." - Sun Tzu

Lawson put his notes and presentation comments in his briefcase. He looked at the sequence of his presentation realizing he lacked some key information from the other items he discovered but did not reveal to anyone but Admiral Roedl. He checked his appointment calendar to confirm the time of the presentation to be made to the Joint Chiefs of Staff that evening. As he did so, Myers looked on. Something caught Myers attention but not so much that it raised any flags in his thought process. It was a passing notion as he saw one of the lines in the appointment page showed the organizer of the meeting as Rod Lavlery. The realization made him feel uncomfortable but he didn't know why. He watched Lawson put his phone away, check his weapon and leave the room.

After Lawson had left to give his presentation to the Joint Chiefs, Myers went back to the computer to assemble all the information they had into a formal report of the mission. The courier had not shown up that afternoon which made Myers' job more difficult to finish the report as he didn't have all the information. Whatever the courier was supposed to bring, Myers felt the lack of having that information left a large hole in the report based upon the significance Lawson placed on it.

Putting his concerns aside, he searched through files they had made for the first message they found, 'OUT FEB 1'. Not able to find the document with the ASCII code and the message breakdown, Myers went back to the original photo of the code sheet and, using the photo software, circled the code area in question to get a copy of the code on the sheet. As he did so, much to Myers' dismay, the code sheet disappeared. Below it appeared a page of computer code written in html, the coding used by web designers to display data and give commands to a web page. The display of the code caught Myers by surprise. A fifth layer to the photo was present that they had no idea existed.

Myers began to look through the code comments. What first caught his attention was a reference to the USS Louisiana, a ballistic missile submarine carrying nuclear warheads. What would the messages sent to North Korea have to do with a U.S. nuke sub. Panic began to settle in on Myers as he continued to read the comments. It identified the scheduled time and location of the submarine for today, February 7, 2016. There was a section of the html code with the identification, 'Launch code' that gave a sequence of letter and numbers. Having been in practice runs to exercise the sequence for a potential order to launch missiles, Myers recognized the pattern of letters and numbers were similar to those used for launch codes. More panic.

Another section identified as 'Secure communication protocol for submarine' gave the frequency and the sequence for opening the communications link to the submarine with an alert message. Myers computer programming skills told him that all of the programming was there to open a secure channel to the submarines EAS alert system.

Then there were comments in the html program for 'code transmission sequence' and 'Presidential authorization code'. Myers looked closer at the html code. In a moment, it was real. The html code was activated by someone being on the internet and bringing up the translated code from the Big Ben picture to activate the html code. Lawson would be doing that when he brought up page seven of his presentation slides during his presentation to the Joint Chiefs and he would be on the internet when he did so. Clicking on the picture in his presentation to show the layers of the picture and the code page would activate the program Myers was looking at. He would be launching eight ICBM missiles but to where.

Reading more of the code he found coordinates for the first missile. Getting the coordinates, Myers looked at the map on the wall. The coordinates looked to be somewhere near Pyongyang, North Korea. In a moment, Myers realized that Lawson's presentation would start World War III and the U.S. would be blamed by the world for starting it.

He grabbed the computer and his key card, rushing out the door to the Department of Defense, thinking all the time that he was the only person able to stop a war. As he hailed a taxi, he realized he had to get there before Lawson hit the page that would result in a holocaust and time was not his friend.

Jumping into the back seat of a taxi, he slammed the door and tried to catch his breath. In a panic he told the cab driver, "If you want to wake up tomorrow morning, you'll get me to the Pentagon as fast as you can!" The driver stepped on the gas, racing down side streets and past cars moving slowly on that Saturday evening. It was dark as night time was several hours old. Even in Myers' panicked state, his mind was analyzing his surroundings. He looked at the driver's face in the rearview mirror then looked at the cabbie license on the passenger side sun visor. The pictures didn't match. Looking down at his computer, he began to put the pieces together. Seeing the driver make some move with his hand away from the steering wheel, Myers thought quickly.

He swung his computer up toward the back of the driver's seat, striking the driver's right hand as it swung back to maneuver the pistol into Myers' chest. The pistol was knocked to the floor as Myers dropped the computer and pulled his .38 caliber pistol. Falling backward toward the back of the rear seat and in one motion, Myers pulled the trigger of his pistol with the round hitting the driver in the side of the head. At the same time, Myers pulled the seat belt across his body and latched it, seeing the running lights of a stopped semi-truck ahead and that the car was about to hit it. As the taxi approached the truck, Myers laid down on the seat, still strapped in with the seat belt. The front of the car came in at a forty-five degree angle, going under part of the trailer and hitting the back wheel. Part of the roof of the taxi was torn off but was intact where Myers was laying. As the car struck the tire of the trailer, it bounced backward, slamming Myers into the back of the front passenger seat, causing him to drop the pistol on the floor. The seat belt didn't hold which, much to Myers' surprise, may have saved his life. Feeling groggy from the impact, Myers picked up his pistol and the computer and rolled out the rear passenger door as the car kept rolling slowly backward. Kicking the door closed, he started crawling toward the tractor-trailer.

Stunned but alert, he crawled in the dark about twenty-five feet, getting under the rear of the trailer while the taxi burst into flames from an apparent gas leak. As he got under the trailer, he could hear the sound of automatic gunfire and could see people running in all directions. The gunfire appeared to be focused on the taxi from the side opposite from where he had gotten out. As gunfire continued into the taxi, he watched in the light from the flames as those that had been firing their weapons ran back to a vehicle, jumped in then the vehicle sped off. As this was going on, he felt dizzy and fought the sense of losing consciousness. He felt the hands of a person reach under both his arms and drag him out from under the trailer. Myers thought this was his time to die as he had no more strength to fight back.

"Don't fight me son," The voice of a man spoke to him, "I'll get you to safety." Myers went limp as he finally lost consciousness.

Myers didn't know how long he was out but as he came to, he found himself in a sitting position leaning against the tire on the opposite side of the trailer from where all the activity was taking place. He looked back under the trailer and could see policemen and fire trucks around the taxi. He looked at his watch then realized he had been out for about ten minutes. His computer was laid next to him and his pistol was back in its holster. No one else was around. As he was on the other side of the trailer, no one saw him sitting there so he got up and brushed himself off. His pant leg of his suit was torn with some scrapes on that leg. There were some spots of blood from his shirt which, he discovered, came from some scrapes on his head. Other than that and a ringing in his ears, he seemed to be ok.

Picking up his computer, he slowly walked away from the scene in a direction opposite the activity. Getting to an intersection, he asked a woman where the Pentagon was located. Looking at him, she realized this may be the man she was looking for or he could be one of the shooters. She put the pieces together quickly.

"You were in that taxi accident, weren't you?"

Myers nodded 'yes'.

"Do you have some ID so I know if I'm helping someone good or someone evil."

Myers pulled out his ONI ID and handed it to her. She gasped then said as she handed back his ID, "We've got to get you to the Pentagon! Both sides are searching for you and Commander Norman is in a frenzy looking for you. Did you connect your computer to the internet?"

"No," Myers responded. "Doing so will start World War III."

"I know," was her response. "Get in the car. We've got to get out of here and get you to safety." It was then that Myers wondered if she knew about the program under the picture or if something else was happening that he was not aware of.

"Forget safety," Myers shot back. "I've got to get to the Pentagon now or we're all finished. What time is it?"

"I have 21:35 hours. 9:35 PM if you don't know military time," she said. While Myers was half in and half out of the car, she shifted into gear and stepped on the gas. At the same time she pulled Myers into the car just as the door slammed shut from the momentum of the car moving.

"Do you know what entrance to the Pentagon you need to take?" she asked while taking a left down the wrong way of a one way street. Myers immediately became fully conscious as the adrenaline coursed through his system. He just escaped one near death experience and she was trying for another. She just turned and looked at him and smiled. Myers first reaction – she was an escapee from a mental institution. After about four blocks she turned down another street, across a couple of green mediums and onto an onramp to I-395.

"The Joint Staff Conference center," Myers remarked while wondering what driving school she graduated from.

"I'll have you there in about three minutes," she said while going over a bridge that crossed the Potomac River. Arriving at the Pentagon, she pulled up to the gate for access. Showing her ID, they immediately waved her through after a Marine jumped into the back seat of the car. His wearing of a Marine dress blue uniform was highlighted by the M4 rifle lying across his chest. "Admiral Roedl wants to see that you have no further interruptions to your drive here," he said while pointing to where they needed to go.

Chapter 15

A Convergence of Events

"It is dangerous to exist in the world. To exist is to be threatened. We must live with threats." - Adam Levin, The Instructions."

The car came to a stop and a small golf cart came out to take Myers to the conference room. The Marine joined him along with the driver. "Once we get to the main door of the conference room, you're to turn your weapon in. No weapons are allowed past the yellow line," the Marine said as they turned down a main corridor to an elevator. Once in the elevator and up to the third floor, they got out and onto another cart that took them to a pair of double doors at the end of one branch of the corridor. The Marine got out and escorted Myers through the double doors to a large desk in a lobby, one of many desks going down the length of the lobby. He handed his weapon to the person on duty and got a claim ticket for it.

"You can't take that computer in with you," the Army sergeant told him.

"This computer goes with me," Myers shouted. "This computer can stop World War III and me not having it will start World War III. What's your pleasure?" As the sergeant was about to protest, a familiar voice came into the picture.

"Ye be listening to what he says, Lad," Gunny said while grabbing Myers by the back of the collar. "That is unless you would like to be vaporized in the next three hours." The sergeant relented. "Myers, you look like crap," Gunny said as he put his arm around Myers while Myers wondered how Gunny would know something about a nuclear attack.

"Gunny," Myers quipped, "Is that a tear in your eye?"

Gunny smiled and pushed Myers forward. "We though we lost ye, good buddy." Myers realized that Lawson's observation was correct. Gunny starts talking with more of an Irish accent when he's stressed. "You be expected inside," Gunny said as he pushed Myers to the door.

Gunny opened the door to the conference room and Myers walked in. The room had high ceilings with lots of oak in the walls, furnishings and floors. There were chairs in rows in a semicircle facing a large oak desk with seven chairs behind the desk and five high-ranking military officers sitting in some of the chairs behind the desk. Lawson was standing in front of a large screen with the picture of the Big Ben picture stripped away to expose the code page underneath. Myers panicked.

"Are you on the internet?" he shouted as everyone turned to see this man with blood on his shirt, scrapes on his face and a torn suit carrying a laptop computer. There seemed to be a lot of confusion at that moment.

"Yes," came Lawson's response. "Welcome back, we were worried about you."

"Then we just started World War III with the launch of eight MIRV nuclear-tipped missiles into North Korea." Myers shouted. "I'm sorry I didn't get here in time to stop it but I was slightly detained." There was immediate panic in the room as people started to get up to run out.

"I was just getting to that part of the presentation," Lawson replied. "No, the missiles didn't launch." Those leaving stopped and went back to their seats. "By the way gentlemen," Lawson said, addressing the Joint Chiefs, "that courier message that you guys sent never arrived and from what I was just told, that almost got Myers killed." They could see there was anger in Lawson's voice and they had heard about his ability to bypass every line of authority to get to the point. It was Admiral Roedl that intervened.

"Maybe we should explain to everyone what happened the past two days," Roedl said as he stepped toward Lawson.

"Ok," Lawson began as his temper decreased, "we discovered that there was a computer program below the code sheet I just displayed on the screen. If I select the original message of 'OUT FEB 1' like this," Lawson said as he selected the area around the message using the mouse, "we see this happen." At that moment, the code sheet disappeared and the page showing the computer program came up. There was a loud gasp from the audience as the program was displayed on the screen.

"From what I see here it looks like the USS Louisiana was to receive orders to launch its nukes," a Pentagon staffer in a suit stated as he read the comments section of the program. "What was the target?"

"The targets were all in North Korea," Lawson answered. "However, we found this program before any of this could happen and ordered all commands to verify launch orders with the Chairman of the Joint Staff before carrying out any order. They had to verify it was him through several different checks, though I can't tell you what the checks were because they are highly classified, so I don't know what they are. As to this program on the screen, it would only work if the computer opening up the picture was tied to the internet, otherwise the program would just remain dormant. So no launch occurred." At that moment a sigh of relief went up from the audience. While Lawson was talking a courier came into the room and handed the Chairman of the Joint Staff a message. The Chairman signed off on the receipt, opened the seals on the folder and read the contents.

"To all personnel, may I interrupt?" He said while looking at the clock. "North Korea launched a long-range ballistic missile Sunday from the Tongchang-ri main satellite launch site near the northwest border with China carrying what it has said is an earth observation satellite at 09:31 North Korean time or one-hour, thirty-one minutes after midnight GMT time." Looking once more at the clock to see it was 10:16 PM Washington, DC time he went on. "Being that it is 22:16 hours our time, the launch happened forty-six minutes ago. It has been confirmed that it was an ICBM. Any comments, Mister Lawson."

Lawson looked at the screen and turned the display of information forward to a slide that showed both messages found in the code sheet. "Well, if you look at the first message, we see 'US NAVY WILL HAVE ALL SHIPS OUT OF YOUR AREA BETWEEN FEB 1 AND FEB 8. BEST TIME FOR LAUNCH TESTS IS FEB 4. DEPOSIT PAYMENT IN GRAND CAYMAN ACCOUNT', which we thought was another red herring to throw us off on the date if we were able to break the code. The important point in the first message is that mention of February 8th, not the false February 4th launch date. Rod Lavlery was thinking that once we got the first message about him being out on February 1st and this message, which would have us focus on the February 4th launch date, we would stop there. However we didn't stop there and were able to find the second message, 'BEST LAUNCH DATE IS FEB 7, WASHINGTON TIME. THEY SHOULD HAVE LOWERED THEIR ALERTNESS FROM FEB 4 DATE IF THEY BROKE THE FIRST CODE WHICH IS ALMOST IMPOSSIBLE.' Now taking into account that we are on the evening of February 7th and North Korea is into February 8th, the two messages were for date verification. So I think the two messages he was sending to North Korea were not red herrings but were real in that the message showing February 8th in the first message and February 7th in the second message were intended to ensure that those receiving the message were aware of the differences in dates. They had to account for the international date line. Everyone with me so far?"

He looked around the room to see that they all were following his logic so he continued, "I am of the firm conviction that the North Koreans knew only about the code sheet and not the program lying underneath the sheet. The two messages were to match up with the ICBM launch we just heard about so that no one would look any further into the code. So that being said, I think that Rod Lavlery expected for us to take much longer to get though the codes we found, which would mean that we would have made this presentation two or three days later. That would mean the USS Louisiana's missiles would be fired two days from now, making it appear that we launched the attack on North Korea as retaliation for the ICBM missile launch. So it appears that Lavlery was really working for someone other than the North Koreans. The North Koreans have very restrictive internet connections which means that if they opened the picture while on the internet, it would not have gone out to initiate the Louisiana's missile launches. Only our opening of the picture while on the internet would have done so. However, there is another piece. Lavlery also planned to have the Louisiana launch its missiles at about the same time as North Korea launched its ICBM if we found the code early. I suspect this as it was Rod Lavlery that set up this meeting for this time. He would know that we would show the pictures you're seeing tonight at this meeting if we found something. This would still make it appear that we launched a nuke strike against North Korea in response to their ICBM launch. Either way, he starts a war."

With that comment the whole room broke out in individual conversations. Myers then realized what was bothering him earlier when seeing Lawson's calendar on this meeting. As Lawson said, Lavlery was the organizer of this meeting.

"What do you base that supposition upon?" the Chairman of the Joint Staff asked. "Let's have it quiet in here. I want Lieutenant Lawson to substantiate his comment."

Lawson stood looking at Myers, motioning for him to come forward. Myers moved up to the podium and the microphone. As he did so, Admiral Roedl picked the microphone sitting on the chair next to him.

"Gentlemen and Ladies," Roedl started, "You've all met Lieutenant Lawson, now I'd like you to meet another expert on my team, Second Class Petty Officer Nick Myers. Go ahead Petty Officer Myers."

"Thank you, Sir," Myers began. "Addressing the reason that Lavlery was working with a group outside of the North Koreans is that it makes no sense for North Korea to assist in their own annihilation. I just found the code this evening and was coming here to stop Mister Lawson from clicking on the Big Ben picture. I didn't know the program under the code sheet had been found."

"I don't understand why you didn't know about the program under the code," The Chairman responded. "I sent a courier to Room 2337 at the Rayburn building this afternoon. The courier was carrying the report on our findings of the program behind the code sheet discovered by Lieutenant Lawson. I had Fort Bevoir intel people analyze the program, modify it to make it inert and create that report. You should have received it."

"It never came!" both Lawson and Myers called out in unison.

The Chairman pushed a button on the desk in front of him which resulted in a clerk in the offices outside of conference room entering the room. "Can I assist you, Sir," he called out as he entered the room.

The Chairman stood up and looked down at a page in a bound set of papers. "I want you to get me the name of the courier that was assigned to take document US201602061434D to room 2337 of the Rayburn Building."

"Yes, Sir. Right away, Sir," the clerk said as he quickly wrote down the number on a pad and exited the room. As the Chairman was talking, Commander Norman came up to the podium and handed Lawson a slip of paper. He, in turn, handed it to Myers.

The Chairman continued," Petty Officer Myers, what other observations do you have?"

"Well Sir, I just got a message from our CAT205 Commander that, I think, bears some impact on this meeting," Myers said while reading the note.

"Well, son, don't just leave us hanging," the Chairman called out as the rest of the people in the room laughed.

"Sorry, Sir," Myers said followed by a whispered exchange with Lawson then continuing. "Again, sorry Sir. Quick analysis from radar and other checks indicate that the North Koreans just put an object into space, estimated to be around four-hundred pounds. This is large enough to be a medium-grade nuclear device. I think from the coding we broke it appears that this launch was significant enough to want to hide the very presence of its existence. Therefore, it is my contention that the North Koreans were hoping this launch would not be detected. One more note, that object they put in orbit could very well be intended as an EMP device meant to be detonated over a large U.S. city which would, from my calculations, render sixty to seventy percent of anything electronic unusable. "

A three star Admiral with the nametag 'Mirkel' stood up in the audience. "What's an electronic technician going to tell us about the depths of cryptographics, the mathematical details of this messaging effort or what an EMP burst will accomplish? I expected a PhD in crypto or mathematics to be the lead expert on this effort and you bring us a Petty Officer trained in electronics."

Roedl held his tongue while the three-star Admiral spoke. Once he was finished, Roedl turned to Lawson and nodded. Lawson smiled and began, "Admiral, I think some additional information is in order. First, this Second Class Petty Officer has a Masters degree from MIT in wave energy generation and energy-based tools. He is also a recognized expert by the Navy, having written several reports on the impact of electromagnetic pulse generation, what you know as EMP, created by nuclear detonation and its impact on micro-circuitry. He is also a math genius, having broken down the methods used by the late Russian Doctor Polevsky in his development of an all-weather penetrating 500 kilowatt laser weapon system. So before you judge a man by his rank, you might try first learning his character."

"Mr. Lawson," the Admiral shot back, "you are arrogant and have no sense of authority or privileges! I don't have time to listen to self-made officers advanced because they happened to get lucky in one mission."

"Thank you, Admiral," Lawson began his retort, "I thought I was slipping but I can see I'm well entrenched." This brought a bout of laughter from the audience which immediately subsided when the Admiral turned to the crowd. "Admiral, you might show some appreciation for us saving your rear. If me and my team had not found the computer program hidden under the code sheet, we'd be facing the wrath of nations at our annihilation of North Korea. As Myers said, we'd be in World War III. Lose the attitude and work with us instead of fighting us. The rank of everyone in this room means nothing if you're dead. We're working to keep you alive and we don't give a damn about your politics, game-playing or desires to make it up the ladder. If you feel that you can do without us misfits in your military structure, every one of us on the CAT205 team can resign based upon our present contractual agreements. We're good at what we do. We may not be the best military examples in the world but, when the chips are down, we are proud to say that we deliver. Sir, what have you delivered in the past thirty days. That question is not an attack, it is a viable question. Don't criticize unless you're absolutely sure that you can do a better job and, if you can do a better job, then mentor those that need the help. Don't just make it another opportunity to condemn someone's efforts. That's both political and petty."

The Chairman of the Joint Staff stood up. "I can see there is some passion in your words, Mr. Lawson. I've been wanting to find the words for my own staff to work together. Can I use your speech?"

Everyone started laughing as Lawson realized the Chairman was giving them both a way out of the contentious conversation. Roedl just smiled, realizing that his effort to wear away Lawson's rough edges was working as Lawson gracefully accepted the offer and proceeded to draw everyone's attention back to the code sheet on the screen.

"Do I need to cover any more on the cracking of the code," Lawson asked.

The Chairman stood up and looked over the audience. "Any questions?" he asked as he continued to scan the audience.

"Can you tell us what the North Koreans are planning, in your opinion," The three-star Admiral that challenged Lawson before asked as he stood with his hands on his hips.

Lawson cleared the screen and brought up a display of a map of the United States. "In my assessment," Lawson advised, "I see them having problems with the development of a missile that can reenter the atmosphere once it gets into space. The heat generated on reentry would be a major obstacle to overcome and that will take them several years to determine an answer, unless they get outside help from China or Russia. That being said, being able to strike a major city would be disastrous but not debilitating to the U.S. It would just put us on a war footing, which is not a result beneficial to North Korea. However, if they were to set off several nuclear devices in space over populated areas of the U.S., due to the EMP effect, they would create significant damage to our infrastructure nationwide that would bring down a significant part of the internet, cut a percentage of cellphone communications, damage the electrical grid and, just as significant, disable many of our satellites, causing loss of GPS, weather satellite and transactional links. The result of this would be catastrophic."

"Explain that internet comment," the Admiral interrupted.

"Well," Lawson continued, "since most of our commerce is done through the internet today, loss of a significant portion of the internet would mean that, in many areas nearest the space-generated bursts, you couldn't by gas or food, shipping of goods would be impacted, communications would be questionable, capabilities for medical treatment would be reduced, billing systems would be off-line, utilities would be shut down and banking would be a question, with many other local and regional impacts not already mentioned."

"So, Petty Officer Myers, how does this happen?" the Chairman questioned.

Myers stepped in front of the microphone and Lawson stepped out of the way. "In simple terms, in an EMP blast, the voltage level on a piece of electronic equipment surges to a level that causes the circuity in the device to melt or separate. An airburst test in a 1962 nuclear project called Starfish Prime damaged electronics in both Hawaii and New Zealand. That's a large area and the electronics of that time had heavier circuitry that could handle more current. An airburst at one-hundred thirty-five miles up could create a brief electrical spike of tens of thousands of volts that could cover a good part of the U.S. That's enough to do considerable damage. Also, it is found that a small nuclear weapon with a yield of just ten kilotons can produce an effective EMP great enough to do significant damage. I suspect that's about the size of the object they put in space. So small fission weapons in thin enclosures can produce EMP events more effectively than large megaton devices. The small devices generate about a thousand volts per meter, more than enough to take out computers, phones, appliances and infrastructure."

"So, Lieutenant Lawson, Admiral Roedl says you have a theory that matches the launch we see today," the Chairman observed. "He said that the launch would happen today, it would include a payload of approximately 400 to 450 pounds and would be put in orbit. You told him that yesterday and today we see that is exactly what the North Koreans did. From notes I just received, analysts are saying that the payload is just a dummy load of approximately 440 pounds. There is no signal being transmitted from the space object and it's tumbling in space. What's your opinion?"

Lawson stepped to the podium, "Well, Sir. My theory is that they will put several of these payloads into space, this is the second one. The reason, I think, that no signal emanates from it is because it's not meant to transmit but rather to receive."

"Why would they do that, it has no value," a person shouted from the audience.

"If I may," Lawson continued, "if I'm dealing with something that I want to behave in a certain way and I don't care if it responds back to me because I'll know it worked through other means, I don't need it to communicate to me. An example of this is a nuclear device that's intended to be detonated at its present altitude. I can communicate to it to tell it to detonate and when it explodes, the whole world will know. It doesn't need to transmit anything." That comment started a loud din of conversation from the floor as discussions between individuals across the audience suddenly increased in intensity. The sense of shock hit everyone as Lawson's comments brought the realization that his opinion was a real possibility.

The chairman let the conversations go on for about five minutes while he conversed with the Joint Staff at the front of the room. They discussed some objectives at length and came to agreement on the next question.

"Quiet down everyone," The Chairman called out resulting in the level of noise radically decreasing. "Mr. Lawson, you and Petty Officer Myers seem to have a handle on this. What are North Korea's next moves?"

"It's just a theory, mind you," Lawson stated, "but I think that if this is a nuclear device, they won't do anything at the present time. One device will do some damage but again, just opinion, I think they will send two or three more of these 'dummy loads' up, stating they are satellites. I think they want to have enough up there to do significant damage. Doing so and putting them up to where they are simultaneously passing over key targets at the same time would allow for the North Koreans to detonate them simultaneously thereby causing the greatest amount of damage."

"So how would you know if that is their intent?" The chairman countered.

"I'll let Myers explain that to you since he's presently doing the math on this part as we speak," Lawson said as he stepped away from the mike.

Myers had been doing calculations while Lawson talked. Taking a moment to finish his analysis he finally stepped to the microphone and looked up at the U.S. map being displayed. "We can get a reasonable determination of their intent by seeing what they do with the next one or two launches. If they place them in an arrangement that places the objects over key major cities at the same time on each orbit, then we can be pretty sure that they are set up to bring down our electronic infrastructure. Other than that, we just have to look for other indicators that can tell us what their target is. One thing we do know, based upon the math I just performed, this newest satellite passes over the San Francisco area and the Silicon Valley every ninety-four minutes." More conversation went on within the audience as the Chairman stepped over to the podium. Realizing that they just crossed from classified possible scenarios into top secret real threats, the Chairman decided that he must immediately to cut off the meeting.

"This briefing is completed. We have other activities directly associated with this operation, so in that sense, Operation Scarborough is still on-going. As such, we ask you to not put any reports or notes on our network at the present time. Everything goes to the SECDAT center so that those involved can see what other team members are doing without informing the rest of the Pentagon. Next briefing will be on February 16th at 19:00 hours at this location. Thank you, Admiral Roedl, Commander

Norman, Lieutenant Lawson, Petty Officer Myers and, out in the lobby area, Master Gunnery Sergeant Glendenning – the CAT205 Team." A round of applause went up as they left the podium and toward the door. Lawson felt nervous that the team's identity had just been exposed to a broad spectrum of Pentagon people.

Chapter 16

Just Like Haman's Own Gallows

"The cause is hidden. The effect is visible to all." - Ovid

"Not so fast, get your team back in here," the Chairman said while putting his hand on Commander Norman's shoulder. "We're not finished here. I have the courier that was supposed to deliver the document to your people last night outside in the lobby and I'm bringing him in." Norman waved at Lawson and Myers to come to her.

When they arrived, Norman looked at Myers, "You look awful. I guess we rescued you in the nick of time," she said while holding back a laugh.

"Nick of time, that's funny," Lawson said while looking at Myers. "Your first name is Nick, the analogy fits." Myers squinted at Lawson and sat down.

"I've been beat up enough today," Myers complained as he rubbed his leg. "This is starting to hurt."

"I've already made arrangements to take care of that," Norman said while ripping Myers' pant leg. "It's just some good scrapes. The medical team will be in here shortly to tend to you."

Lawson sat down next to Myers as Norman sat down to face them both. "Honestly, Nick," she said as she looked at him. "I really thought we lost you. The wreck, the fire in the car, bullet holes all over the car and the dead driver in front, we thought they either kidnapped or killed you."

"They might have if it hadn't been for one of your agents pulling me out from under the tractor-trailer," Myers replied.

"Virginia didn't say anything about pulling you out," Norman responded.

"It wasn't that lady you sent," Myers stated as he was getting irritated at all the drama and mystery. "It was a guy that pulled me from under the trailer. I woke up to find myself lying on the other side of the trailer, next to the wheels where no one would find me unless they were really looking. My computer was lying beside me and my pistol was back in the holster."

Norman was beginning to wonder if there was another party looking out for them in all this chaos. "Honestly, Nick, I didn't have any other person out there except Virginia. I couldn't risk exposing you to more danger if you had gotten clear and more people out there would have pointed Henderson's men to you."

"Henderson?" Lawson called out. "He's on our team! Why is he going after Myers. So the person the Admiral identified you were interrogating was Henderson? Why him?"

"Because he was operating from a different agenda," Norman barked back. "Didn't you realize that when Gunny confronted him in room 2337?"

"If you remember, I wasn't in the room when that happened," Lawson shot back. "I left after Gunny started talking to him about Josh Henry. I had to go as I had to meet with Roedl. So let me get this, if you were interrogating Henderson yesterday, how is it that he was able to give orders today to take Myers out?"

"Here's the sequence, Jim," Norman answered tersely. "I was questioning Henderson yesterday afternoon and most of this evening. Finally, around 9:00 PM this evening, he said that I didn't have to worry about my team any longer because Myers would already be dead, thereby removing Admiral Roedl from any further significant operations."

"That's what would indeed happen," Lawson confirmed.

"So," Norman continued, "Henderson planned to take Myers out at room 2337 then expose you as working as a mole. His team was ready to move in to finish the work against Myers in the room when they saw Myers walking down the sidewalk to the taxi. The taxi was their backup plan. So once Myers got into the taxi, the other Henderson team members got into their car and followed. I got a text from Gunny saying that Myers just texted him from a taxi and said I needed to find some way to stop your presentation before the Joint Staff. I realized then what Henderson's plan was. I notified Admiral Roedl of the need to stop the presentation after I called Virginia, my adjutant in Roedl's office, to get over to the Rayburn building while listening to any activity on the local frequencies. Most of the police and fire have gone over to digital but not the taxi companies. She was able to determine where they were at by the message that another taxi radioed in that one of their taxies was in a collision. That's where she headed. By the way, when I called the Admiral to stop the presentation, he said not to worry about it. It was all under control. So the next thing was the question..."

"I want everyone over here in the front seats," the Chairman interrupted. "Admiral Roedl needs to ask some questions."

Roedl stepped forward as Gunny came in and sat down with the courier that was supposed to carry the documents the previous evening sitting next to him. They were handcuffed together.

"Did any of you receive a document yesterday from a courier?" Roedl asked while looking at each one of them. Everyone nodded 'no'.

"Ok, bring him up," Roedl ordered as Gunny and the alleged courier came to stand in front of the team members. "Which person did you deliver the document to?"

"That one," the courier said while pointing to Lawson. Roedl smiled as he knew the guy was lying and Lawson was the last person to pick for a confrontation. Lawson sat there smiling.

"Well, Lawson," Roedl questioned, "how do you explain his response?"

"Actually, Sir," Lawson snapped back, "I would like to first hear an explanation to his response."

The courier looked at Lawson then at Roedl. "Honestly, Sir, that's the guy."

"Don't use the word 'honestly' and me in the same sentence," Lawson remarked as the others laughed. "Now, since you claim that you delivered the document to me, where's the receipt?"

"I have the receipt right here," came a voice from the back of the room as the person came through the door. It was Colonel Jacobs. The Chairman watched quietly as the scene unfolded.

"Let me see it," Roedl ordered.

"No way," Colonel Jacobs said while handing the slip of paper to the Chairman.

"Well, it does have your signature, Lawson," the Chairman observed as he handed the slip to Roedl. Roedl looked it over and handed it to Lawson.

"Hold it where I can see it," Jacobs shouted. Lawson held it up over his head to see the light shine through the paper.

"This is a forgery," Lawson stated as matter of fact. As he was speaking, another naval officer walked through the door while Gunny announced, "Attention on deck!"

"We don't do that in here, Gunny," the man just entering declared. It was the Chief of Naval Operations, the CNO. "What's going on here? My aide out in the lobby informed me that an inquisition is going on here."

"I'm charging this man with receiving critical documentation and withholding it from his team," Colonel Jacobs responded.

"That's a question still being discussed," the Chairman observed.

"You were mighty quiet during our briefing earlier," Lawson said while handing the receipt to the CNO. "This is the document Colonel Jacobs says proves that I received the document in question."

The CNO looked at the receipt and smiled as he handed the slip back to Lawson. "That's an interesting piece of paper. Interesting, but false." Everyone looked at the CNO as they tried to figure out how he knew that. They waited as they looked at Lawson.

"As they say in the old movies, the jig is up," Lawson said as he sat down. "It's like this, I never sign anything military or civilian with my rank. This is signed by 'Lt James Lawson'. Everything I sign in the military is 'Jim Lawson 9486', the numbers being the last four digits of my social security number. I know there are other Jim Lawson's in the military and I don't want to be mistaken for one of them."

"Yea, right," barked Jacobs. "Like we're supposed to believe that? What a weak argument."

"Weak or not, it's true," Roedl replied. "The CNO has been on my case about Lawson's reports not showing his rank in the document signature area. Lawson doesn't care about rank. He only took the officer rank because I threatened to kick his rear if he didn't accept it. If he's not going to sign his rank on an official document, what makes you think he'd ever take the time to sign his rank on a document receipt." The courier began to squirm as Roedl was talking.

"So, Lieutenant Lawson," the CNO questioned, "who do you think would forge a signature like this?"

"Let's see," Lawson started, "it would have to be someone like Gunny." Gunny gave a surprised stare at Lawson's comment. "Someone who has been in the military for a long time and rank is the currency of the military. Gunny, when you sign something I noticed that you always start off your signature with the letters 'MGS'. What does that mean?"

Gunny looked around at the others wondering what Lawson was up to. Was he saying that Gunny was the suspect? "It means 'Master Gunnery Sergeant'."

"Thanks, Gunny," Lawson said as he walked in front of the others. "To answer your question, Sir, it has to be someone that is long term military and believes everyone carries the value of rank the way he does. Someone that can't think from any other perspective because they can't think outside their own little world. Someone that believes they have to destroy their opponents by any means necessary. There has to be a cruel and selfish characteristic about everything they do. Someone who would bust a Gunnery Sergeant down to a Staff Sergeant for following the orders of the CNO and not the orders he gave. Isn't that right, Colonel Jacobs?"

"Now wait a minute," Jacobs shot back. "You can't pin this on me using your eloquent lying logic. This had to be someone on your team if it wasn't you. Tell him, sergeant," he said while putting his stare on the courier in handcuffs. There was silence while everyone waited for the courier to respond.

"Well, Sir," the courier explained, "I could have been mistaken about the person I gave the document to." A long pause followed then he continued, "Actually, I'm not mistaken. Colonel Jacobs had one of his men put the signature in my courier pad. The guy is an aide with a long military record that claimed he was a forger before he got caught, served some time then joined the military. The Colonel set this all up to bring down Roedl, I mean Admiral Roedl."

Gunny pulled his pistol from its holster and swung it around toward Jacobs. "Ye be pullin that thing out real slow, Colonel,"

Gunny said while he watched Jacobs put his hand inside his uniform jacket. Jacobs opened his jacket slowly to expose a 9mm pistol in his belt.

"I've been in the Marines for twenty-one years," Jacobs lamented. "Guys like Roedl and Lawson cheapen the military with their lack of discipline and disregard for the rules. This is the real America, the military."

"You're wrong, Colonel," Gunny replied. "The military helps America stay the real America. We're only a part of it. Guys like Admiral Roedl and Lieutenant Lawson understand that and also understand that the military may have rules but we're a lot more than that. We're guardians of freedom and, as such, we owe it to the everyday working Joe and Jane to keep the road clear for them to go about their daily lives. We are not a social club to see who can get up the highest in rank and get all the privileges that entails. I wish the lower ranks had all the privileges and the higher you went in rank, the less privileges are given. That would ensure that the only people commanding the troops are the one that want to help them along. I know that thought is unrealistic but seeing what you've become makes me hope something better will come along because of all of the politics I presently see in the upper ranks."

"Well said, Gunny," The CNO responded. "Now disarm him and put the cuffs on him. As for the courier, we'll figure that out later. He may be charged with something but I suspect it will be minor, if anything."

"Master Gunny, you being the senior NCO of the security detail should have known that you don't let someone into the conference center with a weapon without the Head of Security's approval." The Chairman reprimanded.

"That's true, Sir, but Colonel Jacobs is the Head of Security," Gunny advised.

"My mistake, Master Gunny," the Chairman apologized. "A flaw in the protocol."

Gunny took the weapon from Jacobs and handed it to Norman. Then, handcuffing the Colonel, he walked him out of the Pentagon to the security people waiting outside. After Gunny got back into the conference room, he saw that a naval medical team was working on Myers.

"Everyone here," Roedl ordered as they all sat down near Myers and the medics. "They're going to take Myers to the naval hospital for tests and observation as he has to go through concussion protocol. We will all meet at my office at 09:00 hours tomorrow morning as this mission is far from over. Lawson, bring the computer and notes from the Rayburn office building. Norman, I want you to lock down Congressman Latershan's computer. The FBI will join you once we leave here to execute a search warrant to get his computer. They also have a warrant to confiscate Lavlery's computer from secure storage. It better be there as he was required to turn it in when he went on vacation. Gunny, I want you to go talk to Myers tonight once he gets to the hospital so we can find out what happened to him this evening. And Myers, once you give Gunny the information, I don't want to see you until Monday morning. Get some rest. Everyone clear on what they're to do?"

Everyone agreed as they proceeded out of the conference room. Lawson looked at the clock. It was 11:30 PM so he figured by the time they got all this done, it would be close to 1:00 AM.

Chapter 17

Piecing Together a Plan – Day 8

"One is not exposed to danger who, even when in safety is always on their guard." - Publilius Syrus

It was 8:55 AM on Sunday, February 8th when the team assembled in Admiral Roedl's conference room next to his office at the Kennedy Irregular Warfare Center.

The room was the same as Lawson had remembered before. It had a long, highly-polished wooden oak conference table with a number of comfortable looking leather armchairs. At the far end of the room was a large oak cabinet that extended the full length of the wall with a large flat screen monitor at the center of the cabinet. The part of the cabinet that was lower than the monitor had three drawers on each side and underneath the monitor. There were cupboard doors at the same level as the monitor but to the left and right of it. The wall on the right of the room had a couple of pictures and a door just before getting to the cabinet. The wall on the left had three pictures and a fire extinguisher hanging against a red-painted rectangle on the wall near the cabinet. The rest of the room was painted off-white.

Lawson sat down with the computer and notes he had taken from room 2337. Commander Norman sat next to him with Gunny sitting across from them. Admiral Roedl stepped into the room and closed the door.

"Good morning, everyone," Roedl greeted as he moved to the head of the table. "Updates?"

Norman was first to respond, "I have received all of the Lavlery's emails from the archive server and had gotten Congressman Latershan's computer but not without some drama between the FBI and Latershan. We have not been able to find Lavlery's computer. I'm going to interrogate Henderson this afternoon then the fake Marine we caught after that."

"I talked to Myers last night," Gunny offered next. "He gave me a play-by-play description of the events on the attempt on his life. Lawson and I talked about it this morning and we've come to some observations. Lawson has an approach to determining what other people were involved in this escapade and I am already passing some of the ideas past Josh Henry."

"We'll get back to your observations in a minute," Roedl interrupted. "Lawson."

Lawson looked down at his notes then responded, "Well, Sir, Colonel Jacobs talked with me when we left last night. The Marine guards were waiting for transportation to the brig so I had a chance to talk to him. A lot came out of that discussion. Jacobs says he didn't have any action against us that was threatening, acting only to restrict information. Also, it appears that the threats to us are still in action. Last night, when Gunny went to see Josh Henry at the VA hospital, Gunny saw the same guy in the hospital that Gunny and I saw at the Library of Congress. Norman put a Marine security team at his door and only the doctor and assigned nurses can go into his room. They have strict orders to prevent anyone else from going in and, if there is an emergency requiring additional staff, the Marines are to be in the room with the emergency team."

"Ok," Roedl said, "Tell me, Gunny, what is this observation is that you and Lawson came up with."

"Actually, Sir, I'll have Lawson tell you since he's much better at putting concepts in their proper order." Gunny responded as he looked at Lawson.

"It's like this, Sir," Lawson began. "Gunny told me about his visit with Josh Henry last night. In Josh's discussion, Colonel Jacobs name never came up. Everything had to do with Lavlery and Henderson. We came to the conclusion that there were two different parties working against us with different agendas. The first party was Colonel Jacobs and his vendetta towards you. We think he was working against you to make us fail allowing him to point to the failure as a reason you shouldn't remain as Special Operations Commander. The second party was Henderson, Lavlery and possibly the Colonel Chang Sue."

"You mean Colonel Qiang Zhu," Roedl interrupted.

"Whatever, Sir," Lawson responded as the others laughed. "Anyway, the Colonel comes into the picture due to Josh's discovery of a message that has the Colonel, Lavlery and the ship Pacific Jade all in the same message. The other reason why we think it's two parties is that Colonel Jacobs interference didn't appear to include any violent actions while those tied to Henderson did, even up to the attempt to take out Henderson after Norman's interrogation."

Roedl stood up and stretched as he reacted to Lawson's assessment. "You're assuming too much Mr. Lawson. We don't know yet who attempted to kill Myers and the attempt on you and Norman is still being investigated. However, the attempt on you and Norman does appear to have a greater possibility to be

Henderson's work since the attackers all had real DIA IDs. I'll take your assessment under advisement. I'm glad you're all thinking of the possibilities. Now, Norman, what is your plan to get to the bottom of this conspiracy?"

"We should find some things out from Henderson. Lawson has a plan for analyzing any of the communications and Gunny is going to share our findings with Josh to see if he can get additional items from the dark web."

"Lawson," Roedl asked, "your plans for finding other culprits?"

"I'm going to look at Lavlery's emails that we know he sent to find unique words he used in his communications. That should help us in our search to find other hidden emails or threads of emails that can give us other names of people he communicated with."

Roedl seemed perplexed on Lawson's answer. "How are you going to find other players using that technique?"

"It's actually a simple process," Lawson replied. "I check the patterns of groupings. First, I check the emails to see who he's communicated with. Next, I filter out those emails that have to do with people in Latershan's office, removing them since those are normal business emails. Next, from the emails left, I look for groups of emails that match with certain times that communications had gone out to the North Koreans and now, possibly, the Chinese. I figure that other messages would then have been sent to other players around the same time to inform or instruct on actions they should take. Finally, I'll use those communications to get warrants for the emails of those most likely to be suspects."

"Ok, good. Get on it as soon as we get out of here," Roedl instructed.

"One other thing. I need any text messages Lavlery sent. Do we know his cellphone service?" Lawson requested as he picked up the computer and papers.

Roedl looked to Norman, "It's on you, Commander. Get him what he needs." Norman nodded recognition to the order.

"One other note, Admiral," Norman brought up, "Josh said that Lavlery's name came up in a message along with the name of Colonel Qiang Zhu and the Pacific Jade, yet the master manifest for the ship didn't have Lavlery's name on it. It did have a name, Sam Ginty, on the manifest and the passport and access papers were for Sam Ginty. However, the LA port authority says the manifest appears to be either tampered with or a fake. They've got two manifests, the master manifest with Ginty's name on it but no Lavlery and the other manifest has neither name."

Roedl's face suddenly changed to a look of surprise as he heard the name Sam Ginty. "Ginty was fired from the Defense Intelligence Agency several years back for unauthorized activity," Roedl explained. "After that he left he fell off the face of the earth. Now you're saying he suddenly showed up again?"

Lawson interrupted their thought process. "Sam Ginty would not be able to get on board the Pacific Jade without his passport and access papers. So the person who wants to be Sam Ginty had to be a different person."

"A good point," Admiral Roedl agreed.

"There are some other things I need," Lawson said. "I need several documents to verify who Sam Ginty really was on board the ship."

The Admiral questioned Lawson's reasoning.

"Primarily, I want to get a picture of Ginty. Maybe the DIA has a picture from his ID photo," Lawson explained. Roedl immediately understood Lawson's intentions. If he could get a picture of Ginty he could show it to Congressman Latershan to see if Ginty's picture was actually Lavlery. Roedl thought it was a longshot as he thought of what were the odds that these particular people and this mission would be intersecting at the focal point of an international crisis.

"One more thing, Admiral," Lawson added. "The Pacific Jade disappeared from the shipping tracking system. They must have turned off their GPS tracking unit. They've also gone silent and no one seems to know where they are." Roedl swung around to the side of the room, stepping in behind Gunny's chair. They were caught by surprise more by his moves then his words.

"Let me tell you something about Colonel Qiang Zhu," Roedl warned. "He is a nemesis to our intelligence people. He's a Chinese leader in charge of China's foreign intelligence operations. His main job is to find out what we are doing and get people here in the U.S. to turn against our government. If he is somehow involved in this, then he may have had success getting into our intel operations. Now, what concerns me is how does this tie in with the pictures, messages and, particularly, the program you guys found in the London picture. If he is somehow involved in the attempt to override our security measures for launching nukes then what are his intentions and his next moves.

This also makes me wonder if he was the one ordering the hits on each of you."

"Maybe Josh knows what Ginty looks like," Gunny counseled as though they were still on the topic of Ginty. "I'll ask him as they were working at DIA at the same time."

Roedl stopped for a moment, then realizing what Gunny was recommending, gave his approval.

They all began picking up their materials to leave while Norman got on the phone. Roedl had opened the door to get into his office as Norman hung up the phone.

"Henderson is ready to talk, so I'll see him first thing tomorrow morning," Norman said as she was leaving. Roedl nodded his approval and sat down at his desk as Norman left the office.

Chapter 18

Visitation – Day 9

"Of everything we must first ask: is it real or not?" - Mike Klepper

Myers, Lawson and Gunny entered room 2337 while Norman was on her way to interrogate Henderson. It was 07:30 on Monday, February 9th when they arrived in the room. Gunny closed the door as Lawson stepped to the safe and opened it to get the contents.

"Who are you and what are you doing in here?" Gunny exclaimed as he drew his weapon and pointed it at the man sitting in a chair in front of the whiteboard. As he said this, Lawson and Myers also drew their weapons, pointing their guns at the man in the chair.

"I'm unarmed," the voice in the chair responded. "You are probably at the point where you need to find out who is behind the attempts on your lives and the people putting together the plot to destroy North Korea."

They all looked at each other, totally confused as to their next steps with this intruder as they realized they were in uncharted territory. "What do we do now?" Lawson asked as they all were consumed by the unexpected event.

"You're the guy we saw at the Library of Congress," Gunny observed.

"Quite right you are," came the man's response. "I'm also the man that rescued Petty Officer Myers from under the tractor-trailer."

"If that's true," Myers replied, "what did you say to me when you rescued me?"

"I said, 'don't fight me son'," the man answered.

"That's right. Well, he appears to be the same man," Myers confirmed.

"Now, why don't you put away your weapons and let me tell you something about what you're going up against," the man said while taking a sip of coffee from a cup. "It will all become clearer in a few minutes." Lawson and Myers put their weapons back in their holsters while Gunny kept his weapon trained upon the mysterious visitor.

"Do as you wish," the man said to Gunny as he adjusted his chair to face them. "You are not going against one shadow government, but rather one of many," he said while continuing to keep his eyes fixed on Gunny. "There are as many as fifty to sixty different shadow governments here in Washington, each focused on a different venue, cause and objective. Most are weak and ineffective but there are five or six that are organized, well-structured and well-funded. You are tangling with one of those five or six. They have tentacles spread throughout the country backed by lobbyists that are very focused on getting their agenda secured." At that moment, Gunny moved his weapon to the holster and pushed it in until he heard the click of the holster locking the gun into place.

"Why should we listen to you?" Gunny inquired.

The man pulled out a cigarette and lit it up. "I know this is a non-smoking building but, according to their cameras and logs, I'm not even here. Now, where was I? Oh yes, the present administration has no problems with a number of these shadow organizations because the present admin is responsible for putting a number of them in place so that the admin can use them later once the term of office for the present admin is over. Follow me so far?"

Gunny pulled up a chair and sat down. Once Lawson and Myers saw that Gunny was comfortable with the present situation, they followed suit. The man reached into his jacket pocket which caused all three to move their hands closer to their weapons. Once they saw that he pulled out a piece of paper, they returned to their semi-relaxed positions.

"This piece of paper holds the name of a key player and a person of interest in this whole escapade," the man said as he handed the paper to Lawson. Lawson looked at the paper and handed it to Myers. Myers could see a name on the paper that he recognized at once.

"So what does Robert Molliner have to do with all this?" Myers asked.

"So you know who he is?" the man questioned back.

"Yes," was Myers response. "He is CEO of Klyster Technologies, a major producer of artificial intelligence development and robotic systems which also includes weapons development. We had a couple of his systems on board the carrier for testing just before I left to go on the mission to Iran. So again, what does he have to do with this?"

"He is the money man behind the group opposing you on this operation, Operation Scarborough," the man said as he took a drag on his cigarette. "As far as I can tell, he answers to someone else, someone that was previously in congress based upon information I could glean from staff members of congressmen. Nobody wants to talk but they say a lot from what they don't say and from their facial expressions when they don't want to say it. Find this ex-congressman and you'll find the head of this shadow group."

"What's your interest in all this," Lawson inquired.

The man put the cigarette out in his coffee cup as he responded, "My interest is in the survivability of this country. We don't know who is going to be the next President but with the Republicans having a large field of contenders and, with the Democrats having an obvious choice, it's hard to determine where we are going as a country. These shadow organizations only muddy the waters as to what or who will lead after the next general election. Now Lawson, you're a student of history. See anything similar to any other government in history?"

Lawson was taken aback by the man's knowledge of him. He had definitely done his homework. Lawson tried to sort out the thoughts as he focused on the question posed to him. "Well, I would have to say the Roman Empire holds some resemblance to our present day situation. There was expanding corruption within the government, divisions between the leaders and the people, costs of services normally done by the local governments being taken on more and more by the central government, a socializing of the military and greater civil unrest. Finally, the death knell to the empire came when, in 476 AD, Odoacer, a Germanic general forced the Roman Emperor, Romulus Augustulus to abdicate the throne. It wasn't until 493 that the destruction of the Roman Empire, as we know it, came to a crashing end with Theoderic the Great, a Goth, wiping out Odoacer and his cabinet."

"So, based upon your analysis of the Roman Empire's fall, do you see my concern about our situation?" the man asked. Everyone nodded 'yes'.

"One side note," Gunny interrupted. "The fall of Rome happened in a long series of steps that took a couple hundred years. Yes, there were a number of notable events but it was still in a continuous downward spiral. If I look at Rome and where we are today, we have a chance to stop these attempts of bring our country down and keep our country working effectively."

"That's the goal of my effort," the man explained. "I want the rules that effectively made us a unified nation to continue while, at the same time, making small adjustments to meet our needs by way of the Constitution as our founders intended. Doing it any other way brings chaos and the greater potential of opening the door to a manipulating dictator. As Ben Franklin said, 'We have a republic, if we can keep it.' Do you all now understand what I'm focused on?"

"So what is your name?" Lawson questioned.

"I'm not going to give you my name as my value is in keeping as invisible as possible," came the response.

"Then how can we know we can trust you?" Gunny inquired. "For all we know, you might be a member of one of the opposing shadow governments that is trying to bring the others down."

"A fair concern," the man responded. "Supposing I am as you say an opposing group. Isn't the fact that I am working to stop a proven threat worth the risk? After all, if I were an opposing force to the present attempt on the U.S., wouldn't that make me an asset rather than a liability. That being said, I am not joined to any other organization."

"In other words, the enemy of my enemy is my friend," Lawson quoted.

"Close enough," the man acknowledged. "Look, you have a name to start from. I'd check the emails and other communications you guys are going through to see where that name or company shows up. Don't forget texts they may send to each other. Phone numbers and IP addresses may give you additional information as to the source of the communications. These guys are smart but not foolproof."

Lawson could see the value in having this man support them. It was something of a gamble but he was a resource worth listening to. "How can we get in touch with you?"

"You can't but I will feed you information as I find it," the man said in response. "My dark web identifier is 'Excalibur'. Josh Henry knows how to find me, but he is one of the few people I trust to keep my identity secure. I've got to go."

"Thanks for the help," Lawson said as he moved toward the door.

"Oh, one more thing," the man said as he turned to the others in the room. Reaching into his jacket pocket once more, he pulled out an envelope. "This is a high-res copy of Sam Ginty's passport along with a picture of him without all of the passport information as per your request. The passport office wasn't about to give it to you as they have blocked Admiral Roedl's attempts to get information at every turn. However, I have friends inside the office that were willing to help. Show the picture to Congressman Latershan and ask him who this person is. That will help you clear up some questions as I know you were already thinking in that direction."

"Thanks," Lawson replied as he opened the door while wondering how the man got into the room in the first place.

Once the man left, Gunny sat back down and asked, "What do you guys think?"

Myers was first to respond, "I think he's got a hidden agenda but I get the sense he wants to trade information that we've got with info he gets."

"In other words, he's an information trader," Lawson observed. "Part of our value is that we can provide information that he can use to leverage information from others. I'd keep this guy on a very short rope until we have a better sense on what his motives are. Yes, he is a benefit but at what price?"

"Remember," Myers interjected, "Adam and Eve bought into the serpent's lies about the fruit without realizing the vast expense they placed upon humanity. It looked like a good deal until the bill had to be paid." Gunny smiled at Myers' analogy. He was beginning to realize that there were some good examples to reference in the Bible when it came to human nature.

"At this point," Gunny observed, "we don't know if we are dealing with a friend or a serpent. I think it might be a good time for me to give Josh Henry a visit while you guys start filtering through the emails. Also, I haven't seen anything on that request for Lavlery's texts. Have you guys gotten anything?"

Both Lawson and Myers nodded 'no' as they proceeded to open the spreadsheet with the emails provided to them that Lavlery sent. Gunny watched them get down to work and, after a moment, opened the door and left.

Chapter 19

Nowhere to Turn

"Coincidence is merely the puppeteers' curtain, hiding the hands that pull the world's strings." - Kaleb Nation, Harken

Norman arrived at the Kennedy Irregular Warfare Center at approximately 7:35 AM on February 9th. While Lawson, Gunny and Myers were in the process of talking to the man that had entered room 2337, Norman had the Marine guard in charge of Captain Henderson bring him into the interview room. Norman walked into the room and put the file folder down on the table along with her computer after she handed Henderson a cup of coffee. Then she set a microphone on the table and connected it to a cable that went to a recording device in the next room. Sitting down into the chair, she opened the file folder and proceeded to review its contents.

"Captain," Norman began, "Your comments are being recorded. Now, you are presently responsible for the deaths of two cab drivers, five fake DIA agents and the wounding of another DIA analyst. You do realize that I could push for the death sentence for these acts and your obvious act of espionage."

"I did what I did to protect my family," was Henderson's retort.

"I understand that, Captain. How is it you didn't attempt to get someone from the FBI or the NSA to get you protection for your family?" Norman questioned.

"You don't understand," Henderson replied. "Who would I go to? Any person I go to could be working with Lavlery which would guarantee that my wife and daughter would be dead right now. On top of that, the present administration appears to be a part of all this activity or are allowing it. At the very least, I am caught between two battling entities, one that is trying to radically change this nation and the other trying desperately to keep it in its present form. The problem is, I don't know who is who. I've become a pawn that ends up paying the price no matter which way I go."

"So how did you get caught up in this in the first place?" Norman inquired as she took a sip of coffee.

Henderson looked at the file folder in front of Norman as he selected his words. "It started off small. Lavlery wanted me to sign some documents confirming some intelligence gathering. I scanned the documents and felt everything was ok. If I had read the documents with greater attention, I would have realized that I was agreeing that the Secretary of Defense was a spy. By doing so, I would have ended my career right there. Lavlery brought that up a couple of days later and said that he could make the report go away if I were to do a task for him. It was a minor task but illegal. From that point, the things he asked me to do became more and more questionable until I realized that I had dug myself so deep into a hole that he literally owned me. I confronted him with the facts and he responded that if I didn't do exactly as he directed me to do, my wife and daughter would become casualties in the effort. I had no choice."

Norman sat for a moment, realizing that she could be in the same situation if the sequence of events had happened the same way to her. She began to realize that she had to defend his actions in her report. His documented explanation would go a long way to that goal.

"I'm beginning to understand your rationale and reasons for your actions. This will definitely help in your defense," she acknowledged as she focused on the next part of the discussion. "What players do you know were working with Lavlery on this effort?"

"Well," he started, "one name that popped up a couple of times was an alias by the name of 'Prism'. That person appeared to be the main driver in the activities that took place. Man or woman, I don't know, but I do know the person offered Lavlery five million dollars to create some type of computer program. The computer program appeared to be a central focus of the effort and there was a lot of activity around its creation. What it was going to be used for, I don't know. I do know that it was to be an executable file that was to be buried in an electronic document. I suspect that one of the pictures the CAT205 team was to analyze may have been the document they were going to use."

"So you knew that the pictures Lawson, Myers and Gunny got had the program already in it?" Norman questioned.

"Actually, I didn't know," Henderson responded. "I wasn't sure if the program was to be in one of these pictures or some pictures that were to be sent later. The reason I agreed to the CAT205 team doing the analysis is that I was sure they couldn't break even the first level of coding, much less find the program. I figured that, based upon their experiences in Iran, they were good at physical facility entries but not code breakers. They would take too long and, whatever the program was meant for, it would have been activated long before they could find the program. I figured that would take me off the hook. The main concern I had was that Josh Henry could get them moving forward with help to break the code. I was surprised by the fact that Admiral Roedl had been talking to Josh Henry, a fact made known during the inquiry before we started this operation. At the very least, I had to get rid of Henry because, most likely, he would give the team enough information for them to figure out the direction to go."

Norman shifted in her chair. "What about the attack on me and Lawson?"

"That was strictly a capture effort," said Henderson as he took a drink of coffee. "Lavlery disappeared soon after that effort failed. I figure he got the next flight out to some international location. What was it they planned to do with you and Lawson after the pickup, I don't know. I was only to get federal IDs for the people involved in the grab so that they could keep you two in custody if the local police showed up. Failure of the grab effort and the failure to kill Josh Henry is what sealed my fate. I knew it was only a matter of time before the powers that be would be turning their attention to taking me out. I had become a liability to them."

"What do you know about a Chinese Colonel named Qiang Zhu?" she asked.

Henderson rubbed his shoulder as it began to hurt then replied, "I heard his name several times and put together some pieces that gave me a high level of confidence that he was somehow directing the effort. However, I think he was doing it in partnership with someone else. The partner had to be a former U.S. senator or congressman. I'm saying that because Lavlery called a man 'statesman' on one occasion which resulted in some very fierce stares from the man."

Norman wrote some notes then proceeded, "What, where and when was this meeting?"

"It was early last month," Henderson answered. "We were in a restaurant at the Watergate Hotel. I was meeting with Lavlery when the man walked up and Lavlery addressed him as statesman. I wouldn't have thought too much of it except for the look the man gave back to Lavlery. After he gave Lavlery that look, the man looked at me in a manner that I considered quite threatening. I found the confrontation unnerving enough that I went through all hundreds of senatorial and congressional pictures to determine that he was not an active legislator. I could tell that Lavlery feared him."

"Anyone else you can remember that was a part of the shadow group?"

Henderson thought for a moment, "There was one person I know of that was the money man for this effort. His last name was Mollner or Molliner, something like that. He's CEO of a large defense contractor that works in artificial intelligence. Oh, and one more person. Ben Collier is a data analyst at Fort Bevoir. He used to work at the DIA in the pass certification department, checking fake ID badges that were confiscated during arrests. He had to go into the code on the ID cards to figure how they were able to hack DIA systems and use that information to make the pass system much more secure."

"What do you know about Rod Lavlery?" Norman queried.

Henderson leaned back as Norman handed him a pain pill. Henderson took the pill with a swig of coffee then answered, "I know Rod Lavlery is not his real name. I also know that his congressional security check was faked. He told me so. I tried to pull up records at DIA to see if his picture showed up under someone else's name but was stopped by some security rule in the system. It went through a lot of pictures to compare against the picture of Lavlery that I put in. Somewhere around the letter 'G' in the alphabetic search for a matching picture, the screen came up with a security breach message stating I was not authorized to see pictures of field agents. From that message, I figured that he was a DIA field agent though I didn't get access to the name. I was going…" A knock at the door stopped the conversation as the door opened and Admiral Roedl stepped in, thanking the Marine outside the door then closing the door behind him.

"Norman, I have a question for Henderson that needs some explanation," Roedl said as he pulled up a chair.

"He's all yours, Sir," Norman acknowledged.

"Captain Henderson," Roedl started, "there is a man working in the background that contacted my people about a half-hour ago. We don't know his name but he always seems to have the latest information as to what's going on. He even was able to complete a request for a copy of Sam Ginty's passport that the passport office was unwilling to provide. You know anything about him?"

"Sam Ginty, huh?" Henderson questioned as he thought about the Admiral's request. "There's a name I haven't heard in a while. What's Sam got to do with this whole matter?" Henderson paused for a moment but, after looking at Norman's facial expression, decided it was wiser to just answer the Roedl's question.

"Ok," Henderson continued, "If my suspicions are correct, my guess that the person giving your people a visit was the 'Fox'. We at DIA nicknamed him 'Zorro' which is Spanish for 'fox'. He's an information collector that always seems to be up to date on things that are happening, particularly operations. He has a dark web pseudonym of 'Excalibur', you know, the name of King Arthur's sword. The interesting thing about the man is that he not only trades in information but many times, he uses the information to put himself in a position where he can help the party he thinks is trying to do the right thing. I doubt that there are many people that know his name. He apparently has a high-level security clearance and access to some very secure information. He's also a superb locksmith and computer hacker with an ability to bypass security logs, registers and cameras. That's one of the reasons no one seems to be able to find him. He's also very unpredictable. So much so that he never takes the same route twice in a row."

Roedl got up from the table and moved toward the door. "I trust that you can help us get this shadow group and shut down their operation," he stated firmly as he opened the door.

"Only if I know my family is safe," Henderson shot back.

"Fair enough," came the response.

Norman watched as the Admiral left, realizing that he just made Henderson part of the group. This left her interrogation approach up in the air as it was no longer an adversarial approach but rather a cooperative one. "Thanks, Admiral," she complained under her breath.

"Well, things change, don't they," Henderson observed as his comment broke Norman out of her thought process.

"They may change," Norman snapped back, "but before you get too comfortable, you might want to consider how you're going to approach Gunny with that attitude. You may be peeling yourself off of the ceiling."

Henderson's face changed its composure, "I hadn't thought about that possibility, good point."

"Let's get back to our discussion," Norman suggested. Henderson knew it was not a suggestion but an order and he was in no position to debate the fine points.

"We were discussing my search for Lavlery's picture on DIA's internal network and how I was stopped," Henderson continued. "I figured that the next thing I could do was give Myers and Lawson access to the DIA network and let them try to find if Lavlery was another person. That's why I came into the office when I did when Gunny took my shoulder off. By the way, what's Sam Ginty got to do with this?"

"You know Sam Ginty?"

At that moment, Henderson realized that none of the team knew what Sam Ginty looked like and since he didn't either, he had the sense that not knowing could come back to bite them. "I know of him but I don't know what he looks like. He was thrown out of DIA because he seriously violated protocol and was one step away from facing criminal charges if it hadn't been for his commanding officer." Henderson stopped talking at that moment which caused Norman some concern.

"Are you ok, Captain?" she solicited as she looked to see if he was having some type of attack.

"Uh, yes," was his answer. "There is another player in this group I know of. General Blayloc is most likely a prime suspect. I don't know why I didn't realize that before. You see, General Blayloc was Ginty's commanding officer and was responsible for Ginty not being charged."

"So Blayloc is spelled 'Blaylock'?" Norman asked.

"No," Henderson reacted. "It's 'Blayloc'."

Norman entered the name on a government directory page on her computer. "Ok, I think I found him. Since he's the only one listed, it shows him as the Director of the Defense Intelligence Agency East Asia Desk."

Henderson gave it a thought for a moment then said, "That fits. It's a perfect position for the shadow group to pressure East Asian countries into hidden cabals. It's a great place to play intrigue."

"Let's get back to 'Prism'. You seemed to indicate that he might be a top player," Norman posed.

"You're right," Henderson acknowledged. "I'm giving it some thought. See if this works. I know that Prism was a key player, someone giving direction. There are three people now that fit that role. There's General Blayloc, the mysterious legislator and Colonel Qiang Zhu. Now, by a process of elimination, we know that General Blayloc would be too focused on East Asian activities to be involved. Besides, with his support staff, his actions wouldn't be hidden for very long. Then there's the mysterious legislator. He appears to have made a serious effort to remain anonymous which means he's not going to communicate by email but rather by personal courier, so no pseudonym needed. That leaves the Chinese Colonel. He would carry much of the directing responsibilities if he is a part of this group. His role of trying to turn citizens of other countries to the Chinese agenda makes him a perfect person to operate without accountability. We all picked our own pseudonyms so it seems more likely that Colonel Qiang Zhu would pick 'Prism' for his pseudonym than any of the rest of us doing so."

"How do you come to that conclusion about Colonel Zhu?" Norman quizzed.

"It's simple," Henderson explained. "In 2013, Edward Snowden, the NSA spy, was working on a U.S. project called 'PRISM' and claimed that one of the objectives of the project was to spy on Chinese citizens. I figured that it seemed a good match that Colonel Zhu would pick the name 'Prism' as he figured that we would figure that no Chinese agent would be stupid enough to pick that name." Norman laughed at Henderson's explanation then suddenly realized that he may be on to something.

"Ok," Norman stated, "let's get you back into your security area while I discuss your comments with the team." Norman opened the door and waved to the two Marine escorts to take him back to his safe house.

"Thanks, Commander," Henderson gratefully acknowledged. "You have protected me and my family. It will not be forgotten. By the way, Excalibur seldom follows a routine, much like Josh Henry's practices. Maybe Josh knows who this guy is."

Norman thought about Henderson's observation about Excalibur, realizing that he may be right with his opinion.

Chapter 20

Deeper into the Abyss

"In their vanity men focus on what they wish to hear and miss the hidden meaning, the lurking threat." - David Hewson

Lawson and Myers proceeded to filter through the email names on the spreadsheet while Gunny left to see Josh Henry at the hospital. Lawson looked out the window at the late morning sun shining down on the lawns and trees. The areas in the shade had frost on them while the sun had melted the frost in the spaces that were exposed to the light. He mulled over the conversation they had with the mysterious man, wondering what else was hiding below the surface. His thoughts were interrupted by Myers' talking to himself.

"What are you saying," Lawson quizzed as he peered over Myers' right shoulder to see what was on the screen. "That's the code sheet you're looking at. Why? I thought we were finished with the pictures and were focused on the emails?"

"Something caught my attention," Myers immediately flashed back at Lawson. "Now before you go all ballistic on me, you should see what I'm delving into."

Lawson felt the pressure of getting the answers from the emails but something in Myers' voice said to stop and wait for the explanation. So he waited while Myers continued to talk to himself. Finally Myers looked up, "This is the New York picture of the firehouse shows the number twenty-one. I looked at line twenty-one on its code sheet and there are only letters, no numbers. Now, I was at a loss for a couple of minutes but, using your idea of always looking beyond the obvious, I looked at the twenty-one as an ASCII character, as well. The decimal value twenty-one correlates to an ASCII command of 'negative acknowledgement', meaning no message received. At first I thought that might be the message then I took it one step further and tried the hexadecimal value of twenty-one which is an 'exclamation mark'. Following a hunch, I went down the code sheet's first column and found an exclamation mark on the thirteenth line. Now, knowing what I just found, I changed my program to read hexadecimal values which means ASCII characters '0' through '9' are hexadecimal values thirty through thirty-nine. At that moment, Lawson, I realized that the code we broke in the London picture was what they intended us to break. It was too simple."

"So we wasted our time according to you. We had a real message and what about the program we found? That was real," Lawson said as he pulled up a chair.

Myers continued his thoughts, "They intended for us to break a code for information that was to be common knowledge anyway. The real intent on the London picture was to hide the program to launch the missiles. I think this picture of the New York fire station has the real message or messages combined with the messages of the Paris picture based upon what I'm about to show you. What led me to this assumption was that the center of the fire station picture seemed to have some blurriness that I thought was the center of the picture being slightly out of focus. The only problem with that observation was that the front of the fire station was pretty much the same distance from the camera as the corners and top of the building so why would the center be a little out of focus?"

"You've lost me," Lawson objected.

"I figured as much," Myers replied. "As I was looking at the hexadecimal codes for the New York picture, I suddenly realized that each pixel in the picture has a hexadecimal value as well. Normally, for this resolution there would be four million pixels making up the picture, that's how the picture is formed. It's made by ones and zeros that define the color value of that pixel in sets of eight ones and zeros that go all of the way from black to white through the whole color spectrum, which includes reds, blues and greens. Converting each of the red, blue and green color layers we have here gave me twelve million pixels, four million for each layer, which I thought was strange since I could make the whole picture with all its colors with only four million pixels if I just used the full color range for each pixel. Seeing that, I suddenly realized the reason for the blurriness. The values for the pixels in the area of blurriness were off from where they should be. With me so far?"

"I am, so let's just cut to the chase," Lawson irritatingly responded.

"Ok," Myers shot back while trying to keep his emotions from showing his anger toward Lawson's attitude. "I converted each layer's pixels to hexadecimal values then converted those values to hexadecimal ASCII characters once I determined where in the pixel layout the blurred area was and focused on it."

Lawson looked at the screen as Myers continued, "On the green layer I got, 'C   Z   TIN   NS   LIER   T TH VEN   18 AT RE   OU   A   SON   DR   TS' for the area in question."

At this point, Lawson began to see where Myers was going. "So you see parts of a message with each layer."

"That's right," Myers acknowledged. "On the red layer I got, ' APE   ND HU   G W   EN.   TO   EM T   ING F   STAU   TSIDE   FB.   TO H   ONE   ND C'. Now combining the green layer with the red layer gives us, 'CAPE AND ZHU   TING W   NSEN. LIER TO   THEM T   VENING F   8 AT RESTAU   OUTSIDE   L AFB. SON TO H   DRONE   TS AND C," Myers said while Lawson looked at the results of the present combination of letters.

"Then, on the blue layer I got, '   RS A   MEE   ITH GE COL   MEE   HAT E   EB   RANT   HILL HAN   AVE   STAT   ODES'. With me so far?" Lawson nodded yes.

"Finally," Myers explained, "combining the blue layer with the others gives us, 'CAPERS AND ZHU MEETING WITH GENSEN FIRST. COLLIER TO MEET THEM THAT EVENING FEB 18 AT RESTAURANT OUTSIDE HILL AFB. HANSON TO HAVE DRONE STATS AND CODES'."

So, there is a lot of value in this message. We see the names of some of the players and we see there is a meeting of a number of them on February 18th."

Lawson looked at Myers while feeling embarrassed about his earlier reaction. "I owe you an apology, Nick. I should know you well enough by now that if you've got something important to say, I should take the time to listen."

"I know your apology is real, Lawson," Myers said then smiled. "You only call me Nick when you've been a jerk.

Apology accepted." They both laughed as they wrote down the names from the message onto the whiteboard.

Chapter 21

Enemy Identified

"It is possible that a scientific discovery will be made that humans will later regret because it has awful consequences. The problem is, we probably would not know in advance and, once the discovery is made, it cannot be undiscovered." - Paul Davies

While Lawson and Myers were working in room 2337, Gunny had gone to the hospital to see Josh Henry. Josh was eating some oatmeal when Gunny came in.

"How are you doing my friend?" Gunny inquired as he sat down in a chair next to the bed.

"Can they make food any more tasteless than what they do with this oatmeal?" Henry responded while slamming the bowl down on the hospital tray. "You're going to make me work aren't you?"

Gunny smiled and rolled the tray away from the bed. "I have a name that you need to see. A man came into the room at the Rayburn building and talked to us. He wouldn't give us his name but he gave us this name as a possible lead to the people behind the North Korean nuke job." Gunny handed the piece of paper to Henry.

"Robert Molliner is CEO of Klyster Technologies," Henry observed. "This may make some sense. You see, Molliner is known to be the money man for several groups thought to have an interest in Chinese affairs. Let me think how he would fit in this picture." Henry looked out the window then continued, "You said the man got into your room and wouldn't give his name?"

"That's right," Gunny affirmed. "We still can't figure out how he got into the room and without his entry being shown on the security registry."

"Gunny," Henry started as he adjusted his position in the bed, "On your last mission, how did you get into that scientist's office in that facility in Iran?"

Gunny thought for a moment then replied, "I went over the wall by removing tiles from the false ceiling."

"And?" Henry questioned.

"Oh man," Gunny responded, "how dumb of me. That's how he got in." Henry smiled and put his hands behind his head. Gunny felt about three inches tall after missing the most obvious answer.

"Now, as to the name he gave you," Henry continued. "You guys are looking for the top person in whatever organization is working with some foreign entity, that entity most likely being Colonel Qiang Zhu. Am I correct?"

"That is correct," Gunny acknowledged.

"Well, let's do some history on Molliner," Henry recommended. "He started Klyster Technologies about fifteen years ago. Before that he was a senior legislative assistant for Congressman Gordon Capers. It was that relationship with Capers that gave Molliner the contacts needed to get involved in government contracting. If I were to consider a potential leader to this shadow group, it might be Capers."

"Ok," Gunny admitted, "I see where that has a high level of probability. However, there have got to be other people involved in this group. Does Capers or Molliner have any relationships that could point us to other players?"

Well, there is one other person that did technical advising for Capers while he was in office," Henry surmised. "That would be Ben Collier. He was Capers' advisor on all of the highly technical bills going across his desk. I don't know where Collier is now but he might be worth checking into."

"I know where he is," came a voice at the door to the hospital room. Gunny turned to see the man that had visited them earlier that morning.

"Ah, Excalibur or shall I say Zorro," Henry called out as he saw the familiar face at the door. "You seem to be where questions need to be answered. Now here, Gunny, is a man with an inexplicable sense of timing. I'd almost be convinced that he has bugs picking up all of our conversations. Also, how did you get past the Marines guarding my door?"

"Bugs, no. Knowing the human flow of thoughts, yes, Marines, no problem," Excalibur said while pulling up the other chair in the room. "I don't have much time but your questions about Collier can be answered before I leave. He's a data analyst at Fort Bevoir. Anything, any report, any communication would be accessible by him. He still stays in contact with former Congressman Capers and has a lot of communications with a guy at DARPA by the name of Doctor Cole Gensen. He's a DARPA development scientist that develops codes for the nuclear weapons release program for issuing launch orders. By the way, I ordered the Marines to step aside after I showed them my ID."

"What's DARPA?" Gunny inquired.

"It's the Defense Advanced Research Projects Agency, the primary developer of new technologies in the government," Excalibur said. "To put it into perspective, they were the vehicle by which development of the internet was funded and managed. That being said, I know your next question. What is the nuclear weapons release program?" Gunny nodded 'yes' which allowed for Excalibur to continue, "Well, the nuclear weapons release program is the program that determines the coding and coding methods for issuing launch orders to our nuclear commands. And, in light of the past few days' attempts to bypass the launch protocol, I would put him at the top of my list of potential candidates for this shadow group."

Gunny got out of the chair and walked to the window. Looking out over the parking lot, he saw people coming and going. He wondered how many of those people realized all of the intrigue going on in this city. After a few moments of thought, he turned to Excalibur.

"You realize that we may not have seen the end to this whole thing," Gunny said while fixing his stare on the door. "The moment any one of us walks out that door, we are right back in the thick of this activity and I have to ask, where does it end?"

"It doesn't," Excalibur replied. "Once we step out of the picture, someone else steps in. The game continues to accelerate as data becomes more accessible and quicker to get. At some point, the amount of data and its impact will go beyond our ability to manage it. When that happens, just about any trigger can set off a war. Right now, we're fighting for time. The problem is, what will be a working solution to this continual gathering of information. I fear that we will be crushed under the weight of our own curiosity."

Gunny sat back down as he felt the burden of the whole effort and the reality of how big this foreign enterprise might be.

"I must be going," Excalibur said. "Nobody knows where Colonel Zhu is presently. He was last seen boarding the Pacific Jade container ship out of Los Angeles. The problem is that no one knows where the Pacific Jade is now. You guys have fun." Excalibur exited the room as Gunny and Henry looked at each other.

"So what have we got?" Henry asked.

Gunny looked down at his notes and summarized the information. "We have Rod Lavlery, Robert Molliner of Klyster Technologies, Congressman Ben Capers, Ben Collier at Fort Bevoir, Doctor Cole Gensen at DARPA and Colonel Qiang Zhu. Except for Lavlery and Zhu, the rest are longshots at best. Maybe Lawson and Myers can shake out something from their email and text message analysis."

"You forgot Captain Henderson," Henry commented. "Admiral Roedl was in here and left about half an hour before you arrived. He says that Henderson is talking and may help shed some light on the participants in this shadow group. Some of my cohorts are calling them 'deep state'. I don't know if the term is accurate but it does relate better than shadow government because these people are actively entrenched in the government. I can help you in one area. I'll get the IP logs from the servers at the cyber café in Reston. That may help us as we have some of the dark web pseudonyms of the group."

"Be careful," Gunny warned. "They are not a friendly group and, if anyone finds you pulling that information off of the system, it will solidify their suspicions that our team is a dark web hunter-killer team."

"Point well taken, Gunny," Henry answered. "Let Lawson know that I'll feed him the information I pick up. It'll go by courier as I don't want to risk it being discovered on the internet. By the way, here are the master keys you asked for. You're sure that he drove a Volvo because those are the keys I requested."

"I'm sure. Take care my friend," Gunny said as he took the master keys from Henry and walked out of the hospital room.

Henry pulled himself up on the bed to get better support from the pillow. As he did so, he reached under the pillow and checked to make sure where his Maxim 9mm pistol was situated. Satisfied that everything was in order, he picked up his computer from the hospital tray and proceeded to log onto some hidden web sites.

Gunny walked out the door and headed for the airport. "A couple more pieces of information left to get before I report to the team," he muttered to himself as he walked to his car.

Chapter 22

Night of the Long Knives

"Once is happenstance, twice is coincidence, three times is enemy action"
- Ian Fleming

It was later afternoon on February 9th as Lawson and Myers were going through emails, filtering for those names they found in the New York picture when Gunny came into the room. "I got the GPS record off of Lavlery's car. He left it at the airport and it was easy to find as he had the vanity plates showing the name 'HOTROD' on them. Anyway, his car was not too difficult to get to the GPS. Once I did, I selected the send data option and sent it to Myers' email. You should have it."

Myers stopped what he was doing and opened his email. There was a file in GPX format attached to his email. He opened a GPS mapping application and used it to open the file. As he was doing so, Gunny saw the names on the whiteboard.

"Where did you get these names?" Gunny exclaimed as he saw several of the names matching those that were discussed at the hospital.

Myers looked up from the screen. "We found them hidden in the New York picture and it shows Capers, Zhu, Collier, Gensen and Hanson meeting this month on the 18th at Hill Air Force Base. We don't know anything about any of these people except Zhu so we are looking through emails and texts to see if their names show up. Anyway, here's the message from the New York picture," Myers said as he pointed to the screen.

Gunny looked at the screen to see the message, 'CAPERS AND ZHU MEETING WITH GENSEN FIRST. COLLIER TO MEET THEM THAT EVENING FEB 18 AT RESTAURANT OUTSIDE HILL AFB. HANSON TO HAVE DRONE STATS AND CODES.' Opening up his notebook he matched names in his notebook to the names in the message.

"I can give you some basic information on several of these people," Gunny offered as he sat down in a chair. Having both Lawson's and Myers' attention, he proceeded to explain what he had learned about the names from Henry and Excalibur.

Once Gunny finished the explanation, Lawson intervened, "From what you are saying, there appears to be a high level of confidence that Congressman Capers is the 'Big Kahuna'." Gunny nodded agreement. As he did so, he saw Myers on the computer looking at a spreadsheet and selecting filters for different columns.

"What's that you're doing?" Gunny asked as he looked at the screen.

Myers looked up from the screen. "We've got approximately one-hundred thirty thousand emails from the congressional exchange server and eighty thousand text messages. I've put the emails into one spreadsheet and the text messages into another spreadsheet. We've also been able to find some one-hundred sixty thousand emails from a mail exchange server in France that the French government provided. This exchange server is the one that is linked to a Boston server, then links to the server used by the cyber café in Reston, Virginia. I put those emails into a separate spreadsheet. Next, I've been filtering the emails to find names of people we suspect are part of this shadow group using both email spreadsheets. I should have some results on the filtering of Lavlery's emails in a few moments."

Gunny then turned to Lawson. "Where's Norman?"

"You know her," Lawson replied. "She tends to go her own way and suddenly pops up at some ungodly hour with an observation or demand."

"Well, I need to talk to her," Gunny said while he absent-mindedly pressed buttons on the active bug monitor. "I need to update her on Henry's take on things and see what she's found out." Lawson could tell that Gunny was bothered by something. He seemed detached from what was going on in the room.

"You got something you want to talk about," Lawson asked.

"Well, maybe," Gunny responded. "There's a lot of activity going on among us and yet we seem to be moving like we're going through cold molasses. I know we're making progress but it just seems like that, without Henry's or Excalibur's help, we'd still be taking our first steps toward finding out who is involved."

"I understand your feelings," Lawson answered while Myers turned to listen in on the conversation. "You're familiar with laying out a plan, charging into the lion's mouth and getting a victory. You're all Marine. This is a little different. This is more like rolling combat where the plan got changed the first couple of minutes the combat started and the result is having to react to ongoing threats from then on. We are moving according to what is found and some of this stuff includes digging through massive piles of data to find a couple of jewels. It takes time and we don't have the staff that Fort Bevoir has to do this work. So naturally, it's going to take longer. We can't give it to Fort Bevoir because, based upon your input, a potential adversary is there and has access to whatever we provide."

"I take it you're talking about Ben Collier at Fort Bevoir," Gunny observed.

"I am," was Lawson's answer.

As they stood looking at the display on the active bug monitor, Myers interrupted their thoughts.

"I have thirty-seven emails from the dark web that relate to Hotrod Lincoln," Myers stated. "That's Lavlery's pseudonym. I find one message that is interesting, actually it's a thread of the same email being responded to by different parties. The earliest email in the thread is dated February 6th at 19:23, Manila time in the early evening and is from someone named Robert NcNamara. It says, 'AT HOTEL IN MANILA. GINTY DIDN'T ARRIVE. LEAVING TO GO TO TAGUIG'."

"Ok, got it," Lawson said.

Myers continued, "The next email is from someone named PRISM answering the first email from McNamara we just saw. It was sent at 13:46, Honolulu time on February 5th. That means the second email was sent twenty-three minutes after the email we just read and this one states 'DO NOT WAIT, LAVLERY HAD OTHER PLANS'. Then this more recent email about three minutes later to McNamara that said, "CORRECTION, MESSAGE MEANT GINTY HAD OTHER PLANS'."

"Wait a minute," Gunny exclaimed. "How is it that an email sent on February 6th is answered by an email on February 5th?"

Myers looked at Lawson then smiled. Looking back at Gunny he said, "Uh, the Philippines is on the other side of the international date line. It's one day ahead of Honolulu."

"My bad," Gunny replied while everyone laughed.

"So from this mistake by Prism, we now know that Lavlery and Ginty are one and the same," Lawson noted.

"That might be a good assumption," Gunny intervened. "I can give you solid confirmation. I took Ginty's passport picture that Excalibur gave to us and showed it to Congressman Latershan and asked him to tell me who this was. He said it was Rod Lavlery. So based upon these two examples, I would say that Ginty and Lavlery are one and the same."

"So we can note that as confirmed," Lawson acknowledged. "However, I have one question. If Lavlery was on board the Pacific Jade and the Pacific Jade should have only been as far as Hawaii during those emails, then how was it that Lavlery was to arrive in Manila, Philippines at that time."

They all looked at each other in silence until Gunny came up with the most obvious conclusion. "Maybe he was never to reach the Philippines." Lawson and Myers looked at each other on how simple the answer was.

"Then what was this Robert McNamara doing waiting for Lavlery if the powers that be knew that he wasn't going to be there?" Lawson posed as they heard a beep and Commander Norman came through the door.

"It might be that they're cleaning house and tying up loose ends," Norman said as she slammed a file folder down on the computer desk.

Myers picked up the folder and opened it. He flipped through the pages, each one with an information sheet on an individual and a picture of the person. On each of the information sheets was the name, address, department or business and a running description on captured conversations and interactions. There was also a block on the sheets for the person's pseudonym. Most of the sheets had that block blank but four of the sheets did not. The sheet for Colonel Qiang Zhu had the pseudonym 'PRISM', for Rod Lavlery it was 'HOTROD LINCOLN', for Captain Mark Henderson it was 'CAPTAIN CRUNCH" and for someone by the name of Jack Resnick, it was 'ROBERT MCNAMARA'. Across Jack Resnick's information sheet was 'DECEASED' stamped in red letters. Myers held the folder with the sheet out for Norman to see.

"Resnick was found dead a block from the Regency Hotel in Manila on February 6th, Manila time," Norman explained. "It appears that we're getting close to the core group responsible for the launch code fiasco and they may have some other efforts in play to bring down our government. It appears that people familiar with this shadow organization are being knocked off as they are no longer needed."

"So far, this has been like a giant chess game," Lawson stated. "First, Lavlery is working with the North Koreans to give them the best time to launch an ICBM without it getting shot down. At the same time, he appears to be working with China or a Chinese splinter group to take out North Korea and blame it on the U.S. Next, it appears that they are going to meet on February 18th with this Colonel Zhu for who knows what but it appears that drones are involved."

"What February 18th meeting," Norman inquired.

Myers pulled up the message he found in the New York fire station picture. After giving Norman a brief description on how he found the message and what the contents were, Norman wrote down the names and date and got on her cellphone. "Yes Sir, yes Sir," She said as she talked on the phone.

Ending the call, she walked toward the door. "I have to see Admiral Roedl right away. You guys keep working on the emails. Anything else you find, you call me right away. I've got to go." The guys watched the door close as they turned back to the computer. Moments later, Lawson saw that the folder she brought in was still on the desk. Lawson immediately called Norman. She told him to keep the folder and enter information into the information sheets as they find new details on each of the players.

Lawson opened the folder then stopped. "That's unusual," he said while looking toward the door. "When she's talking to me on the phone, she normally says something once she's finished giving instructions, like 'talk to you later' or 'see you in a while'. Something's not right."

"Maybe she was just in a hurry," Myers opined.

"Gunny, with me," Lawson shouted as he ran out the door with Gunny following behind him.

Norman had walked out of the building to the parking lot. As she was talking to Lawson on her cellphone, a van pulled up from behind then a man jumped out and grabbed her while shocking her with a electronic stun device against her neck. The shock caused her face to hit the 'end call' button as she fell to the ground, cutting off Lawson's call. The man was joined by another man that dragged her into the van. Once she was in the van, one of the men went back to the passenger seat in the front of the van while the other man stayed in the back of the van, tying her hands and feet with plastic restraints.

The van driver stepped on the gas, moving forward when another man stepped out from between two cars about twenty-five yards in front of the van. As the driver looked up, he could see the man holding a pistol with a silencer pointed at the driver. The driver panicked and aimed the vehicle for the man standing in his path. The first shot hit the driver in the face followed by a second shot that hit the passenger. In one smooth motion, the man in the path lunged to the side of the vehicle as it was passing him, opened the driver's door and pulled the driver out. Jumping into the van, he swung his weapon to the back of the van and fired once more. The man putting the restraints on Norman looked up just in time to see the gun pointed at him. It was his last moment of realization.

The man hit the brakes on the vehicle, stopping the van inches from the rear of a parked car. Putting the van into park and setting the emergency brake, he got out of the van and opened the side door where Norman was lying. Pulling the knife from its sheath on his leg, he cut the restraints off of her. "Roedl's rule of keeping a knife on the leg finally paid off," he thought while helping Norman up to a sitting position. Still groggy from the shock, Norman shook her head a couple of times then attempted to stand with the man helping her up. They could see Lawson and Gunny about one-hundred yards away, running toward them. As Lawson saw what was going on, he immediately called security to cover Room 2337 as he continued running toward Norman and the man.

"Red, what are you doing here?" she asked the man while he put the knife back in the sheath.

He held her face in his hands while looking into her eyes. "Well, no concussion from what I see in your eyes," He remarked. "I got a message about a half hour ago from Josh Henry that he was getting an eerie feeling something was about to go down. When I pulled in and parked, I saw a van sitting with its engine running and two guys sitting as though they were waiting for something. I somehow knew their presence had something to do with you guys." As he was talking, Lawson and Gunny arrived where Red and Norman were talking.

"It's you again," Gunny said while looking over the carnage Red had created. "Why is it every time something major is going down, Excalibur is there?"

"Excalibur?" Norman queried. "Red, you're Excalibur?"

"Looks like the cat's out of the bag," Red responded while frowning at Gunny. "Yes, I'm Excalibur." Lawson was looking at the man lying on the pavement and the man in the back of the van when Lawson's phone rang.

"We need to get back inside, something just happened," Lawson ordered while Red got on the phone to notify the police of the incident in the parking lot.

"I'll be up with you all in a moment as soon as I get the police up to date," Red declared as he began his discussion with the Capitol Police.

Earlier, when Gunny and Lawson headed down to the parking lot, Myers was busy going through emails when he heard someone rattle the doorknob. Myers pulled his weapon from its holster and grabbed the emergency button off of the desk. As he did so, he heard the familiar beep of someone using a pass card to open the door. Stepping into a position that placed him behind the door once it opened, he pressed the emergency button and watched as the door slowly opened with two men armed with M4 automatic rifles coming through the doorway.

"Where's everyone?" said the first man to enter as he moved toward the computer. "Never mind, we've got their computer."

With the door almost closed, Myers stepped behind the second man and put his pistol to the man's neck. "You move, you die," Myers stated in a whisper. Myers realized that he was standing right behind the man's rifle butt and, realizing the risk, stepped to his left. As he did so the man thrust the rifle butt backwards, hitting only open air. Myers immediately fired at the back of the man's head then swung his weapon and shot as the other man swung around with his weapon, causing the other man to lurch back and fall to the floor. Turning around in quick motion, Myers kicked the door as hard as he could which caused a man on the other side of the door to fly across the hallway and hit the opposite wall. The door swung back open from the impact which caused Myers to fire two shots at the man and seek cover against the wall next to the door. All of this activity took approximately six seconds.

As Myers was ready to meet the next threat, a furious exchange of subdued gunfire from many weapons with silencers could be heard as a raging gun battle ensued in the hallway. After a moment it went quiet followed by a voice saying, "Don't shoot, we're friendlies!" Myers held his weapon pointed toward the door until he saw a friendly face.

"Hi Scott, good to see you," Myers whispered as he collapsed into a chair. The Marine Gunnery Sergeant smiled at Myers then called Lawson and told him that the situation was under control.

Lawson, Gunny and Norman were running toward the main entrance to the Rayburn Building to help Myers after Norman's near kidnapping when the Marine's call was received by Lawson.

At the same time these events were going on at the Rayburn Building, Josh Henry laid in his hospital bed while looking at the data on his computer. His call to Excalibur about the threats was appropriate he thought as he continued to read messages going back and forth on the dark web. Something was going down, but what.

"It's time for you to get another IV," the nurse said while carrying in a saline IV bag and tubing. "The doctor said that you're low on fluids."

"Great," Henry replied. "I already have to use the restroom every two hours as it is." With that comment, he started thinking. "Wait, get the head nurse in here. The doctor told me I was good at 6:00 PM," Henry demanded as he looked at the clock, 8:35 PM. Why would they be giving him an IV at such an odd hour?

"Ok, I'll get the head nurse," the nurse affirmed as she walked toward the door. As she turned back toward him with a .40 caliber pistol in her hand, she saw the Maxim 9 pistol in Henry's hand pointed at her. It was no match. Henry had hit her with two rounds before she was able to get the gun pointed toward him. Moments later, two other nurses came running and the Marines assigned to protect him suddenly appeared. Henry recognized them so he pushed the Maxim 9 back under his pillow.

"What happened here?" one of the nurses exclaimed as they both looked at the body on the floor and the gun laying near the doorway.

"I guess she didn't know the meaning of 'making her rounds' meant," Henry said while smiling at them then let out a laugh. They both just stared back at him as he proceeded to look back at his computer. "Don't you think you should call the police," he continued. "And don't touch anything as this is now a crime scene." The nurses left to make the call while the Marines bagged the weapon the woman had in her hand.

Henry saw a message on the dark web about activity at the Rayburn Building and several people down. He realized that the shadow group was going after everyone associated with the team. Picking up his phone, he sent a text to Admiral Roedl, "The gates have opened. They have a penchant for creating trouble."

Admiral Roedl was sitting in the back of the limousine traveling to the Kennedy Irregular Warfare Center when Josh Henry's text reached him. A sense of panic hit Roedl as he read the message. The word 'penchant' was used. Something was up and Roedl knew it was major effort for Henry to use the 'help' flag. Knowing Henry and his ability to be careful, Roedl knew it was a warning for him rather than Henry asking for help. Roedl looked around at the area he was occupying. Two observations caught his attention – the privacy panel between the passenger compartment and the driver was up and the doors were locked. He was trapped.

Roedl knew that the driver could still see into the passenger compartment because of the camera. He opened his briefcase, took out a piece of gum, chewed it and placed it over the lens of the camera. Then, taking his knife from his leg sheath, he proceeded to work on the passenger door panel.

Norman, Lawson and Gunny were about to go into the main lobby of the Rayburn Building when Norman saw an alert on her phone from Admiral Roedl's emergency alert transmitter showing a map of Roedl's position on Suitland Parkway just outside of the Washington, DC area. His position was stationary.

"Admiral Roedl's in trouble!" Norman shouted as she turned to run toward her car with Lawson and Gunny following closely behind her. Running past Excalibur, she shouted, "Wait for the police to deal with this mess, the Admiral's in trouble!"

"Unlock the car!" Gunny shouted as he stood by the passenger side of the car. Still a little groggy from the shock to her neck, Norman fumbled with the keys and pressed the unlock button. Once the car was unlocked, they all jumped in and headed to the location of Roedl's alert.

They arrived to find several police cars, a fire truck and an ambulance with lights flashing on the road parked around a stretch limo. There was a covered body next to the limo on the ground. Lawson got out and rushed toward the body while Norman parked the car. Lawson came up to the body as a police officer stepped in to stop him. At that moment, Lawson pulled out his ID and pushed the officer aside. The officer grabbed Lawson just in time to have Gunny grab the officer and push him to the ground. Two other officers intervened and, after a short scuffle, Commander Norman stepped in.

"Stop it guys," she shouted as she stepped between one of the policemen and Lawson. "Back off," she exclaimed while facing the closest police officer. "We are operating on official government orders and interfering with these men will only make your lives a living hell!"

The police officers moved to the side as Lawson went to the body. Pulling up the cover, he looked back at the others. "This isn't the Admiral," he observed as he turned to look around at the layout of the rescue vehicles.

"You guys sure took your time," a familiar voice was heard from the back of the ambulance that was sitting next to a firetruck about twenty yards away. Lawson saw Roedl sitting on the back of the ambulance while a paramedic was attending to a cut to the Admiral's head.

"What happened, Sir?" Norman inquired.

"He was kidnapping me," Roedl answered as he winced from the antiseptic the paramedic was putting on his wound. Gunny walked over as he heard the Admiral speak.

"Looks like whoever it is on the ground lost this match with you," Gunny observed, "though he got his licks on you."

"No, he didn't get his licks on me," Roedl snapped back. "I got this cut when I pulled the door panel back to get to the door lock and the knife sprang back and hit me in the face." Everyone, including the policemen within hearing distance, started laughing at Roedl's explanation.

"So what happened to him?" Gunny asked.

Roedl looked at all of them for a moment then explained. "He must have seen the 'door open' indicator on the dash when I finally got the door open. He stopped the car and walked around the front of the vehicle to stop me from leaving. I guess he was startled by the blood on my face and my staggering out of the car which caused him to lower his weapon. I got two shots into him before he could react. He dropped his weapon while crawling to the other side of the vehicle where he died. End of story."

"Admiral," Lawson interjected, "we have all had attempts on our lives tonight. They went after Norman, Myers, you and, from what I just heard coming over here, Josh Henry took out a fake nurse trying to give him a poisoned IV. The 'perps' had probably expected me and Gunny to be in the room with Myers when they went in, which is why we were missed."

Turning to the senior police officer at their crime scene, Roedl queried him as to any other events of significance that evening.

"Let's see, Admiral," the policeman said as he looked at his reporting screen. "There's a shooting incident at the Rayburn Building parking lot, an intelligence incident inside the Rayburn Building that we're not involved with, a shooting at the Washington, DC VA Medical Center, two shootings in the Columbia area, a reported riot that ended up being a celebration at Georgetown University and this incident. All in all, a relatively quiet night."

"Thanks officer," Roedl acknowledged. Turning his attention to Norman, Roedl questioned the progress of the operation.

"We have at least six verified names and four high-confidence ones," she reported. "Myers may have made more progress on the research if he hasn't been weighed down by the NCIS investigation into the shootout at Room 2337. The six verified are Capers, Henderson, Lavlery, Zhu, Collier and someone named Hanson from a message Myers decoded. The four we're not completely sure of are Molliner, Gensen, Blayloc and Mirkel."

"Is that Admiral Mirkel?" Roedl asked.

"Yes, Sir, it is," Norman acknowledged.

"Mirkel," Lawson repeated. "Isn't he the three-star admiral that challenged me during the presentation to the Joint Chiefs?" Roedl nodded 'yes' as he pushed the paramedic's hand away from his face.

"That's enough," he said to the paramedic as he continued his directions to Norman. "Notify the FBI to pick all of them up. I want all of them here by 14:00 hours tomorrow at my office under escort." Norman pulled out her phone to make the call as she nodded her understanding of the order just given.

"Let's get out of here," Roedl ordered.

"You can't leave, Admiral," the police officer in charge commanded.

"NCIS is already here and they will take over the investigation," Roedl answered back. "The senior NCIS agent is over there and don't make any comments like 'where is Gibbs'. They don't see the humor in that. Some issues of grave national security dictates we must leave. The FBI will be here shortly to take over from NCIS."

"Ok, Admiral, but we need an interview report from you on the sequence of events that happened here this evening," the police officer stated as he turned toward the NCIS van. Roedl just waved as they all headed for Norman's car.

Chapter 23

Setting the Stage – Day 10

"My answers are typically 'guesses' cleverly disguised as answers."
- Craig D. Lounsbrough

It was 7:25 AM on February 10th as Myers began to look at the emails using the dates and times from Lavlery's GPS data from his car. Myers filtered the data in the spreadsheet for time, date and the location being Reston, Virginia, location of the cyber café. Checking through each entry taken from the spreadsheet, he listed them in a document with his notes on each entry. Seventeen entries helped him to identify several players in the shadow group that the team came to identify as the 'Mahjong Brigade', named after a popular tile game developed during the Qing Dynasty.

He was going through his second pass of the data when the door beeped and Lawson came walking in. Having the experiences of the previous evening fresh in his mind, Myers pulled his weapon from his holster and picked up the emergency alert button at the sound of the beep. Once he saw that it was Lawson, he holstered his weapon and set the button down on the desk.

"Good morning, Nick," Lawson said as he handed Myers a cup of coffee and a bag of bagels. Myers pushed the trash to the side from previous meals and sat the bag down. Grabbing a bagel from the bag, he took a bite and proceeded to chew as he pointed to the screen.

After swallowing the mouthful of bagel, he turned to Lawson to give his progress of the filtering effort. "I've used Lavlery's GPS data to help identify the people Lavlery communicated with while he was at the cyber café," Myers explained before taking a drink of coffee. "I've identified five people from their emails and locations based upon the IP address." Lawson looked at the screen, looking for a pattern to Myers' notes.

"This IP address is identified as Hill Air Force Base," Lawson observed while looking at five different messages. "Who is being contacted?"

"It's a person with the Pseudonym of 'Hillbilly'," Myers replied. "I think I've discovered who that person is. Look here at the fourteenth message down. It uses the name 'Hanson' and it appears that this message was sent by someone angry at the results of some event happening. Notice the message, 'Hanson, you were given five days to get this done and, as always, you're continually late. This will not be tolerated or we can find someone else'. The person writing the message is Lavlery and he failed to realize that, in his anger, he used the real name instead of the pseudonym. The name 'Hanson' also matches the name in the message in the New York picture."

"So you think you know who Hanson is?" Lawson inquired while grabbing a bagel from the bag.

Myers pulled up a directory screen of Hill Air Force Base personnel and located Hanson on the list. "There are three Hansons. Only one fits the need of this type of shadow organization which is this one here," Myers remarked as he pointed to the name 'Major Harvey Hanson'. "He's the only one that's an officer and his role happens to be Logistics Controller at Hill, the type of person that can get materials for research work being done at the base. The others are junior-level enlisted personnel."

Lawson walked around the room while considering the observations Myers made when the door beeped. They both pulled their weapons as the door opened. It was Norman. As she stepped in, she set her briefcase down and looked around the room.

"This place is a pigpen and you guys are pigs," she exclaimed as she began to pick up trash and place it in the trashcan.

"We're men," Myers barked back.

"That's what I said," was Norman's retort.

With that comment, Lawson started laughing until he saw the look in Norman's eyes. She was not happy. He remembered a quote from an author named Jordan Sarah Weatherhead that seemed to fit the occasion, 'When she's mad, even the demons run for cover' and there was no question about her present condition. Lawson just pulled up a chair and sat down next to Myers. As they both looked at each other, they hoped she couldn't see their expressions of retreat, similar to a two-year old being caught writing on the wall with a permanent marker. Myers continued to look at the spreadsheet while looking back once in a while to where Norman was at that time. Lawson just sat and pretended to be focused on the screen though his first inclination was to bolt out the door.

Norman finished and sat down in the chair. "Where are you guys?"

"Scared," was Myers answer. They all laughed as Myers took another drink of coffee.

"Sorry I jumped down your throats," Norman apologized. "I've spent the last three hours getting FBI agents out of bed to grab the people we already know are part of the conspiracy but you have to admit that you've let this place go to the dogs."

"True," Lawson admitted. "Myers has some new information." Norman turned her attention to Myers as he began his explanation.

"We're pretty sure we know who the person called Hanson is. From the emails, I was able to confirm that Molliner transferred thirty-million dollars to Gordon Capers eleven days before the pictures were transmitted. Lawson has something else concerning Lavlery."

"Well," Lawson started as he clicked on one of the messages on the screen. "You remember this email thread where it appears that Colonel Zhu is telling this guy in Manila that Lavlery won't be showing up. His statement is 'Lavlery had other plans'. Zhu worked in diplomatic circles for years, primarily with Americans. Now, with his knowledge of the nuances of the English language, why would he have said 'Lavlery had other plans'. He used 'had' instead of 'has' which tells me that Lavlery, Ginty or whatever you want to call him is probably dead as Zhu referred to him in the past tense." Norman agreed with Lawson's logic.

Once Myers went through each of the suspected names and they were able to verify the players, Norman called Admiral Roedl with the information. After getting instructions from Roedl, she made several calls to different FBI offices and gave them additional instructions. Myers continued to pull up more incriminating information as he built the list of names of those involved in the conspiracy. Lawson followed the stream of information until he had enough to render an opinion.

"It appears to me that this was a conspiracy to weaken, if not overthrow, the U.S. government. First, launch an attack on North Korea that would destroy its major cities and put the blame squarely on the shoulders of the U.S. Second, bring the UN into the picture by having sanctions put on the US by the other major powers. Third, set up a series of drone attacks in the U.S. to destabilize the major cities. One thing that I find interesting and based upon a couple of these emails, why did Colonel Zhu risk bringing a ship loaded with Chinese antitank munitions into a U.S. port. The only answer to that is that he offloaded a portion of his munitions stash to a group in the U.S. to oppose any military movement the government might use to respond to the destabilization of the country thereby throwing us into the makings of a civil war. Net result, this leaves the U.S. open to foreign invasion under the auspices of the United Nations."

"That is quite a jump of assumptions, Lawson," Norman replied. "However, what I see here on the screen provides some merit to your argument."

While Norman was looking at the screen a beep was heard at the door. Admiral Roedl walked in with Gunny and Henderson in tow. When they all stepped into the room and Roedl was closing the door, another person came through the door. It was Red. Moving to one of the chairs, he sat down and smiled at Norman. Roedl just motioned for everyone to sit down while Red lit up a cigarette. Roedl frowned at Red's activity but said nothing.

"I want to introduce you all to Red Draper," Roedl offered as they turned their attention to Red. "You all probably know his younger brother Colonel Ed Draper of the 25th Ranger Regiment from your experiences in Iran. Red and I have known each other for over ten years and he has helped me in numerous ways. I assigned him to fly cover for you guys because I knew we were dealing with more than one threat. Norman, when I questioned Henderson on Excalibur, meaning Draper, I already knew all about Red. I just wanted to see what Henderson knew. I wanted to make sure Red's identify had not been compromised and, Norman, I knew that you would know Red but not as Excalibur. Any questions?"

"What is your real first name?" Lawson queried. Everyone laughed while Admiral Roedl stared at Lawson with a disapproving glare.

"That's ok," Draper responded. "You must remember that he has to have answers to things that look out of place to him. Let's give him some comfort in answering the question." Roedl nodded his approval.

"It's short for Reddick," Draper announced. "My parents were fans of old English names."

"Now, if there are no other questions, can we begin to update what we've got?" said Roedl.

Norman and Lawson looked at each other then turned to Myers. Myers pointed to himself with the unspoken question of 'What, me?'. They both nodded 'yes'.

"Hum," Myers started, "let me see. We've confirmed that former Congressman Ben Capers is leading this whole group.

However, he is being directed by someone else which we suspect to be Colonel Qiang Zhu. That being said, it appears that the Chinese government is as surprised as we are about Colonel Zhu's activities. They are searching for him as well as he took off with a massive amount of antitank weapons and has disappeared. Rod Lavlery is obviously another confirm and Lawson feels strongly that Lavlery is dead based upon the language used in an email from Zhu to his agent, Resnick, in Manila who was later killed. Robert Molliner of Klyster Technologies has been confirmed to be the money man. He was picked up by the FBI early this morning and is in transit to Washington, DC. Ben Collier was picked up at Fort Bevoir and Doctor Cole Gensen at Hill Air Force Base. According to Norman, Gensen was caught with Major Harvey Hanson at Hill Air Force Base along with some rather revealing documents. That confirms what Lawson and I determined this morning. General Mark Blayloc of the DIA's East Asian desk and Admiral Mirkel, the guy that challenged Lawson in the joint staff meeting, are both in custody. As we all know, Captain Henderson was already in our custody and has been helping us. There may be others but we're not sure at this point.

"Can we have everyone in custody in my office by 16:00 hours tomorrow?" Roedl asked.

"Everyone but General Blayloc," Norman replied. "His plane lands at 18:20 hours tomorrow evening from Japan. There's also Colonel Zhu and Rod Lavlery that aren't in custody."

"Ok, then we'll set the meeting time for 20:00 hours tomorrow, that's 8:00 PM for you Lawson," Roedl stated while everyone laughed. With that order, Norman got on the phone and proceeded to give FBI agents in different offices the instructions and timing for the U.S. Marshals to bring their detainees into the Kennedy Irregular Warfare Center.

Chapter 24

The Trap – Day 11

"Good character going bad is like a beast escaping its cage; it will be hard to capture it again!"
- Israelmore Ayivor, The Great Hand Book of Quotes

The CAT205 team was present in Admiral Roedl's office as Gunny Glendenning stepped out of the conference room as Roedl entered his office. Gunny looked at the clock as he went through a last minute checklist in his mind of the preparations for the meeting to be held at 8:00 PM. It was now 7:45 PM on February 11th. Seeing Gunny come out of the conference room, Admiral Roedl could see Myers sitting in the conference room and wondered what Gunny and Myers were doing.

"Just checking security," Gunny said in anticipation to Roedl's obvious question.

Roedl looked around to see four armed Marines standing in his office, ready for the evening's activities. Norman and Lawson were sitting on chairs in front of his desk while Red Draper leaned against the wall close to the door. He nodded at Gunny as Gunny nodded back. Moments later, three white-dressed servers rolled in serving carts with coffee, donuts and fruit. One of the Marines motioned for them to wait in the corner of Roedl's office as the Admiral sat down at his desk.

"I want all of my people sitting in the conference room closest to the door to my office. There are to be no Marine guards in the conference room as I've ordered that no weapons are to be in the room unless I call you," Roedl instructed the senior Marine. He acknowledged the order.

Norman walked over to where Red Draper was standing. "It's funny that you would come back into my life at this particular time," she noted as she positioned herself next to him.

"When I heard you had been assigned to this operation, I knew you were thrust into a threatening situation. I couldn't leave you hanging out there," Red responded. "You know I've always had a place in my heart for you."

"I know, Red," Norman whispered. "When you proposed marriage, I wasn't ready to settle down. Then after I left DIA, I lost contact with you."

Red adjusted his position as he watched the people in the room. "Beth, I moved on to other agencies and other responsibilities. I saw your name pop up a couple of times in messages I was evaluating but I figured that you would have found someone to share your life with by this time."

Norman looked at the Admiral talking on the phone and Lawson sitting in the chair in front of the Admiral's desk.

"A lot of things have changed since we dated at DIA," Norman reminisced. "I always thought of you as a dear friend and, if conditions were right, I might have considered your proposal later. I'm not talking as though this was some business transaction but rather my affections of the heart. You're a good man and a rare person, Red. I love you for your compassion and dedication to keeping the innocent safe."

"Look, Beth," Red interrupted, "I have deep feelings for you but I know we're not a good match. I see how you and Lawson get along. He's a good man and you two seem to click better on all levels, not just professionally. Don't throw away something hoping for something better. You may never find one like him again."

"I know," Norman affirmed. "He has one flaw that concerns me. He is rather cavalier about taking lives when there may be other options. He doesn't do it in anger, just the cold, calculated response he has is what concerns me."

"I think you doth judge him to harshly," Red replied. "His ability to not hesitate but to make a quick decision is what has kept him alive. It's not coldness he's showing, it's survival."

"It sounds like you want me to spend my life with him," Norman observed. "That's not like you. You get what you go after and it sounds like you're still in love with me, so why the change of heart?"

Red fumbled with the change in his pocket while he thought out his answer. "Your happiness and future is more important to me than my possessing you and sharing my life with you. I've had serious changes in my life since we were together. Changes that taught me that there is an eternity out there and my responsibilities here have a direct relationship to giving people a chance to realize that as well."

"You're beginning to sound like Myers," Norman teased.

"Myers is a good man and, in some ways, way advanced beyond where I am in life. He has a calmness is the mist of turmoil that tells me what he believes is real. It's hard to ignore," came Red's retort.

Norman was surprised by Red's analysis but recognized he was correct in his observation. "There is something definitely deeper about Myers that seems real. There's nothing fake about him." They both stood looking around the room as she slipped her hand into his and squeezed it. They both looked at each other and smiled, recognizing the depth of their friendship.

Moments later, U.S. Marshals came into Roedl's office while escorting the detainees one by one into the conference room. Once they sat their charges down into assigned seats, they exited the conference room by another door near the front of the room where the cabinets and large digital video display where installed. Each person was brought in and placed in their seats as Gunny and Myers watched the detainees.

Capers, Collier and Gensen were brought in first, being placed at the end of the table closest to the cabinets. Mirkel, Blayloc, Hansen and Molliner came in next and were directed to the right side of the conference table closest to the cabinets. Henderson came in last without escort and sat on the right center part of the table.

There was some conversation in Admiral Roedl's office followed by the door opening and the next group came in. Lawson was startled by the officers that entered. He expected to see Admiral Roedl but was surprised to see the Chairman of the Joint Chiefs of Staff and the Chief of Naval Operations (CNO) take seats to the left side of the table. There was an uncomfortable tension in the air as Lawson observed the facial expressions of both parties. Red Draper walked in and sat down next to Commander Norman to the right of her. As soon as he entered, former Congressman Capers protested but immediately stopped when he saw the expression on the CNO's face. It was then that Lawson realized that Capers knew that Draper was Excalibur.

Roedl began the meeting to the proceedings as an unknown two-star Admiral came in. "I would like to introduce you all to Admiral Johns. He has first-hand knowledge of the conspiracy we are about to address today."

"Just what conspiracy are you talking about?" Capers questioned.

"Let's start with the charges," Roedl began. "First, attempts to bypass nuclear protocols to launch an attack on North Korea. Second, planning a drone attack in major cities to incite chaos in those cities and third, illegally negotiating with UN delegates to create an excuse for several countries to intervene in the U.S. under UN auspices. Then there are the charges of attacks on military personnel investigating the conspiracy and, finally, the charge of treason. Have I missed anything, Commander Norman?"

"I don't have anything," Norman replied. "Lieutenant Lawson may have something."

All eyes turned to Lawson as he looked at his notes. "There is also money laundering, payoffs to foreign agents, in particular, Colonel Qiang Zhu and the threats on Captain Henderson and his family. I might also include the unauthorized hiring of mercenaries using U.S. federal monies to use against other U.S. federal officers and the illegal issuance of government IDs to persons not cleared for such activities. I would also like to add the discrepancies in Congressman Latershan's office that allowed Sam Ginty to come into Latershan's office under the name of Rod Lavlery." At that comment, an uproar ensued around the table. Roedl slammed his hand down causing everyone to quiet down.

"Those charges match with the experience and attempts to recruit me," Admiral Johns affirmed after everyone stopped talking.

"What do you mean Rod Lavlery is actually Sam Ginty?" The Chairman of the Joint Chiefs asked.

"We have undeniable evidence that Ginty and Lavlery are one and the same," Roedl responded. "Congressman Latershan confirmed it for us."

"You realize that Sam Ginty was thrown out of the Defense Intelligence Agency for attempting to hack into and launch a Chinese missile?" the Chairman noted. "He could have been charged for espionage and given twenty years instead we discharged him and put a 'no-government association allowed' flag on his personnel file. So how is it that he ends up working for a congressman that's on the House Intelligence Committee?"

"He was recommended by Congressman Capers," Lawson responded.

The Chairman became even more agitated. "Even if he was recommended by Capers, he would still have to go through fingerprinting and background checks. So how did he pass all that without being found out?"

According to the email chains we've researched, it appears that Ben Collier used his position at Fort Bevoir to stamp approvals for Lavlery, thereby bypassing the needed security checks," Myers interjected.

"This is almost as bad as the Walker espionage situation," the CNO observed, referring to the 1980's John Walker family spy ring that sold damaging information on the U.S Navy to the Soviet Union while John Walker was able to delay his security checks.

"It may be worse," Henderson added. "The Chinese got a lot of information through Colonel Zhu by way of Lavlery on our technology and methods. Even though Zhu went rogue, he was still providing information to the Chinese as a façade to keep them from suspecting his true intentions. It is…"

"That part I know," the CNO interrupted. "It's not the information that's got me worried, it's the level of depth you people have embedded yourselves into the …" The CNO stopped as the three servers rolled their carts into the conference room, rolling them to the right side of the room behind the chairs.

As they did so, Gunny noticed something black flash for a moment behind the white cloth that covered the lower portion of the cart. Tapping Lawson on the hand to get his attention, he moved his hand to his lap and pointed under the table. Lawson felt under the table and found a pistol taped to the underside of the table. Gunny tapped Lawson's leg once more and pointed to Norman. Lawson grabbed Norman's hand under the table and moved her hand to the pistol taped under her position. Both of them slowly pulled the pistols from the bottom of the table and removed the tape. Lawson checked for a round in the chamber then cocked his pistol while waiting to see what got Gunny's attention.

"Norman right, you center," Gunny whispered. "Only move when I do." Lawson moved the pistol to his lap as he saw Norman do the same thing.

Leaning over to Norman, he whispered, "You take the guy on the right when Gunny makes his move." Norman leaned back in her chair with the gun in her lap as she checked for a round then cocked her weapon and waited while watching Gunny out of the corner of her eye.

The three men laid coffee cups in front of each of the attendees and placed plates of donuts, bagels and fruit in the middle of the table while everyone remained silent. After laying out the refreshments, they positioned themselves next to their carts. In one synchronous act, they moved in unison, reaching behind the cloth draped over the lower half of the carts. Swinging up with automatic weapons from their hiding places, they were half up when Gunny jumped up. As he did so, Lawson and Norman jumped up, each firing their weapons at their respective targets. The assailants slammed against the walls and back cabinets of the room as the rounds hit their marks. Blood splattered the walls as they fell to the floor.

When the shooting started, everyone else dived under the table. They were all met by Myers pointing a pistol at them under the table with a smile on his face. They knew not to challenge him. Once the shooting stopped, Myers informed them, "Slowly get up into your chairs. There may be some blood in the area but don't let that concern you."

Seconds after the shooting started, the Marines out in Admiral Roedl's office came running in and placed themselves around the Chairman and the CNO. "The situation is secure.

They're all dead," Admiral Roedl stated as he quickly checked each of the deceased on the floor.

"You think you had this escape all figured out, didn't you Mr. Caper," Myers stated as he adjusted himself in the chair while Roedl took the weapon from Myers' hand. "Well, you didn't count on one thing. You had arranged to take us out, then take out the Marines and finally the U.S. Marshals in the adjoining room to enable your escape. The problem with your plan was, according to Josh Henry based upon a message he captured on the dark web this evening, that the assassins had orders to take everyone out. That included all of you as well. No honor among traitors, huh."

Capers looked at Myers then at Gunny. Gunny nodded affirmative to Myers comment. Capers knew he had run out of options.

Roedl got up and opened the side door and motioned the U.S. Marshals to come in. Lawson wondered why they didn't come into the room at the sound of gunshots. Giving it some thought, he figured that the reason Red was late getting into the room was that he had used that time to instruct the Marshals to not respond if something happened.

"Mr. Capers, Hanson, Collier, Mirkel, Blayloc and Gensen. You six are being sent to 'Gitmo', better known to us as the Guantanamo Detention Center," the Chairman instructed as he began the judgment. "The evidence against you six is overwhelming. I could take you into court and demand for each of you to be executed for treason and that would be the outcome. However, doing so would put the U.S. in a precarious position with the exposure of the information on what you did that would cause us to lose the confidence of our allies. It would also force us to expose to our enemies the level of damage you have done to our national security. So, the decision was made to declare you all as terrorists and hide you away for the rest of your lives."

"You think this is over, Roedl. Well it isn't as you'll soon to find out," Capers said while the Marshals escorted him out through the side door.

"You can't do this," Admiral Mirkel complained. "I demand a Courts Martial. You have nothing on me! I'm an Admiral with …"

"Admiral Mirkel," Lawson interrupted. "You sent information you received from General Blayloc of the East Asian desk to Colonel Zhu concerning the plans for the U.S. Navy's John Stennis Carrier Group. The message was intercepted which included the details for close passage around South Korea. We also found that you both were paid $25,000 for the information. A Courts Martial would result in a death sentence for you for treason. Do you deny any of these charges?"

"I thought that information was safely hidden," Mirkel responded. "I guess I have no defense left on the subject. I gambled and I lost. What else am I to say?"

Admiral Roedl saw to the escorts of each person. The Marshals turned their charges over to Marine guards to be escorted to planes waiting at Andrews Joint Base for transfer to Gitmo. Captain Henderson, Admiral Johns and Molliner remained in the room with the CAT205 team, Roedl, the Chairman, the CNO and Red Draper.

"Mr. Molliner," the CNO addressed, "you will be turned over to the civilian courts for money laundering, giving aid and funding illegal international activities along with conspiracy to defraud the U.S. government. None of the documentation we have found can be used in your defense since it has been classified as being too damaging to release. So you are on your own and any attempt by your defense team to obtain the information that came out of this conspiracy will result in you being declared as supporting international terrorists which will result in your immediate transfer to Gitmo. Do you understand these conditions?"

"Yes, Admiral," came the dejected reply after which Marshals escorted him from the room.

"Now we get to you, Captain Henderson," the chairman said while looking at his notes. "You had joined up with Capers and his group and even attempted to kill Mr. Joshua Henry. You almost succeeded and, if you had, we'd be having a different discussion right now. So, here is what I see. You were acting on behalf of Capers as a result of first, being trapped by small offenses and second, by threats to your family. I also understand that you didn't know who to turn to or who to trust to help you so you felt you had to go along with the conspirators' plan. Is that your defense?"

"It is, General," Henderson acknowledged.

"Ok, I've given this a lot of thought and believe I have a solution that will satisfy both of us," the Chairman offered. "I am willing to give you an honorable discharge which means that you can keep your pension and benefits. No charges will be filed and no courts martial will be demanded. In other words, your record will be clean. However, you are restricted from ever working in any U.S. agency, service or contractor. In order to provide you with this outcome, I need to have your letter of resignation presented to me personally tomorrow morning at 10:00 hours. Are these terms agreeable?"

"Yes Sir, thank you, Sir," Henderson exclaimed as he realized that he had just escaped the judgment that the other members of the conspiracy had received.

"By the way, Captain. Your wife and daughter will be in my office when you deliver the letter. They have already been informed of the situation. Admiral Roedl believed that this was the fairest action we could take, based upon your situation," the Chairman said.

Roedl walked up to Captain Henderson and put forth his hand. "You made mistakes, Mark. The aid you gave us after you were freed from the conspirators was key in helping us put this to bed. Thanks for your help. Good luck and God bless you on your journey."

Henderson took Roedl's hand and shook it. "Thanks, Admiral for all you've done to get me out of this mess. And a special thanks to you, Commander Norman, for rescuing my family." Norman smiled at him as he was escorted out the door. At that point the Chairman of the Joint Chiefs of Staff and the CNO got up to walk out the door.

"Keep us posted on any new developments," the CNO advised as they opened the conference room door to leave. "You all did a good job."

After they left, Roedl motioned for his people to sit back down. Lawson, Gunny and Norman cleared their weapons and laid them on the table. A Marine opened the door to tell them that the NCIS crime scene people were here at which Roedl motioned for the Marine to close the door.

"I should have known that you four can't follow orders," Roedl admonished. "I said no weapons in this room and what do you all do? Every one of you brings a gun in direct violation to everything I told you."

"But Sir, you brought a gun," Norman observed.

"I can because I'm the Admiral," Roedl snapped back. "How did you get the weapons in here?"

"I brought them in, Admiral," Gunny admitted. "Josh Henry texted me that a three-man team was coming in to take us out during the meeting in the conference room. He said that the order he saw on the dark web was there was to be no survivors. I tried to get in contact with you but you were not available so I had to come up with another plan. Myers and I ran over to the weapons supply space in the basement, checked out four weapons and some duct tape and brought them up here. I gave the weapons to the four Marine guards to bring into your office as they were the only ones that could have the arms. Then we got them back once we were inside. Myers helped me tape the weapons to the underside of the conference table."

"I know, Gunny," Roedl remarked. "I got a text from weapons supply telling me something was going on. I decided to let things go their way as I figured this team saw a threat and was preparing for it. I just didn't know what it …" At that moment the Marine guard opened the door again.

"Sir," the Marine pleaded, "the NCIS guys are impatient and need to get in."

"Ok," Roedl responded, "send them in."

Turning back to the CAT205 team, Roedl said, "I'm not making any case for you violating my orders. I've come to the conclusion that you all will do things your way no matter what I tell you to do. That being said, don't press your luck too much. You might catch me on a bad day." Everyone laughed as the tension left the room.

"I need to get statements from you, Admiral, as to what happened here," the head NCIS agent said.

"Ask them," Roedl advised while pointing to his team. "They did the shooting, let them do the answering." Roedl walked out of the conference room into his office as Lawson sat down to receive the grilling by the NCIS people that he knew was coming.

As he sat, he noticed that Norman's weapon was no longer on the table and she was gone. Grabbing his weapon, he stepped out of the conference room into the Admiral's office. Looking up from his desk, Roedl saw the concern in Lawson's face while hearing a voice from inside the conference room saying, "You can't leave, Lieutenant. We haven't interviewed you yet."

As Lawson moved toward the entrance door to the waiting room that people used to enter Roedl's office, Roedl jumped up and was right behind him. Two shots were heard coming from the waiting room. Both Lawson and Roedl opened the door at the same time to see Norman on the waiting room floor, obviously wounded. The security vault door to the hall was closed with the entry door from the security vault to the waiting room open. Norman motioned to where the shot came from. Lawson bolted to one side of the waiting room near Norman and fired into the security room. A man in a Marine uniform staggered into the opening as Lawson attempted to unjam his weapon. Norman fired from her lying position, hitting the man in the head.

Lawson dropped down to where Norman was lying. Her blouse had blood on it but from what Lawson could see there was not a lot of blood. Ripping her blouse he saw the entry point of the bullet had hit her in the side and went through. Being concerned with internal bleeding, he felt her side to see if there was any swelling. Meanwhile, Roedl had gotten on the phone to get the emergency team up to his office as Gunny was checking on the dead man in the security vault.

"What were you doing," Lawson asked while pressing on Norman's side to cut down on any bleeding.

Norman smiled at him. "I realized that the three shooters had to get their weapons past the Marine sentry's position in the vault. The only way they were able to get the guns in is if the sentry let them in. I then realized that if he was still here, he was operating with another objective. That had to be taking out Admiral Roedl. I didn't have time to tell you guys what was happening as the Admiral was getting ready to leave."

At the moment, a knock on the outside vault door led Gunny to press the button in the security area that caused the inner door to close and the outer vault door to open. Moments later, the inner door opened again and three medical responders came into the waiting room.

"Thanks, Jim, for your quick attention," Norman said to Lawson as the medical team moved to take over from Lawson. "Hi, Sam. I think I'll pass out now," she said to one of the responders then closed her eyes. The medics started working on the wound and getting her vitals.

"She's going to be ok, Lieutenant. She hasn't lost much blood and her vitals look good," the man Norman addressed as Sam said while he prepared her to be transported to the hospital.

"I heard," Roedl stated. "It looks like this conspiracy has some long tentacles. I guess this was the threat Capers was referring to. I'll take Gunny with me to the hospital. Lawson, you should come too. Myers can answer the questions for the NCIS team." Lawson saw Myers standing in the waiting room doorway to Roedl's office. He acknowledged, gave Lawson a thumbs-up and went back to the conference room as Lawson, Gunny and Roedl prepared to exit through the vault door.

Chapter 25

Inquiry – Day 15

"Where is all the knowledge we lost with information?" – *T. S. Eliot*

Lawson looked around the inquiry room as everyone sat waiting for the inquiry board to start. Admiral Roedl sat in the front row with Commander Norman as Gunny, Lawson and Myers sat in the second row and Red Draper sat in the back of the room with Josh Henry. With both Henry and Norman bandaged up, the room began to look like they all came out of a war zone. Lawson looked at the clock, 8:59 AM. Roedl turned around to Lawson.

"I'm counting on you to lay out the details as they request them. Commander Norman would normally do so but she is just a little drugged up," Roedl ordered as Norman listened.

"I think the Admiral has a point," Norman added. "Right now, the pain medicine is kicking in and I may say something that could embarrass us all. I'm not thinking clearly." Lawson gave her a smile as the yeoman called the attendees to rise. Moments later, a General and two Navy Captains entered the room and moved to the inquiry board table. Everyone stood until the board members sat down. Once they did so, everyone else took their seats.

"This is an inquiry into the events surrounding Operation Scarborough," the General called out. "Let the record show this meeting started on February 15, 2016 at 09:00 hours. The witnesses are Admiral Evan Roedl, Commander Elizabeth Norman, Lieutenant James Lawson, Master Gunnery Sergeant Arnoud Glendenning and Second Class Petty Officer Nicholas Myers. Let the record show that Admiral Roedl has requested that Lieutenant Lawson present the final report as Commander Norman was wounded during the operation and is on pain medications. Thank you all for coming." They all replied an acknowledgement to the welcome.

"Here is the final report," Roedl stated as he laid the document on the table.

"Report has been received and shows it was properly sealed as per operational requirements. I am breaking the seal," the General stated as he broke the seal to the document and opened it to look at its contents. Looking up he saw those sitting in the back of the room. "Red Draper, is that you?"

"Yes, General," came Draper's response.

"I don't see you on the witness list for this inquiry. What are your reasons for being here?" the General inquired.

"Well, Sir, I have a personal interest in this operation," Draper answered.

"What interest would a senior agent for the CIA have with this operation?"

"This operation has major international implications that may include the exposure of CIA field agents due to the nature of the information being passed around," Draper explained.

"Fair enough," the General replied. "You have access and clearances that allows for your presence. I couldn't throw you out if I wanted to, though I don't want to. I see that Josh Henry is also here. Based upon Admiral Roedl's report, you had a significant role in this operation. Thank you, Josh, for the assistance you gave. Now, one other item of interest. I received a report this morning that you all were aided by an agent known as Excalibur or the Fox. Does anyone have an idea of who this person is?" As he looked around, it was obvious he was not going to get an answer.

"If I might, Sir," Lawson interjected. "Even if we had an idea of who he is, we wouldn't expose that information as his value is based upon his ability to remain anonymous. That ability was a significant weapon in our arsenal as we worked to break the code and identify the threat. Without him, some of us might not be alive today."

"Point well taken," the General answered back. "His identity will remain undisclosed. This inquiry is for information only. As such, no sworn testimony is required. Now, let's get to the casualties of the operation. I count nineteen dead and two wounded. Of the dead, there are the six on Pennsylvania Avenue, the taxi driver that Myers stopped, the three men that tried to kidnap Commander Norman at the Rayburn Building, the six men that tried to storm room 2337 at the Rayburn building and the three that were killed in Admiral Roedl's conference room. The two wounded were Josh Henry and Commander Norman. Did I miss anything?"

"There was also the man killed in Admiral Roedl's security vault and we believe that Sam Ginty, also known as Rod Lavlery, was also killed. One other addition, Captain Henderson was also wounded," Lawson added.

"Thank you, Lieutenant, that helps," the General noted. "Have we determined the name of this shadow group you brought down and the extent of their influence?"

Lawson opened his copy of the report as he began to answer, "The name, no. Their influence, unknown but suspected to be significant and international. We believe we have accounted for everyone but Colonel Zhu. According to Chinese intercepted transmissions, the Chinese government is also vigorously looking for Zhu. He appears to have gone rogue with a large stock of antitank weapons and around thirty million dollars in cash and bonds. He remains a threat to both us and China. All of the ongoing investigations here in the United States have been turned over to the FBI. Any international investigations are being handled by the affected countries in a joint effort with the DIA and CIA. I must point out, Sir, that we came close to a nuclear war due to the actions of a few people. Our recommendation is that there be a second level of coding used to authorize nuclear launches and, from what we have been informed, all previous launch codes have been changed. Also, we want to note that former Congressman Capers escaped from custody due to the help of another person on the day he was being transferred, that being February 11th."

"Excellent report," Mr. Lawson, the General commended. "Now, I've been informed that this team has come up with a viable scenario on North Korea's intentions with their missile launches."

"That's true, Sir," Lawson concurred. "I will ask Petty Officer Myers to address the question."

Myers leaned back in his chair as he contemplated his answer. Gathering his thoughts, he began his explanation, "North Korea put up two satellites that the experts say are just dummy loads for the North Koreans to see if they can get objects of around four hundred pounds into space. My assessment indicates that, based upon the path of these two satellites, they may be Trojan horses. By that I mean that they are about the size of ten kiloton nuclear devices and they are positioned to pass over highly critical U.S. infrastructures. Their ability to generate an EMP burst with that size of a payload does put us at a level of risk. The problem we have is that we don't know if these are real or not. That's the risk."

"What if we were to take them out with antisatellite missiles," the General asked.

"The problem with that solution is the debris issue," Myers replied. "It is the same issue we have if they do create a nuclear detonation. The debris coming off from either destroying the satellites or from a nuke detonation would throw debris out at hyper-velocities. That would mean that any satellites, space stations or space vehicles in the direct line of sight to the blast would be in jeopardy of being hit by the debris resulting in damage or destruction."

"Thank you, Petty Officer Myers," the General remarked. "Not what I wanted to hear but definitely what I needed. Now, Mr. Lawson, I also see from reports and messages that the dark web has become a supermarket for government secrets. Your opinion, please."

"I believe that Mr. Henry should be able to give you a better answer on the subject than I can," Lawson responded.

Josh Henry immediately sat up in his chair as he heard his name mentioned. Seeing that everyone was looking his direction, he proceeded to answer the question. "The dark web is the digital marketplace that replicates the earlier 20th Century markets for illicit information trading that once were Geneva, Paris and New York. Every legal marketplace, whether physical or conceptual, has a hidden market within it that trades in the more suspect products that may not be allowed by some countries. These are still called 'black markets'. The dark web is no different. It is an offshoot of the internet and is a natural outgrowth of a market society. The advantage of the dark web market over previous markets is that information can be bought and sold in seconds rather than days. This means the information is fresh and reliable. It also means a country can respond to a threat or create a barrier to an action before the threat has a chance to be implemented. That being said, it can also initiate a threat more rapidly, making some of our threat response protocols outdated."

The General turned his pen in his hand then posed his next question. "So what type of information is bought or sold on the dark web?"

"You can buy individual pieces of information or blocks of it," Henry instructed. "The methods of selling and buying information has become so advanced that it resembles the trading of home mortgages. Information vendors will take large blocks of information and package them as a single entity for sale. In a block sale, they will put some significant information like names and social security numbers, corporate trade secrets and intercepted government communications in with less valuable information such as individual's purchasing preferences and internet browsing sequences. Similar to what mortgage lenders do by mixing good loans with bad loans in a loan derivative sale.

For sales involving valuable, selected and focused information, certain dark web information providers may even have their own team of agents going into different countries to gather secret and top secret information to sell. It's a very lucrative market."

So, how do we protect ourselves and our information from this type of threat," the General asked.

Josh Henry looked at Red Draper then responded. "You can't fully protect yourself or your information from these people. Having extensive encryption, trusted personnel and strong procedures will help. However, encryption can be broken, trusted personnel in the size of the organizations that make up the U.S. Government is a dream or more likely a nightmare, and strong procedures will always have some chink in the armor. So what I am saying is, the best protection is not to document anything that can be dealt with by other means. You can't use yesterday's methods for today's problems. You've got a million different avenues for the hackers to come through whereas we have security being a secondary concern that takes us away from our jobs. Our focus is very general with a lot of different areas of concern. Their focus is very narrow with only one or two concerns, mainly to find some way to get into our information. They have a significant advantage."

"Petty Officer Myers," one of the Navy Captains of the inquiry board began as the General received a note from one of the Marines in the hallway, "I'm Captain Spencer and my question to you is simply what access do you think the North Koreans have into our classified data?"

"Well, Captain Spencer. I think they have had enough people working indirectly for them within our government that all classified information is exposed."

"What do you mean by 'working indirectly'?" Spencer queried.

Myers took a drink from a soda can then spoke, "Individuals may receive a request from someone internal to an organization that is cleared for classified information and respond to that request thinking that it's legit. The request may seem innocent enough but may be one of many requests sent out by the same individual. Taking these multiple responses, the requester is able to put the pieces together from the several requests in which responses were returned, helping the requester to identify a top secret item from lower level classified information."

"For your information that stays in this room," the General began. "We came to the same conclusion and have people at Fort Bevoir working on the problem to determine our level of exposure. Now, you have noticed that none of you have been put under oath. The reason is that you had significant transparency in this operation due to Admiral Roedl's and Commander Norman's reports to the Joint Staff. There are other activities within the Operation Scarborough effort that are still ongoing. However, from what we can see today, the CAT205 team's involvement appears to be completed. I also received a note updating us on Congressman Capers escape during the transfer of custody from the U.S. Marshals to the Marine contingent. Apparently, there was an attempt to run the whole group down in the garage of the FBI building by a person in a limousine. As you know, the driver was caught but Capers escaped in the confusion. This update bulletin out on him says to assume he is armed and dangerous. The update says that one of the Marshals weapons, a pistol, is missing but they're not sure if he took it. So, to be on the safe side, they're considering him armed."

The General nodded to Admiral Roedl at which point Roedl turned to the others in the room. "That finishes this inquiry," Roedl said while moving to the front of the room. "We are evaluating other operations that may involve this team. You all have fifteen days of leave to recover from this effort. I am modifying an agreement previously made to the Joint Staff. Due to the Capers escape and the fact that someone aided him in his escape, I want all of you to keep your weapons on you until further orders. Keep them concealed but loaded, even while on leave. Now let's all head back to my office."

They all got up and left as a group to the exit to the facility. They retrieved their weapons from the security officer at the main desk of the building then left the building. Walking along the length of the parking lot, they followed Admiral Roedl to their cars while discussing the conversations of the inquiry. Norman saw movement out of the corner of her eye as Lawson turned to see what Norman was looking at.

"Roedl," came the shout of a voice at the other end of the parking lot, "You're finished!" It was Capers.

Norman jumped in front of Roedl as Lawson turned to the sound of the voice. Lawson saw Norman's move as he turned, pulling his weapon from its holster. Realizing there was no time to get between Capers and Norman, he leveled his weapon at the man with the gun. Both men fired simultaneously with Lawson's shot hitting Capers, causing him to stagger and drop his weapon as he fell to the ground. Panic set in as Lawson turned to see where Norman was, knowing the shot had to have hit her. Norman was holding onto the Admiral, wondering if the shot had hit her and, with the rush of adrenaline, maybe she didn't feel it. Thoughts raced through her mind. "He missed," she realized as she took stock. It was then she grasped that Red Draper had stepped between her and Capers as she saw him lying on the ground. Lawson ran over to Red and knelt down beside him while checking to see where he had been hit.

"Red, no!" Norman screamed as she ran to where he was lying. "What did you do that for?"

Red smiled at Norman as Gunny joined Lawson to tend to the wound. "The same reason you stood in to protect Evan?" Red told Norman as his breathing was becoming more labored.

"I've called for the LifeFlight helicopter," Roedl said as he joined the others. "Gunny, go check on Capers and make sure he can do no more damage."

"Will do, Sir," Gunny obeyed as he jumped up to go where Capers lay. Myers grabbed Red's hand as he smiled at Red.

"No greater love does one have than to lay down their life for another," Red stated as he gripped tighter on Myers hand. Norman grabbed Red's other hand while tears ran down her face.

"I've heard that before. Where did you get that saying?" Norman asked, her emotions now in full disarray.

"It's from the Bible," Myers answered. "It was Jesus' statement to amplify on what was the greatest act of love." Norman looked at Myers while Lawson continued to work on Red's wound. The bullet hit next to the heart and Lawson was beginning to comprehend that the shot was fatal.

"As I told you, I had some life-changing experiences that brought me to this point," Red whispered. "I am now going to meet my Lord and Savior in a few moments. Thank God I'm forgiven for all of my past offenses, not because of this act but because I gave my life to Jesus." Norman was taken aback by his comment but it was now obvious to her about his faith, he was a changed man. "Nick, thanks for your friendship, my brother." Myers just smiled as tears rolled from his eyes.

"Red, don't go," Norman pleaded as the sound of a helicopter could be heard approaching.

As Red's life was ebbing away, he pulled Lawson down to where Lawson could hear him, "Marry this lady," he whispered. "She's the best thing that could ever happen to you." He looked at Norman, lovingly smiled while gripping her hand and closed his eyes. "I'm coming, Lord," he whispered as he let out his last breath.

Roedl put his fingers to Red's neck. "He's gone," he declared as Lawson got up and pulled Norman close to him as both of them felt the tears flowing. Gunny came back and stood for a moment, feeling the loss of a close friend but he still had other responsibilities to care for. Moving to an open area of the parking lot, he directed the helicopter to land.

"I'll take care of notifying his brother," Roedl stated.

"Where is Colonel Draper now?" Lawson asked.

"He's still in the Kurdish mountains of Iran," Roedl answered. "I'll send him a message once we get back to the SAL center at the Kennedy facility." The coroner arrived a few minutes later and examined Red's body. After he signed the death certificate, they all stood watching as the medics from the helicopter put Red's body into a body bag and moved him to the helo.

Beth Norman had a sense of peace come over her as she saw the helo take off. She remembered a quote that said something like 'grief is the last effort we make of saying I love you to someone lost'. She had truly lost a dear friend that day.

Chapter 26

Transitions

"A single event can awaken within us a stranger totally unknown to us. To live is to be slowly born." - Antoine de Saint-Exupéry

They all stood outside of the chapel as everyone was exiting the memorial service for Red Draper. Lawson stood holding Norman against him as she just watched and breathed, taking in all of the unreal events of the past two weeks. Myers was looking at the forested area to the side of the chapel while deep in thought. Lawson looked up to see Colonel Ed Draper and Admiral Roedl walk out of the chapel door and approach the group.

"It was a very appropriate service for such a good man. It's hard to believe he died a week ago as it seems like only yesterday we lost him," Lawson said as Draper approached them.

"Good to see you again, Lawson, and thanks. Hi, Beth. I know it's been tough for you with the history and friendship you and Red had," he lamented as he pulled her to him and hugged her. She gave him a kiss on the cheek while fighting to keep the torrent of tears to a manageable flow.

"What are you going to do now, Colonel?" Lawson posed.

Draper looked down at Norman's face as he contemplated his answer. "It's more important to ask the question of what are you and Beth going to do? Red told me about your relationship. I agree with Red about your character, Lawson, knowing the experience I had with you in Iran. You were a fresh breath of air.

As for me, I've got to get back to Kurdistan and Bahram Khaliqi's tribe. There are tensions developing between the Kurds and the Iraqi government. The tribes are being pressed by both the Iraqis and the Iranians and it's not a good situation. By the way, Khaliqi said to tell you 'Hi' or I think that's what he said. It was actually 'good man, wise man', which for him is the same as saying 'Hi', if you know what I mean."

Lawson nodded he understood then looked at Gunny as Gunny was motioning to him about something. Excusing himself from the conversation, Lawson walked over to Gunny as Gunny held out a piece of paper in his hand.

"It's from Josh Henry," Gunny said as he handed the note to Lawson. "Apparently, Colonel Zhu wants to talk." Lawson read the note and thanked Gunny for the information. Turning, he walked over to Admiral Roedl and handed him the note while the Admiral was talking to the CNO. Roedl read the note then turned to Lawson.

"Your take on this, Lieutenant," Roedl requested as the CNO looked on.

"I think he's trying to get us to go neutral so that we won't be bothering him while the Chinese are searching for him," Lawson advised.

Roedl looked at Lawson then the CNO. Handing the note to the CNO, Roedl said, "He is offering a very tempting carrot. A list of all the players in the top shadow groups in the U.S."

"This looks fantastic," the CNO exclaimed. "We can put a number of spies out of business with this."

Roedl looked at Lawson then the CNO as Colonel Draper and Commander Norman came over to see what was happening. Lawson motioned for Myers to come over while Gunny approached Lawson from the back.

Roedl chose his words very carefully, "This may look like a gift of significant value but I'm reminded of a snake that offered some fruit to a woman with a great promise that turned out to be a trap. This has all the makings of that story all over again." Norman stood wondering why the same story of the snake in the garden came up again. Maybe Gunny was right. Maybe that Bible Myers had was a good source of understanding how people behaved.

"You do what you seem is right," the CNO instructed Roedl then continued, "Mr. Lawson, your take on this, in depth."

"Yes, Sir," Lawson answered as he formed his thoughts. "Colonel Zhu knows he's being hunted. He's looking for a safe port in a storm and the most opportune way for him to do that is to negotiate a level of protection by us in exchange for names. He knows it will take several months for us to verify, document and capture those involved. Meantime, while he's in our custody, he is out of reach of the Chinese government and the sale of those weapons he's holding can still be carried out giving him a heavy cash input. It would also give him time to plan how he is going to stay out of the Chinese government's reach."

"As long as he is hunted he doesn't have time to organize or set things up," Myers added.

"Commander Norman, your thoughts?" the CNO asked as he handed her the note. She wiped the tears from her eyes and read the contents.

"I think you are walking into a trap if you accept this offer," Norman stated as her voice quivered from the events of the day. "Colonel Zhu is always making sure that loose ends are removed. He may very well be making this offer in order to remove those loose ends out of his reach that can tie him to the whole North Korean incident, not to mention also removing some of our good people or, at least, creating distrust so that we remove their input from consideration."

"Still tough Beth. That's what I like about you Commander," the CNO commended.

"I'm not as tough as I was before this mission," she admitted.

"You're tougher than I've ever seen you," Draper shot back. "Don't ever mistaken tears for weakness. You're merely showing that you're human. You can still fight and give advice even when your thoughts are consumed with loss." At that, Norman leaned against Lawson as he held her and nodded to Draper. Draper patted Lawson on the shoulder then put his hand on Norman's head. "I lost him too," he said as he turned to go. "He's finished his race, now I have to continue mine. Beth, Jim, make a life for yourselves."

"We'll let Zhu stew in his own problems," Roedl told the CNO as he shook Draper's hand.

As Draper left, everyone else gave their hugs, said their goodbyes and went their separate ways leaving Lawson and Norman standing alone in the parking lot listening to the silence around them.

"Are you hungry?" Lawson asked. He looked at her face as she nodded 'yes' and realized he was seeing the depth of her beauty in her most vulnerable circumstance. In that moment he fell in love with her.

Lawson grinned at her which caused her to change her expression from one of grief to curiosity. "Let's get some Chinese," he suggested. At that they both laughed through the tears as they turned to go to his car. It was then that she knew.

About The Author

Mr. T. James LeDoux is a U.S. Navy Vietnam veteran, having worked on river operations on the upper Mekong River with the Mobile Riverine Force and, at times, supporting the Office of Naval Intelligence in Vietnam in 1969 and 1970. His military experience extends from years 1968 to 2000, in both active and reserve service in the Navy, Army, Air Force and Coast Guard. In Coast Guard Reserves, he was part of the Coast Guard security team for former President Nixon's residence at the Western Whitehouse at San Mateo Point in California.

During his life, as a design engineer and manager, he has designed numerous defense and commercial systems and products in both the high-tech hardware and software disciplines as well as managed many product development projects. His last 10 years were dedicated to training, mentoring and aiding technical leaders in managing high-tech development projects and people.

He also spent time as a technical investigator, investigating patent infringement claims and acting as an expert witness in court cases involving development processes in both hardware and software development projects. Along with Warren Yates, he developed the 'Control-Feedback-Abort Loop' concept for problem solution analysis being used in a number of high-tech companies to aid in determining how people will use products to solve problems.

He and his wife presently live in Colorado Springs, Colorado writing books, doing research on high-tech development and historical events, analyzing present international events and providing consulting assistance to up and coming design engineers in managing their teams.

He is author of several books on business management and historical subjects such as 'The Barbarians Guide to Management' (2012), 'Amateurs With Egos' (2013), and 'Trouble on the Grand Canal' (2013).

His novels include 'The First Real Christmas' (2012), 'Unsanctioned Protocol' (2017) and 'Breaking Protocol' (2018).